I AM DRAGON

A RANDALL ERIK DDRAIK NOVEL

BRIAN J. GREEN

HALK-KIN PUBLISHING | GRASS VALLEY, CA

Library of Congress Cataloging-in-Publication Data
Names: Green, Brian, Author

Title: I AM DRAGON

LCCN 2024917660
ISBN 979-8-9913806-1-4| ISBN 979-8-9913806-0-7 (ebook)
Urban Fantasy
Editor: Grant Skakun
Half-Kin Publishing
Grass Valley

Book Cover Art by Brian Castleforte - castleforte.com/animated-bookcovers/

Book Cover Design and Interior Formatting by 100Covers.

Welcome to the world of I Am Dragon, I hope you become a fan. My goal is to create a big world for Randall to live in, and for every reader to have a bloody good time immersing themselves in it, as it grows.

You can discover more of it by going to my website, iamdragonbook.com, for character art by Brian Castleforte, Randall's Blog, and new information about current and upcoming books. You might even find a surprise short story from the world of I Am Dragon, from time to time. Join the mailing list so you'll always be up to date and the first to know about the latest releases and happenings.

Thank you for reading!

To Joe, Jean, and Tami Green.
I wish you could have been here to see this book published.
You're loved and always missed.

To Elizabeth Keyes-Blanchard.
My heart.
Yours.

To Dave Brownlee and Erik Seversen.
For showing me how to get this
Self-publishing done.

To all the OG writers of the
Speculative Ink writers group in LA, who
Helped me through so many iterations of this book.

THANK YOU ALL

CHAPTER ONE

My name is Randall Erik Ddraik.

I'm a Dragon.

I'm currently falling from the top floor of a forty-story hotel in downtown Los Angeles, after being thrown off the balcony of my client's suite.

I really don't want to die.

Why don't I just glide gently to the ground, or fly away into the night? Because I'm also half-human. A brief description is probably in order.

I'm six foot five, weigh in at two-twenty, blessed with a strong jaw, sharp nose, and high cheekbones. My hair is a dark reddish-brown and my eyes are emerald green. The color of a Scottish hillside my mom used to say... sorry, not relevant now. The important point you need to take away here, I don't have wings.

But I digress, I was falling to my death I believe.

Time slowed to a crawl as I sailed over the railing, and every detail snapped into sharp focus. I saw the faces of the men hurling me to my death, all of them sharing the same look, warrior's courage and righteous triumph. They're Vanatori Drakon. Literally translated, Dragon Hunters. They're assholes.

I saw my client, Annalisa VanSusstern, watching in horror as I was launched into the night sky. Her dazzling amber-colored eyes wide with confusion and fear. A man's hand clamped over her mouth to suppress the scream trying to escape it. She's not just a client, she's in my care, which meant I had taken an oath upon my life as a Dragon to keep her safe and free from harm. Yes, I do realize I'm doing a suck job of it right now. Shut up.

The last thing I saw as I pinwheeled into space and the balcony disappeared from view, was the man holding her. He was tall, wrapped in a long black trench coat. His skin was porcelain pale, and his eyes were white. All white. They seared into my memory like a red-hot brand. Not their lack of color but the look in them. It was sadness.

I should have sensed him long before I saw him, because he wasn't like the other men. He was Half-kin, a Dragon, like me. What in the name of bloody fuck all was a Dragon doing with Vanatori, and why hadn't I sensed him?

I didn't have time to think about it though, because falling and all.

I dropped past the thirty-seventh floor.

My mind was consumed by a single screaming thought: *I don't want to die!*

As I passed the thirty-fifth floor, I twisted and flipped over in midair, assuming a skydiver's free fall position. Arms out and bent up at the elbows, legs bent up at the knees. If I was gonna die I would damn sure face it head-on. Far beneath me, but rapidly approaching, the water of the pool sparkled from underwater lights. I was going to smash into the concrete deck surrounding it.

I don't want to die.

Involuntarily, a primal scream began building deep inside me. My Death Roar. I tried to fight it back, hoping that if I could prevent it from escaping my mouth, I could somehow prevent myself from said smash. My mouth wouldn't listen to my brain, and my lips began to part on their own, a low growl emanating from my throat. Stupid lips.

Goddammit… I don't want to die.

Before my mouth opened completely, I caught a glimmer of light rocketing towards me from below. As I dropped past the thirty-third floor I focused on the light, revealing the tiny form of Tatiana Fynfire. A name right out of a Tolkien book I know, but her name, nonetheless.

Her long bluish-blond hair whipped wildly around her head, and her large eyes were lit bright orange, matching the sparkling glow surrounding her body. She shot towards me like a tiny glowing missile. Her teeth bared in a snarl, her eyes narrowed and blazed like hot coals.

Tat's a Fae of the air, commonly known as a sprite. I'd had her tailing Annalisa and me while we were out for the evening. She'd been in a holding pattern outside, waiting for me to come out on the balcony and give her the all-clear sign. Being thrown off was not it.

With a high-pitched yell that would have been cute under any other circumstance, she slammed into my stomach with a surprising amount of force. Tat's significantly stronger than her just-over-a-foot-tall size lets on, and I felt ribs break as I folded in half around her tiny form.

She'd hit me at an angle, and I felt my straight downward trajectory slide sideways. She was trying to push me toward the pool. She had a ton of momentum behind her when she hit me. Add to that the lack of resistance a free fall provides, and you've got a recipe for some serious midair movement.

As I hurtled past the tenth floor the deep end of the pool slid into my view and my thought suddenly changed... I might not die today! My building Death Roar turned into a mad cackle of survival.

"Roll!" she screamed.

I flipped to my side as best I could. I had been folded over Tat, trapping her with my body. The move created just enough space for her, and she broke free and streaked skyward.

As the fifth floor flashed past my periphery I screamed to myself, I am not going to die today! I willed for it to be true with every fiber of my being as the water became my worldview.

I snapped into a fetal position, trying to avoid the mother of all face plants, and in defiance of every natural instinct to tense my body, I forced it to relax. Have you ever heard of drunk drivers surviving accidents that should have broken them to pieces? It's because their bodies are so loose and fluid that they unconsciously move with the momentum and motion of the crash instead of fighting against it. I tried desperately to apply the same principle here. I failed a little as I clenched my jaw. I'll call it a win.

I hit the water.

Hard.

I felt more ribs break. The water twisted me wildly, something in my left shoulder snapped as I slammed back first into the bottom of the pool, and my head cracked into the plaster. A universe of stars erupted in my sight. A split second later the stars winked out as my vision narrowed to a pinpoint of light, and darkness flooded in. Despite my best efforts to hold my breath, I screamed and immediately sucked in what felt like half the pool.

I flailed weakly, trying to swim upward toward the tiny point of light still left in my vision. I became dimly aware of feeling a rough surface on my face. Bloody hell, I was swimming down not up. The white I had thought was light was really the plaster of the pool bottom. I grinned insanely as the thought 'death by pool' bubbled through my head, then everything faded to black.

CHAPTER TWO

I don't know how long I was out, but the next thing I remember was lying on the pool deck retching up all the water I had swallowed, along with the remnants of an exceptionally good steak tartare from dinner. It was much better going down. My chest felt like a hammer had been beating on it. It hurt to breathe. It hurt period. It was a glorious feeling. It meant I was alive.

I'm not going to die today.

Two men, their black suits soaking wet, were kneeling over me. One, a rough-faced young man in his mid-twenties, well-muscled with brown eyes and hair. The other, a short, fat guy who must have been at least sixty, judging by the wispy strands of grey hair wetly plastered to his mostly bald head, and his thick grey mustache.

"He gonna be all right?" the old guy asked.

"He's breathing," the young one said, with a strong southern accent. "I'll settle for that right now."

"How's he even alive after that fall? I mean, how many floors do you think…" said the older man, trailing off as he looked up at the hotel.

"Forty stories," I slurred to the older man as I pawed at him weakly, trying to answer his question.

His hand recoiled from mine. It must have freaked him out that I could even move.

"Jesus! Sorry mister wasn't expecting that," he said apologetically, then placed his hand on mine and pushed it gently back to the ground. "Forty stories? Christ, best if you don't move, I think." He patted my hand awkwardly, then moved his away.

"Not gonna die today," I rasped, more to myself than to them. My voice sounded strange, distorted. Oh yeah, my nose had been shattered by a heavy blow from something as I'd walked into the hotel room. That was fun.

"You owe that to the kid," said the older man, hooking his thumb at his young partner. "That was some great work, Kevin."

"Great teamwork. All the CPR in the world wouldn't have done him any good if we hadn't got in and hauled him out so fast," Kevin said.

His voice sounded as if it were coming through wet cement. My vision was swimming in and out of focus, and I was seeing things in triple. Kevin snapped his fingers in front of my face several times.

"Hey! Stay awake man!" he shouted.

My eyes popped open. I hadn't realized I'd closed them. The rest of my body felt like it was somewhere in South Dakota, trying to figure out its way back to LA to meet up with my eyes.

"That's better, sir," he said, "We've got paramedics on the way. Stay with us."

For some stupid reason, I tried to sit up.

"Whoa, hold up! Where you tryin' ta go? Just lay back and take it easy." I felt him gently press back on my shoulders.

Normally I could've tossed him off of me like a wet towel. All two hundred pounds of him. I wasn't normally half dead. I went back down like a newborn kitten... er, tiger.

"Don, grab a pillow off one of those lounge chairs to put under his head," Kevin said to the older guard. "Can you tell me your name, sir?" he asked me.

"Annalisa!" I blurted out. I had to get to her. They had her. Then I cackled crazily. That wasn't my name. Hey, you try falling forty stories and then think straight. Go ahead, I'll wait. I grimaced and inhaled sharply as the laughter hit my broken ribs.

"What is it? What's wrong, sir?" Kevin said, sliding the pillow under my head.

"Ribs... broken," I rasped.

"He works for Mrs. VanSusstern. He's her bodyguard I think," said Don.

"Knew he looked familiar. Can you tell us what happened?" Kevin said.

If I answered truthfully, it would mean cops. I don't like to involve law enforcement of any kind in my business. Considering my nature and often the nature of my clients, it can get complicated if they start asking questions. Then again, I knew Annalisa was in the hands of the Vanatori and the Dragon who was with them. I wasn't going to be able to start looking for her anytime soon in my current condition, and the longer I was on my back the colder her trail would get. I needed the police for now, until I was back on my feet.

"We were attacked. They took Annalisa," I wheezed. Speaking was an effort.

"By who? Where?" asked Kevin, still not moving his eyes from me. The kid was cool, calm, and professional. I could tell he had training, beyond the lame ass hotel security kind.

"Presidential suite," I said, trying to sit up again. Kevin pushed me down just as easily as the first time. Dammit.

Don spoke into the radio mic secured on his lapel. "Don to base, Don to base. I need a couple guys to meet me at the Presidential suite ASAP. And call the police, we've got a possible kidnapping."

There was a burst of sound and motion as paramedics and firemen came rushing onto the pool deck, pushing a rattling gurney with them. They dropped equipment boxes around me.

Don stood and backed off.

"We need room to work, man. You gotta move," one of the paramedics said to Kevin as he knelt down in Don's vacated spot.

Kevin hesitated. "Can you describe the men to me?" he asked.

"Six men, wearing all black. One had an eye patch. That's all I remember," I lied. I remembered every detail about them. Honestly, I didn't want anyone else finding them. I was going to hunt them down and take them apart on my own.

As Kevin started to rise, I jerked my head up and grabbed his arm with all the strength I could muster. "They're probably armed. Wait for the police," I said with intensity.

As utterly unlikely as it was that someone was still in the room, I didn't want them taking chances. Something no Dragon ever takes lightly is a debt of gratitude, and I owed both of them now. I wouldn't be able to settle up with them if they got themselves killed.

Kevin nodded, "Understood, sir," he said, then he and Don hustled into the hotel.

My head lolled back to the pillow from the effort. I looked up and saw Tat hovering high overhead, smiling down at me. Eagles and owls have got nothing on a Dragon's eyesight. If she'd been half a mile up, I could've seen if she had spinach in her teeth. Which she didn't. I don't think she even liked spinach. Where did that come from? Bloody hell, was I loopy.

She was barefoot and wearing what basically amounted to a white bikini. Sprites aren't big on a lot of clothes. Think Tinkerbell without the wings, plus a whole lot of sexy.

She pointed at her eyes then made a 'follow' motion with her hands. She'd seen something, hopefully the Vanatori, and was going after it. I weakly gave a thumbs-up sign. My thumb felt heavier than a truck. She streaked away, leaving a glowing orange trail in her wake. Go get 'em, you little badass. Tat's my girl Friday. Friend, confidant, voice of reason, warrior, among many other things.

The blue-eyed face of a young paramedic loomed into view over me, blocking out everything else. "How you doing, buddy?" he asked.

"All things considered, just peachy," I replied, "It's not every day I survive a forty-story fall."

His eyes bugged. "You what?" he practically shouted.

"Fell. From up there," I tried to point up to the suite with my left hand. I was rewarded with a searing bolt of pain that blurred my vision. I was in shock, and I'd forgotten about the wrenching it took when I hit the pool. I clamped down on the sound that wanted to escape my lips.

"Easy," he said, as he gently lowered it. He began feeling around on my shoulder. I sucked in air through my teeth.

"Sorry," he said, "Your left shoulder is really badly dislocated. Probably got some torn tendons too. All things considered, I'd say you're pretty damn lucky." He shot a quick look back up to the hotel room and then returned his gaze to me, shaking his head as he did. "Man, this is one for the Guinness book."

I nodded and bravely held in a whimper. I'm a Dragon, we don't whimper.

"How about something for that pain?"

"Bloody hell yes," I said.

The shot was a good one. The next thing I knew I was bandaged, neck braced, in a sling, on the gurney, and in the back of an ambulance with its sirens wailing. All with a huge shit-eating grin on my face. I passed out somewhere along the way to the hospital.

CHAPTER THREE

As I floated in the darkness of unconsciousness and the bliss of painkillers, the faces of the men who'd thrown me off the balcony burned through my mind. You'd think that they'd have worn masks to hide their identities, but they'd wanted me to see them. They'd gotten the drop on me and wanted me to die humiliated and beaten. Probably why they hadn't just shot me point blank.

Though the presence of the other Dragon could just as easily have had something to do with that. I couldn't wrap my head around it. Vanatori and Dragons have thousands of years of bad blood between us. Seeing them working together defied all logic. I had to find out why.

I focused my willpower and began pushing away the darkness, clawing my way toward consciousness. The black slowly turned to grey, and the silence was broken by a distant, rhythmic beeping. The sound was accompanied by cold and pain. My eyes snapped open.

I was in a dimly lit hospital room. The EKG machine I was hooked up to breaking the silence with rhythmic beeps.

My nose and ribs were tingling so strongly it felt like a hive of bees was crawling on them. A sign from my body telling me that I was already healing, a benefit of having magical lizard DNA. When I was two hundred and six, I regrew a hand that I'd lost in a sword fight. It only took a month.

I inhaled quick and sharp, flexing my abs at the same time. All I felt was mild soreness. I touched my nose. It was covered with a thick gauze bandage, but it felt fine when I squeezed it. My left arm was in a sling. I slowly tried rolling my shoulder and was met with a stab of pain. Nowhere near as blinding as it had been but still bad. That was gonna take more time to heal.

I lifted the sheets to see that I was wearing a hospital gown. My clothes were draped on a chair across the room. I got up and detached myself from the EKG which promptly flatlined.

I glanced in a small mirror hanging on the wall. My eyes, which should have been horrible shades of black and blue and swollen shut, had only small black marks beneath them.

I shrugged out of the gown. Putting on damp pants with one hand is tricky business. They were still somewhere south of my thighs when a panicked female nurse came bursting through the door.

She was a dark-skinned, short, plumpish woman. Her face flashed panic, relief, then mild amusement when she saw what was happening.

"Hi," I said, grinning.

"You shouldn't be out of bed. What are you doing?" she said with a thick Filipino accent.

"Trying to put my pants on. Little help?"

She hustled over to my side and helped me keep my balance while pulling up the left side of my pants, as I got the right.

"Why are you getting dressed?"

"I figured walking through the hospital naked would be frowned upon," I said.

"You shouldn't be leaving."

"I've got a lot to do. I'm a busy guy."

"You're a foolish guy," she said sternly.

"Yeah, it's a bad habit of mine."

"You need to stay in bed and rest. You should be here for at least twenty-four hours of observation. You took a nasty whack to your head."

"I've got a really thick skull." So my mother used to tell me. Constantly.

"Head traumas can have serious ramifications. They often don't manifest symptoms until hours later."

I fought one-handed with my zipper and buttons and finally beat the stubborn bastards, getting them fastened. On to the belt, victory shall be mine!

"Monica," I said, reading her nametag, "You're very helpful, very professional, and probably right, I should stay and rest but I can't. There's a woman out there who hired me to protect her, and right now I can't say I'm doing a very good job of it. I have to go." Did I just admit that out loud? Maybe I do need to be observed.

"You won't be able to do the job at all if you keel over from an aneurysm," she said firmly.

"I'm pretty tough, I'll be okay," I said with a grin, as I grabbed my shirt and jacket.

I draped the tattered garments around my shoulders as Monica stood blocking the door, scowling at me. Her hands planted firmly on her hips.

"You gonna tackle me if I try to leave?" I asked, turning my grin into a smile.

"No, but now that you're awake there are a couple of officers out there who want to talk to you. They've been waiting for you to regain consciousness. I told them to stay put when you flatlined. I'll send them in." She strode out, shaking her head.

A clock on the wall said it was 5 in the morning. I had gone over the balcony at about 1, so Annalisa had been taken four hours ago. The longer I was stuck here answering questions the colder her trail was getting. Unless they were going to tell me they had found her and she was safe in protective custody, I didn't have time for their questions right now.

For the record, I like cops. They have a swagger that I respect. The man and woman who walked into the room weren't cops. They were Feds. Cops have swagger, Feds have polish and arrogance.

He was pale, bald, and stood about five-eight. There was more to him but I didn't really notice, because I was looking at her.

She was tall. About six-three, two inches of which came from her boot heels. She was very pretty, though trying hard not to show it. Minimal makeup, her long brown hair pulled back into a tight ponytail. Her eyes were bright blue and stood out against high cheekbones, accentuated by tan skin that smelled like coconut oil and jasmine.

Dragon nose, as good as the eyes. Even wrapped in gauze.

She wore steel grey pants that were tight enough to show strong, well-defined legs that led up to a slim waist. A matching jacket covered a black shirt, only partially hiding the swell of her breasts which I could tell were impressive.

I immediately wanted to see her naked. I took a silent breath to regain my focus. In my defense, very few things are as distracting for Half-kin as beautiful women. We have a genetic predisposition to want to breed and have children, even though we can't. It didn't help that it felt like she was radiating pheromones. That could have been me still being loopy from the fall, but I doubted it.

They flashed their IDs. He smiled, she didn't.

"Mr. Ddraik, I'm Special Agent Hooper. This is Special Agent Buck. FBI," he said. He stepped over to me and stuck out his hand. I shook it. His grip was intentionally strong. What he lacked in height he made up for in muscle, the tailored lines of his black three-piece suit showing off an athlete's frame. A grey tie with a perfect knot laid against a white shirt. Black shoes gleamed on his feet and wire-rimmed glasses covered his brown eyes.

"Sorry to barge in on you right after you wake up. I gotta tell you, I'm amazed you're alive after that fall."

"It's actually unbelievable," Buck said, her voice deep and husky.

"Yeah, I'm pretty sure I used all nine of my lives."

Buck raised an eyebrow at that.

"You've got to teach me that trick," Hooper said.

"Sure, but practicing is a real bitch."

He laughed as he retreated a few steps.

"You fooled the nurse," I said to him.

"Excuse me?" his smile faltered.

"She thought you were cops."

"Life would be easier if we were," he said, his smile coming back. "Less politics and paperwork."

"The police are investigating the men who tried to kill you. We've been assigned to a joint task force to assist them with the investigation of Ms. VanSusstern's kidnapping," Buck said.

"Why are you involved at all?" I asked, "The same men committed both crimes. Neither of which is in federal jurisdiction."

"A woman as wealthy as she is has a lot of powerful associates," she said.

That was true. Annalisa is one of the five richest people on the planet. She owned a financial empire with interests in almost every kind of industry imaginable. That kind of money commands a lot of influence.

"When her CEO learned what had happened to her, he made a direct call to the head of the Bureau and raised hell," Buck said.

Hooper cocked his head and gave a small shrug. "Politics. The end result is, here we are," he held out his hands to indicate both of them. "Hope we can work together on this."

"Sure," I said. Bloody fat chance, I thought. I work alone.

He clapped his hands together and rubbed them vigorously for a second. "All right then, let's get to it," he said, pulling a notepad and pen out of his jacket.

Buck hadn't moved since she'd walked into the room. There was something odd about how still she stood, like a statue. Nothing about her moved except her eyes. It was even more pronounced compared to Hooper, who practically vibrated like he'd mainlined coffee.

As if to prove my point he clicked his pen several times before asking his first question.

"Hotel security told us you work for Ms. VanSusstern. Bodyguard, right?" he said.

"Right," I replied.

"For how long?" he asked.

"Just under three weeks."

"You ever work for her before?"

"First time," I said.

"Where was the rest of your security detail?" Buck asked.

"I work alone."

Hooper looked at me over the rims of his glasses. "Seriously?"

"Yes." It was a lie, but I couldn't tell them about the rest of my team. Like me, they weren't human, but unlike me they couldn't pass for it.

"That seems strange, for a client of her caliber."

I said nothing, just looked down at him evenly.

He held my gaze for a few seconds then clicked his pen rapidly again and jotted something on his notepad.

"Doesn't seem to be working out too well for you," he said.

If he'd still been looking at me, he would have seen the growing smolder in my eyes.

"Had she received any threats in the time you were with her?"

"No, but she had before I came on board. That's why she hired me."

"Any idea who from?" he said.

"Nope. Anonymous letters, no prints, untraceable. I've got them at the hotel. I'll get them to you."

"Have they produced any leads?"

"Anonymous. No prints. Untraceable," I repeated flatly. I was getting annoyed at my time being wasted, and not trying very hard to hide it.

"You think they have any correlation to the attack and kidnapping?"

"Possibly. Not enough information to answer that right now."

"Do you know the men who attacked you?" he asked.

"I didn't get a good look at them. They broke my nose as soon as I walked into the suite. I couldn't see much after that."

"Ouch. That must have hurt," he said, writing more notes.

"Not compared to a forty-story fall into a pool," I said.

"Yeah, not your day."

Buck cocked her head and stared at my face, the rest of her remaining motionless.

"Your nose was broken? Doesn't look like it."

There was something in her tone that raised the hairs on the back of my neck. Her sex appeal faded into the background as my instincts shouted out a danger warning and I put myself on guard.

"Fast healer. Runs in the family," I said.

"Fortunate," she replied.

Hooper scanned his notepad then continued. "You told hotel security there were six of them in the room?"

"Yep," I said with a nod.

"How do you know that, if you couldn't see?" he asked. He was getting less friendly with each question.

"I said I couldn't see much."

"Police found no sign of forced entry. Any idea how they got in?"

"I don't know but bet your ass I'm gonna find out, and I need to get started."

I moved toward the door. Hooper didn't get out of my way so I stopped and purposely towered over him, letting him feel my height advantage. "We done here?"

"For now. You're not planning on leaving town, are you? Cause that wouldn't be a good idea." He craned his neck to look up at me, still smiling but it was decidedly unfriendly now.

"Are you telling me I'm a person of interest in Annalisa's kidnapping?"

"Everyone is. Until they aren't," Buck said.

She didn't sound friendly, then again, she hadn't from the start.

"It's just a little suspicious," Hooper said, "You're her newly hired security. You're working alone. No forced entry into the room. You identified six assailants, but you said your nose was broken and you couldn't see. Except your nose doesn't look broken."

"I was also nearly thrown to my death."

"There is that," he said, staring up at me over the rims of his glasses.

"Yeah. There is," I said, my voice cold as an ice pick.

"Here's the thing, though, you're still alive. Up and walking no less. It's unbelievable."

"So, if I'd died, you'd think I was innocent?"

"Not necessarily," Buck said.

I shot her a glare as cold as the ice pick of my voice.

"You don't know me, so you have no idea how ridiculous what you're suggesting is. The last thing I'm going to do is leave town. The men who did this, I'm going to find them, and I'm going to bring Annalisa home safe." I left out the part about killing them.

"It's gotta sting, having her taken from right in front of you like that," Hooper said. He'd officially moved from unfriendly to asshole.

"I've got work to do. I'm leaving."

I sidestepped around Hooper and found myself almost eye to eye with Buck. She'd covered four feet with silent, casual speed. Sexy.

"We expect your full cooperation in this investigation."

I smiled, flashing my well-developed incisors. "I'm sure I can live up to any expectations you have, Agent Buck."

Her expression didn't change a hair. "I doubt that, Mr. Ddraik. Most men can't."

"I'm not most men," I said, retracting my smile. If she was going to be a bitch, I could easily be an ass. "We want the same thing, don't we? Annalisa's safe return. It's why you're here, isn't it?"

"Yes, it is," she said.

"Then I'll share any information I find if it will help your investigation."

She tucked her card into my jacket pocket.

"Be sure you do."

I strode around her toward the door.

"It wouldn't be wise to be uncooperative, Mr. Ddraik," she said. It was a warning and a threat.

I slammed the door in response. Childish I know but hey, I'm only five hundred.

CHAPTER FOUR

Outside the hospital I grabbed a cab and headed back to the Saint Marque. My damp clothes clung to my skin uncomfortably. I prided myself on looking sharp, a holdover from growing up a raggedy peasant. Right now, I looked like a half-drowned rat. Embarrassing.

I stared out the window and mulled sourly over the mess of the situation. What the bloody hell was a Half-kin doing working with Vanatori? Their sole mission is to try and kill my kind. You'd be more likely to see a python playing with a puppy than a Half-kin and the Vanatori working together. How do I get Annalisa back safe and fast? Why did the Feds think I might be involved? Who did that short, bald, shit stain Hooper think he was, questioning my competence?

I've seen more combat than any soldier on the planet. I've fought in every major war since the Hapsburg-Valios Wars in Europe, right up to recent combat in the Middle East. I've done mercenary and black ops work the world over. I'm an expert marksman with every type of gun you can think of and a master of every kind of martial arts system you can name, plus a few you've never heard of. If it rolls, floats, or flies, I can pilot it. I can bench press a car. Like a Honda Civic, but it's still a bloody car. I'm Batman on steroids for Christ's sake.

How the hell did I get ambushed in the room? I remembered walking in and the crack of my nose breaking as something heavy hit my face, but everything before that was vague and blurry. With my heightened senses I should have heard or smelled the Vanatori in the room as soon as we got off the elevator. Long before that though, I should have felt the presence of the other Dragon. All Half-kin have a kind of Dragon radar, and mine should have lit up like a flash-bang before the elevator even reached our floor.

Then there was the most important question. Why did they take Annalisa in the first place?

It had been a horrible end to a great evening. After two weeks of non-stop business grinding she'd wanted a quiet night with minimal company. She'd asked me to join her for dinner, and I'd been happy to oblige. She was the rare client whose company I actually enjoyed without it requiring a paycheck.

She'd regaled me with stories of growing up as a child of the world. Never attending a formal school, but tutored by the finest teachers, which her parents' immense wealth made accessible. After getting a doctorate in economics at Harvard she spent five years traveling the world on her own, just to experience it, usually with not much more than a backpack. When she stepped into the corporate dynasty that was her birthright, she improved every division, subsidiary, and acquisition she touched. When she took over the company, she had earned it, and the admiration of everyone in it. She had a huge set of balls and wasn't afraid to swing them. I respected the hell out of her for it.

Just the idea that they might hurt her had me wanting their heads on spikes. Killing her hadn't been their objective though, she would have gone off the balcony with me if it were. Ransom was a possibility, but I doubted it. Not with the players involved.

The hairs on the back of my neck stood up. I glanced out the back window. It took a few seconds, but I spotted the tail. Grey sedan, hanging back about three car lengths. The Feds I'd bet. I focused on the license plate and committed it to memory.

"Eighteen even," said the cab driver, breaking the silence.

We were back at the hotel. I must have hit my head a lot harder than I thought. I had just missed most of a twenty-minute cab ride lost in thought. At least I'd spotted the tail. I wasn't completely off my game.

I handed the driver a twenty and got out. As I strode across the lobby toward the elevators, someone called out to me, sounding very surprised.

"Mr. Ddraik?"

Kevin the security guard headed toward me from the front desk, looking as shocked as he sounded.

"What are you doing here?"

"I'm staying here. It's where my dry clothes are," I said, as I punched the elevator call button.

"No… I mean, yes, I know that. I mean, shouldn't you still be in the hospital?"

"People keep asking me that," I said, "I can't figure out why."

"Maybe cause you fell forty stories into a…"

"That was sarcasm, Kevin," I said dryly.

The elevator pinged and the doors opened.

"I don't have my key. Could you get me into the room?"

"Sure," he said.

We got on and he slid his key card into a slot on the panel. He punched the fortieth-floor button and the elevator hummed upward.

"I'm just amazed you ain't hurt, sir."

His drawl sounded much more pronounced now that my hearing wasn't so fuzzy from smashing my head.

"A little," I replied, indicating my sling-clad arm. It had finally begun a steady tingling.

"After the fall you took? That's it?"

"I've got a killer headache," I said with a grin. "I want to thank you for saving my life," I stuck out my good right hand and we shook. "I'm in your debt, Don's as well, and I take that seriously."

"I was just doing my job," he said humbly.

"Well done. Are the police still in the room?"

"No, they left about an hour ago. Room's still sealed as a crime scene though. We moved all your stuff to the suite across the hall, hope ya'll don't mind. We transferred your old room's phone number into the new suite. Detective told me to inform you that they put a trap and trace on the line in case the kidnappers call with demands."

"I need to see any security camera video you have," I said.

We stopped outside the door to the new suite, "I already went over the footage with the cops. We didn't see any of the men you described."

"I still want to see it."

My description of the men had been intentionally vague. They hadn't seen those faces, which were so clearly burned into my memory. It would've been easy for the cops to miss them.

"I might find things they missed."

"No problem, but it's boring stuff," he said as he raised his key toward the electronic lock.

"That a master key?" I asked.

"Yes sir, opens every door in the hotel. All security have 'em. Way ahead of you on this one. We ran a computer interrogation on the lock. Only people who'd used keys were you, Mrs. VanSusstern, and housekeeping. Cops questioned the housekeeper for a good hour, maybe more. Sent her home around two am."

Kevin was still ranking high on my professionalism scale. He slid his key into the card slot and unlocked the door. As it opened, I heard four distinct clicks from inside the room, faint but clear to my ears.

It was Shrill. As happy as I was to hear him and know he was inside, the clicks were a warning signal. They meant 'intruder in the room.' I switched to battle-ready caution in about half a second.

I stepped in front of Kevin and practically forced his hand off the doorknob. It was abrupt and disrespectful. He stepped back with a surprised look on his face.

"I'll call your office when I'm ready to start going over the footage," I said dismissively. I held the door open just wide enough to fit my body through it. I was positioning myself as a shield, not wanting Kevin to be in any danger from what might be inside if it jumped me. My debt of gratitude to him hanging heavy over my head.

His expression went from surprised, to angry, to stoic all in a matter of seconds.

"Affirmative, sir."

There was condescension in the way he said sir. I knew immediately the kid had been military. He backed away a few steps with a bit of chest out swagger before turning and walking away.

I closed the door and looked around. The suite was almost identical to the one we were in before. The living room was large and elegantly decorated. The master bedroom was down a short hallway to my left, the second bedroom and dining room were to my right.

I inhaled deeply. The whole place was permeated with an earthy, sharp odor. There was a sweetness that lay on top of that scent, like it was trying to cover or mask it.

"Hurry along Randall. Chop, chop!"

The voice came from the master bedroom. It was male, nasally, and high-pitched. The kind of voice that gets annoying fast. The bedroom door was ajar, a sliver of light coming through the crack.

Battle-adrenaline dripped into my system, pushing my pain into the background. I rolled my shoulder, it still made me grit my teeth and wince. If this was going to be a fight, I would be doing it with a bum wing. Bloody hell, I hadn't even gotten to change my clothes yet. My muscles coiled and ready to move, I braced myself and pushed the door open with my foot.

I blinked a few times to make sure I was seeing the man in front of me correctly. Flamboyant would have been a massive understatement. Mind you, I lived through the French Baroque and Renaissance periods, so that's saying something.

He was straight-up Adonis beautiful. Standing about six-seven, his overly tan body was all steel-braided muscle with not a lick of body fat. I could tell this because his outfit consisted of white leather thigh-high boots with five-inch heels, extremely small and obscenely tight white booty shorts, and a white leather trench coat, which was adorned with a plush white fur collar. Tight around his neck was a diamond choker necklace at least two inches wide and probably worth more than the gross domestic product of some small countries. Matching diamond bracelets adorned his wrists. On his head was, I kid you not, a tall white stovepipe hat with a blood-red rose pinned to the side of it. Cause sometimes a giant stovepipe hat just isn't flamboyant enough on its own. Long blond hair pulled into a tight ponytail draped down his back. Several strands of it were woven into thin braids and tucked behind his long pointed right ear. He stared at me with large blue eyes that were so bright it looked as if there was light coming from behind them.

I would have called him a gay elf, for the outfit, but an elf's sexuality is an amorphous thing. Not easily categorized, changeable on a whim, and ultimately self-serving. My immediate guess was that he was from the White Clan of elves, but I was doubtful. The Whites are very pale, surprising I know, so the tan didn't make sense.

He stood with his right hand resting gently on his hip, his thumb hooked inside the seam of his shorts. Dangling from his index finger was a glass sphere about the size of a softball, which hung at the end of a diamond-encrusted chain.

"Hello Randall, we've been waiting for you. So thrilled you're finally back! Oh darling, what happened to your arm? Soooo sad," he said, devoid of any real sympathy.

One sentence was all it took for his voice to annoy me.

In his left hand he held Shrill by the throat. He's part of the inhuman team of mine that I couldn't tell Hooper about.

Shrill's a drake, distant cousins to Dragons. They're born looking like big lizards but eventually sprout wings and grow to about the size of a Clydesdale. They have the chameleon-like ability to blend into their surroundings, rendering themselves effectively invisible, and can also emit ear-splitting howls loud enough to easily shatter glass. It's why I named him Shrill. I'd hatched him from his egg myself.

"Put him down," I said, taking a step forward.

He put a finger to his lips and pursed them exaggeratedly, as if actually thinking about it. "No, I don't think I will."

Shrill's normally black scales were mottled through with white, and the ridge of spines that ran down his back was flattened against it. Both signs of pain and distress. I kept my face calm but inside I was furious. My circle of trusted friends is very small. If you hurt them, you better bloody believe I'm gonna hurt you back.

"I won't ask you again," I said, taking another step.

"Please don't. You'll bore me. I hate being bored."

Everything about him changed in an instant. The high pitch left his voice, replaced by a hollow, cold tone. His skin darkened to a deep shade of blue, covered in swirling grey tattoo patterns across his chest and arms. He wasn't a White, he was a Blue.

The muscles of his forearm rippled as his grip tightened on Shrill's throat. His clawed hands grabbed helplessly at the elf's forearm, and his long prehensile tail thrashed in the air.

"Snapping his neck might ease the boredom. It would be easy to do. Quick too," his eyes narrowed, daring me to move.

"You're a Darkling," I said, taking a step backwards.

There are four major elf clans. White, Red, Green, and Blue. Darkling is slang for the Blues. In general, elves are smart, strong, fast, magically adept, and very secretive. With the Blues, take all the aforementioned then throw in deceptive, violent, and occasionally batshit crazy. They're dangerous as hell.

"Indeed I am... Dragon."

He said the word slowly, drawing it out. At least his voice was far less annoying now.

"Good, you know what you're dealing with," I said.

"Why do you think I have such a firm grip on the little dear's neck?"

"Why the glamour?" I asked.

"Please, darling. I can't walk around with blue skin and not draw attention to myself, now can I?"

"Yeah, you're the picture of subtlety. Why the glamour for me, I mean?"

"First impressions are ever so important," he said, blasting me with his smile. "Be honest, I look smashing!"

"You really don't want me to be honest. Who are you?"

"Nerufane, of the Wight."

That caught my attention. The Wight is just one house, within the Blue Clan. They make their home in the UK, where I grew up.

"You're kind of far from home."

"Oh, you know luv, just on holiday. Checking out the local sights and hot spots."

"My hotel room is a hot spot?"

"Hardly, dumpling, but I hear you know the most fabulous people," his voice rose back into the annoying zone as he relaxed.

"You wanna maybe close your coat," I said.

If you think 'hung like an elf' is supposed to mean small, think again. Trying to talk to this guy with his junk staring me in the face was off-putting.

"Jealous?" he replied, swishing his hips.

"Not even a little. What do you want?"

He didn't close his coat.

"So pretty, yet so dense. I should think it would be obvious. I want Annalisa."

"Come again?"

His smile bloomed back into full wattage. "I want you to get her back, then give her to me."

"What makes you think she's missing?"

I wanted to see how much he knew. Not that I could trust it. When it comes to manipulation and deceit there are few better players amongst the supernatural than the Blue Elves. Even the greater Fae are wary of dealing with them, and they're legendary for their trickery.

"Come now, Randall, do you think me a fool?"

"You probably don't want me to be honest about that either."

Shrill choked again as he retightened his grip.

"I was here when she was taken by the White Dragon."

He knew a lot.

"And Vanatori, no less. Such wonderful madness, isn't it? It truly boggles the mind."

"You were here when they came into the room?" I said.

"Just before. I chose to leave when they arrived. Unfavorable odds. I did get this dear as consolation though," he shook Shrill a little.

"And you think you could have taken Annalisa, from me?"

"Well, the Hunters did it, cupcake. So how hard could it be?"

Mother fucker! Before I could stop myself, I'd taken three steps towards him.

He backpedaled and dropped the glass ball from his hand. It fell to the end of its short diamond chain, liquid sloshed inside it.

"This is Eriel glass, Dragon. Renowned for its ability to hold intense heat when brought in contact with an open flame."

I put the brakes on my forward motion.

"This sphere is enchanted to burst into flame should it be broken. Combined with its natural properties that's enough heat to vaporize water almost instantly. If a naiade happened to be trapped inside…" he let the words hang.

"Drop," I said.

Drop's a water sprite or naiade. He's the other part of my non-human team. His normal state is basically a solid humanoid puddle, but he can take any form of water he wants to, from ice to vapor.

He and Shrill were always somewhere in the room watching Annalisa, with her being none the wiser. Shrill disappearing into the background, Drop hiding in one of the plants, or a sink, or toilet. He's kinda weird like that. She had eyes on her 24/7, even if it wasn't always my eyes. This gaudy fuck-tard was the reason neither of them had been able to warn me about the attack, dammit.

"Is that the little puddle's name? He didn't have a chance to tell me before I put him in here."

He began to swing the sphere around his finger in a looping circle.

"I want Annalisa. You are going to find her and bring her to me. If you do not your companions are going to die."

This is why I preferred to work alone. Friends can be used against you. He had two of mine. Fuck me. At least I knew he didn't have Tat. Something didn't make sense though, he'd come to get Annalisa on his own originally, why was he trying to force me to do it for him now? Unless...

"You're limited," I said, narrowing my eyes at him as I took a few steps back.

He'd played his hand. It was stronger than mine but now that I'd seen his cards, I knew I had some leverage.

"You don't have what it takes to get her yourself, now. If you did you wouldn't be blackmailing me to do it for you."

His smile faded.

I pointed at Drop and Shrill, "If you kill them, you'll owe me blood debt. Your payment for that will be steep." It would be his death and he knew it.

"I'll play your game for now, but if you seriously want an exchange for them when I do get her, you're going to tell me why you want her."

It was the only card I had to play. He furrowed his brow in thought and frowned. Then he pursed his lips and let out a high-pitched peal of nasal laughter.

"Now, now, Randall. There's no need for us to be enemies in this venture."

"I'm inclined to disagree," I said.

He caught the looping sphere in his hand and cradled it gently as he lowered Shrill and eased his grip on the drake's throat.

"Consider them insurance. I mean them no harm, so long as you assist me."

My face revealed nothing, but I breathed a sigh of relief on the inside.

"Why do you want her?"

"Oh, muffin…" he said with a sigh and condescending smile. "You don't know who she really is, what she is?"

I didn't hide the confusion on my face, or the gears working in my head too well, apparently.

"You really don't. Randall, Randall, Randall, it's so sad."

My temper flared, and I took a step forward in spite of myself. I stopped short as his diamond necklace and bracelets started to glow with a soft orange light.

"Oh bollocks," he said, his eyes narrowing in frustration, "I have to go. You must find out what she is on your own, I'm afraid. I will tell you this, she's not human."

Say what?

He pulled the rose off his top hat, pressed it to his lips, and then tossed it to me. As it sailed through the air it began to change shape. What I caught in my hand was a red crystal rose.

"When you have her, Randall, speak my name to the rose, and I shall come to you."

The glow from his jewelry began to pulse, getting brighter on each beat. The light flowed inward across his body covering him in an orange cocoon.

"You have three days, and then it will be too late. For her, and for your friends."

The light completely enveloped him, retracted in on itself to a tiny pinpoint, and disappeared with a small flash.

CHAPTER FIVE

That was different.

Wherever he'd gone, I was almost certain it wasn't into one of the realms. I'd never seen a doorway that looked like that.

The realms are where most of the supernatural live, and there are a lot of them. Wyrm, home of Full Blood Dragons, Sidhe, the Realm of the Fae, Asgard, Olympus, the Circles of Hell (ick), just to name a few.

Earth and the Material Plane are separated from the realms by a barrier that is either razor-thin or oceans-wide, depending on your perspective. Walking through it is no more difficult than thinking about it, if you know how. If you don't, you might as well be standing on Earth trying to jump to the Moon.

Nerufane had been taken somewhere by that orange glow, but my gut told me he was still on Earth. He probably used the same trick to get into the room as well.

Three days? There was something significant happening then, but I couldn't remember what. I closed my eyes to focus, and it hit me. Annalisa's fiftieth birthday.

The porno-elf had said I didn't know what she was, and as much as I didn't want to admit it, he might be right. With all the supernatural players interested in her all of a sudden, I had to consider the very real possibility that she might not be human.

When I take on a client, I always spend a week or more looking into who they are and the job they want me to do. The research I had done on Annalisa... I grimaced. Don't kid yourself, Randall, you slacked. It only took me a day to take her on, and it wasn't because of the job, that was for damn sure. Babysitting a human wasn't exactly exciting, or any great challenge... ahem, usually. It was a big payday, and while I'm never one to turn down adding to my hoard that didn't really matter, I'm already rich. Most any Half-kin my age is.

Honestly, this was my mother's fault. Not literally, the woman's been dead for hundreds of years, but Annalisa reminded me of her, and that's all it took.

On the surface they looked nothing alike. Annalisa was a petite five-six, and olive complected. She was pretty but not beautiful. My mother was the product of Scottish genealogy. She had been unusually statuesque for her time, five-eleven, and shaped like a proverbial hourglass. Her stunning porcelain face topped with a long, wild mane of dark red hair.

Both women held themselves with a confidence bordering on regality. For Annalisa, that had as much to do with her upbringing as it did her current station in life. For my mother, whose station hadn't been much higher than poor country girl, it was just an intrinsic quality. She had a spirit that made her a force of nature. That similarity hadn't caused me to make such a haphazard decision, though. It was something far simpler.

"The eyes," I said out loud, surprised by how wistful I sounded to myself.

They had the exact same eyes. Pale amber, almost gold. Shot through with blue streaks and so piercing they could make you feel as exposed and vulnerable as a baby, or as calm and safe as if you were wrapped in a warm blanket on a cold winter night. One look into those eyes had made me ache with loss, and all I wanted to do was protect her and keep her safe, because I saw my mother in them. That's why I'd done such a piss-poor job of vetting her.

In my defense, if you knew my mom, you'd cut me some slack. Go ahead, call me a momma's boy, I dare you.

Ok, what did I know? Annalisa was the only child of Carlyle VanSusstern IV and Kali Dagher. He was Norwegian and a shipping billionaire. She was Indian and of equally impressive wealth, owning an electronics conglomerate. When she was twenty-six, her parents died in a plane crash over the Aegean Sea, and Annalisa inherited the family fortune. Now forty-nine, she controlled an empire with additional interests in global real estate, mining, and banking. What had I missed? A lot it seemed.

I stepped out onto the balcony, put my fingers to my lips, and whistled three short blasts. If Tat was within a mile or so radius, she would hear it and come back. It's old-school, but it's not like she can carry a cell phone. I waited a full minute but she didn't show. I knew she'd seen something, or someone, that she felt was important enough to follow, and gone after them. I wasn't worried, at least not yet. If she hadn't come back, she had good reasons for it, and she could handle herself. I wouldn't bring her into the field with me if she couldn't. Obviously, I couldn't tell short, bald Fed man about her either.

I had to get out of these stupid wet clothes. In my room, I threw the ruined suit in a pile on the floor, took a quick shower, then went to my closet. I put on a black Hugo Boss three-piece suit, over a white Brunello Cucinelli dress shirt. No tie, too easy to use against me in a fight. A white silk handkerchief went into my jacket breast pocket, and black socks and gleaming black Ferragamo oxfords went on my feet. I looked at my reflection in the mirror, running my fingers through my hair with a little gel to style it just right. If I wasn't me, I would have wished I was. The green eyes looking back at me were more angry than cocky though.

I found my leather weapons case leaning against the wall in the closet. I thumbed the lock tumblers to their proper numbers to open it. My thoughts turned with the tumblers to the White Half-kin. That was the only thing I knew for sure about him.

Dragons come in two major orders, Chromatic and Metallic. Each order has different families. There are seven families in the Chromatic order, Red, White, Black, Green, Blue, Yellow, and Orange, and each family has traits or abilities specific to its color. His all-white eyes were a trait unique to his family line and a dead giveaway.

The lock popped open, but I just sat there, stuck in churning, angry thoughts. *He had taken someone who was in my care.* My anger was directed at myself, far more than at the Half-kin or Vanatori. I'd failed in my oath. Being in a Dragon's care is no small thing. You're protected by him until the job is done and the agreement is formally ended, or he's killed protecting you.

I jerked open the case and pulled out one of the many guns inside it. A Sig Sauer P226 40mm pistol. It was shiny stainless steel with custom red ivory grips. I took out three magazines. One I slapped into the gun, racking the slide to chamber a round. The other two went into holsters that I slid onto my belt at the small of my back. I took off my jacket and shrugged into a shoulder holster, grimacing through the pain in my protesting shoulder. I slid the gun home and put my jacket back on.

I took out a small, hand-carved wood ring box. Inside it, resting on a small red silk pillow, was a thick, black-metal ring, inlaid with tiny runes, and set with a large yellow gemstone. The gem sparkled when it caught the light just right because of a tiny living flame that danced inside it. I'd named it Incindis. It could blast a jet of white-hot flame two or three times per charge, depending on how long each blast lasted. I'm overanxious for the cooler Dragon things that come with becoming a Full Blood, and breathing fire is pretty damn cool. Just because I can't do it on my own yet didn't mean I couldn't resort to alternative means. I slipped the ring on my right index finger.

The last thing I pulled from the bag was a Ka-Bar five-inch throwing knife. I slid it into a slim leather sheath and strapped it to my left ankle.

I picked up the crystal rose Nerufane had given me.

"If you're listening," I said to it, "If anything should happen to my friends, you'll never be able to run far enough, or fast enough, to escape me."

I don't have a lot of friends, it's safer that way. I'd learned the hard way over the years that friends can be used against you in my line of work. The ones I do have I hold very close to my heart. Woe be to you if you fuck with them, and the porno-elf had gone way over the line of fuckery.

I put the rose inside the case and locked it, then put it back in the closet. I called the security office and told Kevin I'd be down in about thirty minutes.

"Ready whenever you get here," he said coldly, and hung up.

I couldn't blame him for being short, I'd been an asshole at the door. He hadn't known it was for his own safety.

I pulled a black-wood walking cane out of the closet. It hid a hand-forged Wakizashi sword, basically a short katana, that was over three hundred years old. It was sharp enough to slice through bone as if it were soft butter.

Well-armed and looking like a million bucks I headed out of the room and up to the roof.

CHAPTER SIX

There had been no sign of forced entry into our old room. So how did they get in? They didn't fly in for Christ's sake. I had a theory.

I took the stairwell up to the rooftop access door. Ignoring the 'Authorized Personnel Only' sign I shouldered through the door and stepped onto the roof, into cool morning air. I spotted a camera mounted above the door in a little bubble casing. I gave it a quick wave and noted the time, 8:32 am.

In its early life the Saint Marque had been an office building, it was gutted and remodeled to its current status as a hotel less than ten years ago. The roof was an open, flat expanse, covered with AC units and exhaust vents. It was strictly utilitarian and not for guests.

The rooftop walls rose up about four and a half feet above the floor, forming a structural abutment that doubled as a designed guard rail. The top of the abutment angled up into a point to prevent anyone from standing on it, for further safety.

I found the spot above our original suite and stood still, opening up all my senses and taking everything in for a moment. Then I turned in a slow circle, inhaling deeply. I caught the acrid smell of burnt tobacco. I let my nose lead my eyes to the smell. I spotted the butt jammed against the wall of the abutment. On the ground around it there was a mass of different footprints. Not enough for five men, looked more like three judging by the different shoe patterns.

I picked up the butt. Marlboro. I stood and was about to stretch over the abutment and look down toward the suite, when I saw that the paint on the wall had been scored away, revealing grey stone underneath. There were two marks about an inch apart, each about a quarter inch wide and covered in rope fibers. I looked behind me. There was a metal ring drilled into the wall of the elevator shaft structure, directly across from where I stood. It was dull grey, thick rolled steel, a loop about three inches in diameter. I walked over and gripped it with my good left hand and pulled, not with everything I had but still more than a normal man could muster. It held firm. I put a lot more oomph into a second yank, and it still held.

I swiped my foot across the ground at the base of the wall, and it left a mark through fresh cement dust accumulated there. This thing had been drilled in recently. Like last night recently.

I went back to the abutment wall and craned over it to look down to the suite's balcony, about twenty feet below, tops. The ring was a perfect anchor point for a climbing rope. Easy to throw it over and rappel down onto the balcony. Smart, though it still didn't explain how they beat the security cameras.

I was about to pull myself back over the abutment wall when I saw something fluttering in the wind. A hair was caught on a piece of framework about two feet down on the outer wall. I stretched for it and grabbed it gently in my fingers. It was dirty blond, long, and straight. I put it underneath my nostrils and inhaled, closing my eyes to better focus on the smell. An acrid, sharp stink. The smoker. I dangled it close to my eyes. It still had a root. Gotcha. I pulled the handkerchief out of my breast pocket and put the hair securely inside it, then refolded it and placed it back in the pocket.

I headed toward the stairwell door but stopped before I went through, staring at the camera with a frown. How the bloody hell did these guys go ghost on every camera in the hotel?

There was a plastic ring at the base of the bubble that covered the camera. It screwed onto a plate that was drilled into the wall and kept the bubble covering in place. I reached up and unscrewed the ring, then removed the cover. Inside was a small high-end camera. Piggybacked on top of the camera body was a cylindrical metal device. It had a wire trailing off of it which had been spliced into the camera's power line. Two little lights were on the top of the device, one pulsing a steady green, the other dark. It was getting power but apparently not doing anything if the dark light was any indication. I had a guess as to what it did.

I reached up to touch it. This proved to be a mistake.

I don't know if I screamed, or if it was the shrieking sound of electricity surging through my ears that I heard. My body convulsed, my vision went white, and I was hurled backwards.

When my head cleared, I could smell charred skin, and tears blurred my vision. I wiped them away and found myself flat on my back blinking up at the sky. I was about four feet away from the door. The skin on my left hand was a raw angry red. This was really not my day.

I took a few deep breaths then pushed myself to my feet. I wobbled for a moment until my equilibrium steadied, and then I moved back to the camera. The device had fried itself and melted the camera to slag. Booby trap and self-destruct all in one. I don't know how many volts I had been hit by, but I knew a normal man would be in the hospital after the jolt I had just taken. I needed to make sure that didn't happen. I had to warn Kevin and his staff in case there were more of these devices on other cameras around the hotel.

CHAPTER SEVEN

The security office was down in the basement of the hotel, two floors beneath the lobby level.

It looked like almost every other hotel security office I'd ever seen. A large storage locker stood against the far wall, flanked by a shelving unit next to it. A desk sat next to the door, cluttered with two computer monitors and random office supplies. An old couch and small coffee table took up the middle of the room.

Kevin stood from his seat at the desk when I entered.

"Mr. Ddraik," he said curtly.

"Two things," I said, looking him in the eye, "First, back at the room, I was a dick because I thought I heard someone inside. I didn't want to put you at risk. That's why I gave you the quick brush-off."

His eyes got a little wide.

"Was there?" he asked, genuinely concerned.

If only he knew.

"No, I was just being paranoid, but after the night I've had I'm sure you understand why."

"Understandable, sir," he said, nodding. He relaxed his shoulders and deflated his chest, his pride soothed.

"Second, I think your cameras have been compromised."

He frowned, "About the cameras, sir…"

"Three, stop calling me sir," I said with a slight grin.

"Sorry si… Mr. Ddraik," he countered my grin, "Southern raising. Force of habit."

"I was guessing Marine habit."

"Army, Airborne Ranger," he said, chest puffing with a different kind of pride. "About the cameras. They stopped working about ten minutes ago. At least a bunch of them did. They just went black. I've rebooted the software three times since, but it hasn't worked."

My getting flash fried was the reason for that I was fairly sure.

"It won't," I said.

I quickly explained to him what I had found on the rooftop camera.

"Is the stored footage still accessible? Can you pull up the feed?" I asked.

He sat back down at the desk and used a mouse to open a window for the feed. It was all black, as he'd said.

"Yes si… yes. It's stored on the hard drive."

"Rewind the rooftop camera to about 8:45," I said.

With a mouse click he brought up a twenty-four-hour time bar and rewound it to the right time. The black was replaced by recorded footage. On the screen, my recorded image was just unscrewing the camera cover. Kevin clicked on the small camera feed window and dragged it over to the second monitor, where it filled the screen. Several seconds later, we watched me take the electric jolt. The image lasted long enough to show me flying backwards in midair, my face contorted in pain. Pretty sure I was screaming.

"Holy Jesus!" Kevin blurted, "Are you all right?"

"I'm fine. It was like a Taser." If a Taser and a lightning bolt had an evil bastard child.

"Oh shit!" he blurted again, a sudden panicked look on his face. He grabbed for a radio sitting on the desk. "Kevin to Don, Kevin to Don!" there was a silence. "Don!" Kevin shouted into the radio.

"What's up partner?" came Don's voice through the receiver.

Kevin exhaled, relieved. "Don't touch any of the cameras."

There was a brief pause, "What? Why not?" Don replied sounding confused.

"Just don't! They might be booby-trapped!" Kevin almost shouted.

"What are you talking about?"

"Just come back to base, I'll explain when you get here. On the hustle, buddy."

"Copy that, en route."

"I sent him to take a hands-on look. He'd have a heart attack if he got shocked by one of those things," Kevin said, looking at me with relief.

He rewound the footage and we watched it a second time.

"Damn. What zapped you?"

"A device attached to the camera. I wanna check something, can you view multiple camera feeds at once?"

"Yeah. Lower quality cause they're small though."

"Doesn't matter. Do it and rewind to thirty seconds before I got zapped."

He did and then let the footage play. As I'd guessed, all the feeds went black at the same time. The only cameras still working were in employee areas. Places where guests would never go, or need to worry about being seen.

"Were your cameras serviced recently?" I asked.

"Lemme check."

He rolled backwards in his chair to the storage locker and pulled out a white three-ring binder. He flipped through a few pages and then stopped.

"Two weeks ago, our vendor came out and installed a software upgrade on the office computer here," He nodded toward the system on the desk. "They also did a routine hardware check on all the cameras and the power supply and router downstairs."

Routine my eventually scaly ass.

"You got a service invoice for the job?"

He flipped to the back of the folder and shuffled through some papers, pulling out a yellow sheet.

"Here it is. That's weird," he said with a frown as he scanned the document.

"What's weird?"

"This isn't the normal vendor for our security system," he said, his brow furrowed. "Oh, here it is. Dyna-Tel Security subcontracted out the job due to a manpower shortage. They gave us the software upgrade for free because of it."

"Who was the subcontractor?"

There was a business card stapled to the invoice. He pulled it off and handed it to me. It read: *Sword & Shield Security*.

Don hustled into the office. "Hey buddy, what's the story?"

Then he looked from Kevin to me, with a shocked face. Probably because he couldn't believe I was standing in front of him, not still in the hospital. Not to mention looking so damn sharp.

"Mr. Ddraik?" he said.

"Surprise," I said, grinning. I extended my good hand, "Thanks for saving my life."

He took it hesitantly at first as if he thought I might break, then shook it firmly.

"Well sure. I mean, somebody falls in a pool you go in after them, right? It's what you do."

"I'm in your debt. I intend to make good, we can talk about how later."

I tried to release his hand, but he held firm for a second, looking up at me.

"I don't mean to tell you your business Mr. Ddraik, but you sure you shouldn't have stayed in the hospital?" It was said with fatherly concern. I'm sure he thought he was older than me, which was cute.

"I'm all right. I'm tougher than I look."

He held our grip for a beat longer and then nodded, apparently satisfied.

"Can you show me that power supply and router, Kevin?" I said.

"Yes, sir," he said. He sprang to his feet and grabbed the radio off the desk. "We'll be in the basement, Don. Tell the next shift not to touch the cameras if they come in while I'm gone. Call those Feds, tell him we found something they need to look at. This way, Mr. Ddraik."

I followed him out. Don stuck his head out of the office door behind us.

"You still didn't tell me what happened?"

"I'll show you when I get back," Kevin said over his shoulder.

He opened a stairwell door and we went through, descending four flights to the bottom of the stairwell, exiting into the lowest level of the parking garage.

The ceiling-mounted fluorescent lights were muted and dim. Several of them flickering weakly in a losing struggle to stay alive. Two were out completely.

Thick concrete support columns rose from floor to ceiling, running across the length of the garage. There were ten cars parked randomly around the floor in numbered spaces. It could have held about forty, so it felt empty.

Kevin led me toward the far side of the garage, where we turned a corner and entered a small alcove that wasn't visible from where we had entered, a lone door stood in front of us.

Kevin fished in his jacket pocket and came out with his master keycard. He swiped it through the lock and opened the door. The tang of burnt metal and plastic hit my nose, along with the unique smell left by an electrical fire.

"Oh shit, you smell that?" Kevin said, yanking a fire extinguisher off the wall.

"Yeah, but don't worry, it's out already." My nose told me.

He lowered the extinguisher but didn't put it back until he was sure. The power room was about ten by ten and full of computer equipment. A portable AC unit sat on the floor next to the server racks, blowing cold air onto the system.

"Power box?" I asked.

"Over yonder," he said, then shook his head, "Man, I'm never gonna make it as an actor until I get this damn twang under control. I mean, over there."

He pointed at the far wall, where the smell was coming from. It was lined with three large electrical boxes. Big metal conduits ran out of the boxes and up through various holes in the ceiling.

He moved to the biggest electrical box and opened it. It was filled with wires, switch boxes, and circuit breakers. In the bottom right sat another rectangular-shaped box. Metal conduit snaked out of the top of it and up through the larger electrical box.

"Camera power's in there," he said,

I jerked it open. Inside was a long row of circuit breakers, ten of which had been tripped to off positions. The main power junction box, sitting below the circuit breakers, was covered in black soot. It had come from the fried, blackened mess of the device that had been wired into the top of it. It had been bigger than the one that zapped me. At least three times the size.

Maybe the Fed's techs could figure out something from the smaller devices on the other cameras. It didn't matter though, I was fairly sure that they were remote-accessible flash drives, used to store camera footage. When the Vanatori had entered the hotel, they had turned them on. The stored footage took over the live feeds and they walked right through the hotel without ever being captured on camera. They wouldn't have needed more than five minutes with a coordinated effort. It was military-level tech. Especially that lightning bolt booby trap feature.

Kevin whistled under his breath when he saw the damage. "That dog won't hunt," he said.

"What?"

"Sorry, southern expression. It's FUBAR."

I didn't respond. My nerves had begun to vibrate, the way they only did in the presence of another Dragon, and a strong scent hit my nostrils, something foreign that I couldn't identify.

Kevin mistook my silence for confusion.

"It's Army slang. Means, Fucked Up…"

"Beyond All Recognition," I said, finishing his sentence for him.

There was a pulsing sound that seemed to come from everywhere at once, like a giant single heartbeat. All the lights in the garage went out.

"What the hell's going on?" Kevin said from behind me.

"Things are about to get FUBAR."

CHAPTER EIGHT

The power room was still lit by a dim glow coming from all the computer equipment. Just enough to see clearly by. Darkness wasn't much of a problem for me though.

I stepped out of the power room into the garage and began closing the door.

"Hey!" barked Kevin, "What the hell are you doing?"

"Stay here," I said quietly, "It's for your own safety."

"I'm a goddamned Army Ranger!" he snapped back but in a lowered voice, probably instinctual because of his training. "I don't need you to protect me!"

I turned and put a hand on his chest, hitting him with an icy fighter's glare. If you're a UFC fan you know the look. I've had over four hundred years to practice mine.

"Stay. Here," I said.

Kevin didn't flinch, but he did look down. It was only for a second, but that's all it took. When he looked back at me his resolve had withered.

"Affirmative," he said, resigned but angry about it.

I pulled the door shut. The air had a faint hum to it that tickled my skin. There was magic at work, some kind of suppression spell was keeping the lights off. Noise was being damped along with the lights. My steps made almost no sound as I walked out of the alcove, and I couldn't hear the voices or moving cars coming from the upper garage.

I blinked twice, lowering a secondary lens over my eye. The pupil on this lens was vertical, like that of many reptiles. My sight snapped into the infrared range. All blooming heat sources and cold spots. It's another unique trait inherent to my family of Red Dragons.

I drew my sword from the cane and leaned the sheath against the alcove wall. My mind and body went into battle mode. Battle-adrenaline dumped into my system, and my already heightened senses became razor sharp. The pain in my shoulder didn't exactly stop but it became very distant. My movements became lighter and feline smooth as I glided into the garage, sword held ready and loose. A pulsing excitement surged through the pleasure centers of my brain. Like sex only better. You heard me, better. I lived for this.

Standing at the far end of the garage bathed in a fuzzy, shimmering corona of yellowish light was the White Dragon. He was giving off enough to see by, so I blinked back the infrared lens.

His long black hair draped across half his face. He wore a long white leather jacket with an untucked white button-down

shirt underneath it and black jeans and boots. A competi-
tion-grade composite longbow was in his hands, knocked with a
nasty-looking razor-tipped arrow.

I stalked to the middle of my end of the garage and faced
him, at about thirty yards apart.

"You gonna tell me your name?" I asked.

"Alamander. Well met, Randall."

His familiarity made my skin crawl a little. I wanted no
association with a Half-kin who would sell out his own kind and
work with Vanatori.

"Surprised you have the balls to face me alone. Where's
your posse?"

His body language changed. He seemed to sag in on himself a little, and his expression took on the same sad look I had
seen when I was going over the balcony.

"I am truly sorry for what the Vanatori did to you."

That surprised me. I hadn't been expecting an apology.

"What the hell were you even doing with them?"

"They believe I am something that I'm not. It was necessary
for me to allow it to happen, to maintain the ruse. I'm happy you
did not die."

"You really shouldn't be," I growled. "It means things aren't
going to go well for you. I want Annalisa back."

He sighed. "I know, but I cannot do that. I've come too far."

I took a few steps toward him.

"I'm not here to fight," he said calmly.

"Boy did you come to the wrong place."

I took another step as my right hand drifted down toward
my gun. I barely felt the protest in my shoulder as my blood sang,
ready to fight. He raised the bow in response.

"I've come to ask you to join me."

I stopped in my tracks. "Come again?"

"As an alternative to enmity, I propose alliance."

"Alliance in what?"

"Changing the destiny of Half-kin forever."

"How do you propose to do that?"

"I'm going to put an end to the senseless slaughter we inflict upon one another. In three days, a metaphysical door will become visible, and there will be a once-in-an-eon opportunity to rewrite our history and fix the unforgivable wrong done to us by our ancestors."

"What in the bloody hell are you talking about?"

"Annalisa is the key to unlock that door. I'm going to use her to undo the magic that binds us to the Test and destroy it forever."

"What?" I said. It was all I could get out of my mouth. I was dumbfounded almost beyond words.

"Every Half-kin will be able to take his birthright and become a Full Blood Dragon."

"You can't be serious." My voice sounded very small in my own ears.

I couldn't believe what I was hearing. Unbind the Test? Destroy it? That was impossible... wasn't it? The confusion was written all over my face.

"I have never been more serious. I'm going to free us all from our slavery to the Test and the unspeakable horror that it truly is."

My mind raced. It had to be bullshit, but... what if wasn't? Could I really become a Full Blood Dragon without the Test?

Every fiber of my being was screaming to hear him out, and he could see it.

"An amazing prospect, isn't it?"

I can't lie, it was, but I was miles away from believing him.

"How is Annalisa the key?" I asked.

"Imagine what we could accomplish together as a race," he said, ignoring my question.

That's when I saw it. The dangerous gleam in his eyes. Something I'd seen in the eyes of countless soldiers. Men who'd been pushed too far and crossed an inner line there was no turning back from. It was the gleam of madness.

"Imagine the worlds, the entire realms we could bring under our heel," he continued, his voice rising.

Madness combined with the mindset of a tyrant, fantastic. Full disclosure, the thought of becoming a Full Blood without having to take the Test was heady and intoxicating. It was also epically, disastrously stupid. The planet would be overrun by Full Blood Dragons, fighting each other for power and territory without a care for the devastation and death they were causing around them. Yet I was still rooted to the spot thinking about it, when I should have been attacking him. What if it really was possible?

"Annalisa, what is she?" I asked.

"All you need to do to find out is join me. If not, it must remain my secret."

I stared into the mad gleam in his eyes to keep my rational mind focused, fighting back the part of my brain that wanted to hear more.

"Let me get this straight. You want me to ignore the fact that she's in my care and join you in a plan that sounds like the mother of all fantasy stories, married to the father of all bad ideas, and just... trust you. The guy that helped get me thrown off a roof?"

"Yes," he said simply.

"No," I replied.

I jerked my gun from its holster. His bow came up in response, drawn and ready.

"You're insane. The Test exists to prevent exactly the lunacy you're describing. However sweet you try to make it sound, it's poisoned fruit. No deal."

"Pity," he said sadly, "You would have made a formidable ally."

"I make a worse enemy. Return Annalisa or die."

"I cannot."

His movement was so fast it was a blur. The arrow streaked at me in razor-tipped silence. I sidestepped and flicked the blade up, cutting it in half before it hit me. A second arrow was already on its way as I launched myself into the air towards him. It whistled beneath my feet, his aim too low for my leap.

I aimed at his center mass and fired three times. What should have been the echoing thunder of gunshots was muted down to almost nothing by the magic he was using. He was fast. I missed all three shots. My mind may not have been registering the pain in my shoulder, but it was still being affected by the injury. If I was at a hundred percent I wouldn't have missed three times, no matter how fast he was.

He dove, tucked, rolled, and came up with his bow knocked, firing as I landed from my leap. I ducked as the arrow streaked silently over my head then sprang upright and batted another out of the air before it pierced my chest. I had a fierce smile on my face as I raised the Sig to fire.

Alamander bounded up onto a car, leaving a white glowing trail from the aura surrounding him. As he moved, he fired another arrow and buried it in the barrel of my gun before I could pull the trigger. Son of a... Robin Hood, eat your fucking heart out. Respect.

I dropped the gun as he leapt from the car, trying to hit me with a flying side kick. I caught his leg and used his speed against him. Spinning him through the air, I flung him back across the garage toward the alcove. He hit the ground hard, his bow skittering away from him as he lost his grip. He slid across the floor and cracked his head against the bumper of a car.

The aura surrounding him flickered off when he whacked his head. The lights in the garage came back on and sound rushed back into my ears in a roar. It felt like the mother of all ear pops. Magic can play havoc with the laws of physics, but it can't entirely negate them. All the energy he'd pulled from the environment to mute the sound and light had to go somewhere. He'd surrounded himself with it, causing the glow. Conking his head had disrupted his concentration and stalled the magic.

It was all the opening I needed. As he tried to regain his footing, I leapt at him and slammed my elbow into the side of his head. As he crumpled I caught him by the lapels of his coat with one hand and hoisted him into the air. That's when I saw the necklace and pendant underneath his shirt. It was a large white stone set onto a silver backing, faintly glowing the same color that had been surrounding him. The source of power for his sound and light tricks, I was sure. I wasn't going to be able to hold him up and try to get the pendant without dropping my sword, and I wasn't doing that.

Instead I spun around and hurled him at the wall with all my might. It was about twelve feet behind us, and he cracked the cement when he hit it, then crumbled to the floor onto his hands and knees. He was gasping for breath as I stalked toward him.

"Where is she?" I growled. "I have no problem carving it out of you."

"She is beyond your reach," he spat. The glow drained from his pendant like liquid mercury and coalesced onto his right hand which he threw forward at me. I raised my sword at the last second.

The bolt of energy he unleashed slammed into me with brutal force. It hurt. A lot. I was thrown backwards, almost into the alcove. Stars swam in my vision and my teeth felt like they were vibrating in my jaw. I couldn't breathe.

I had dropped my sword, and it lay on the ground, just out of reach. The runes running the length of the blade, invisible before being hit by the blast, glowed vibrant green, having absorbed a lot of the energy. I might have been burnt to a crisp if they hadn't.

My brain screamed for me to get up, but my body wouldn't listen, it wanted to take a nap. I tried to rise but was stopped by Alamander's boot slamming into my chest. Breathing got a whole lot harder.

He reached down and lifted me, then slammed me into the wall and slammed his fist into my face. My head rebounded off his fist and cracked into the wall. He let me go, and I collapsed to my knees. My vision was ten shades of blurry, as blood ran from my mouth and nose.

"This saddens me. I would have preferred you by my side."

"It's not too late for you to give up," I rasped, blood spraying.

He raised his fist and energy began to swim around it, flowing into it from the pendant, building in intensity. I was rethinking my decision not to take it from him.

"Your defiance is admirable, but useless."

I managed to focus my vision and look him dead in the eye. *Go to hell*, it said.

"I had not wished for things to end this way. I will savor your Death Roar."

"Choke on it, you son of a bitch."

His fist crackled with energy as he drew it back, aiming at my face.

Before he could throw the killing blow, Kevin slammed into him with a brutal full-body shoulder tackle, cracking his elbow into Alamander's neck, while screaming at the top of his lungs.

Alamander flew backwards into the corner. His hand whipped over his head and smashed into the floor. The coalesced magical energy exploded into it, gouging a deep scorched hole in the concrete. He howled in pain as the magic backlashed, sending blue-white energy crackling up his arm to the pendant, shattering it to pieces.

Both of us stared at the wild-eyed Kevin for a beat as he stood between us. I moved first.

"Hit the deck!" I yelled.

Kevin reacted with a soldier's instincts and dropped flat on the floor. I raised my hand at Alamander as the word *Incindis* flashed from my mind to the ring and a gout of fire erupted from it, roaring over the prone young man.

Unfortunately, my warning shout gave Alamander time to react as well. He crossed both arms in front of him and hissed a word that I didn't understand. A black, round portal opened beneath him, and as the fire engulfed him he fell through it, taking the flames with him. I couldn't tell what effect they'd had on him, it happened so fast. As the flames subsided Kevin raised his head, looking at me with eyes as wide as saucers.

"Jesus H. fucking Christ a 'mighty!" he whispered.

If I hadn't shouted out a warning Alamander would be flambé and Kevin would just have been collateral damage, the price of a battle won. But I owed him a debt of gratitude, there was no way I could've allowed myself to be responsible for his death. I couldn't believe he'd had the stones to attack Alamander, not if he'd seen any of our fight. Now I owed him twice.

"What the fucking hell just happened?!" he blurted, his voice a shaking mix of shock and disbelief.

I flopped over onto my back and groaned. This was going to be one mother of an explanation.

CHAPTER NINE

Kevin stood up and stepped cautiously over to the spot where Alamander had been, peering at the crater left by the energy from his hand. He was mumbling under his breath and moved as if the floor might fall out from underneath him at any moment. I suppose in a way it just had. His mind was trying to process the impossibility of what he'd seen with the fact that he'd just seen it.

"I hit him!" he said, "He was right there! Where the hell'd he go?" his drawl was heavy now as panic overcame his vocal training. He whirled toward me. "And where'd that fire come from?"

I stood up slowly. My body shouted at me to leave it alone and stay lying down. I ignored it.

"This is gonna take some explaining," I said. Not to mention some serious suspension of disbelief on your part, I thought.

"So explain! Where did he go? Why was his hand glowing like he was holding a... a... ball of lightning?" A confused look snapped across his face as the words came out of his mouth. He was already starting to doubt his own eyes and hear how crazy he sounded. To himself anyway, not to me.

"Seems impossible, doesn't it?"

"It is impossible!" he shouted. "Was it some kinda military Taser or something?" He said it more to himself than to me.

"You saw it, didn't you?" I said calmly, looking at him with a level gaze.

"Yes. No! I mean... I don't... maybe?" his wide eyes pleaded with me as he stood there, helplessly confused.

I walked over to him and put a hand on his shoulder. "Breathe. Nice and slow. You saw what you think you saw."

"I did? Yeah, I did," he said, a little more calmly. "You saw it too?" he asked, losing the look of wide-eyed panic.

"Yeah," I nodded, "I did."

"So where did he go?"

I sighed and released his shoulder. "Good question."

"Man, I got no idea how to explain this damage to anyone," he said, running his shaking hands through his hair.

"Let's get out of here and you won't have to, no one will be the wiser," I gave him a grin, trying to calm him more. "I can expense it to Annalisa when I get her back."

"Yeah, sure," he said, still struggling to process what had happened.

"You said you were getting off shift soon, right?"

He looked at his watch. "I'm off now, actually," he said, nodding.

"Good. Go upstairs, get some air. Wait for me out front, and I'll do my best to explain to you what just happened."

His eyes locked on mine.

"I'm not crazy, right? We both saw that shit?"

"We did and you're not. Go."

I pushed him toward the stairwell door. He walked through it in a daze. As soon as he was gone, I slammed my fist into the wall, cracking the cement. *Fuck!* I just had my ass handed to me. I lost focus when Alamander started talking about unbinding the Test. It was a nearly fatal mistake. One that put me twice in debt to Kevin. I'm not gonna lie, that was kind of embarrassing.

Get your shit together, Randall. I moved, quickly clearing the garage of the remnants of our fight. Arrows, his bow, and my ruined gun. Then I grabbed my sword sheath and hustled back up to my room to change out of my second ruined suit in less than ten hours. I had to get the hell out of this hotel. The damn place kept trying to kill me.

Alamander's words kept running through my head like a freight train. *End the Test. Become a Full Blood.* I couldn't quiet them, or the undeniable lure of the possibility.

The Test is what every Half-kin spends his life fighting for. Killing for. Earning the chance to take it is the reason for our existence, and only one from each Family of Dragons will get that chance.

Tens of thousands of years ago Dragons created the Test to regulate their own numbers. There were too many of them, causing too much chaos and destruction, and they knew it. Wyrm was a constant battleground as Dragons fought each other for everything. It had made them and their realm a pariah to all other beings of the supernatural.

Through the Test, Dragons bound all their future offspring to what they considered the weakest realm. Earth and the Material Plane. Only allowing themselves to breed with mortal creatures of the planet. That meant almost exclusively humans, but there were a few exceptions.

The magic used in that binding fundamentally changed what we were as a species. Before the Test, Dragons were asexual. Full Bloods of the right age would self-impregnate, generate a clutch of eggs, lay them, hatch them, and protect their young for a time. No mating necessary. Eventually the parent would leave their young to fend for themselves and survive, or die, on their own. The problem was they were great survivors, which is why there were too many of them. After the creation of the Test there was only one Full Blood Dragon of each Family who was capable of breeding.

We Half-kin kill each other to keep our numbers down, only the eventual survivor gets to take the Test. It's not fun having to kill my own kin, but the reward is more than worth it. The last one of us standing will get to enter Wyrm for the first time in his life to take it. The Test itself, what taking it entails, is the most guarded secret in all Dragondom. All we know is, pass and transform, or fail and die. The one thing we do know, if you pass you stop shooting blanks and can finally have sons of your own.

Could Alamander really unbind us from it? There was a part of me, larger than I'd care to admit, that wanted to believe it was possible. My rational mind knew it would be insane to do, my lizard brain, however, that deep-seated, instinctual animal side, was hungry and salivating at the thought.

I pulled a black T-shirt over my head and stood in front of the mirror. The reflection staring back at me looked shaken. Failing Annalisa and almost getting killed twice in less than twenty-four hours isn't what had me rattled. It was that hungry part of my brain.

CHAPTER TEN

I emerged from the hotel dressed for action not style. Black biker boots, black jeans, and a black T-shirt. An armored, high-tensile strength nylon motorcycle jacket covered the T-shirt. Black, of course. I still looked great, but it was function over fashion.

I had the jacket zipped up slightly to conceal my shoulder rig. It housed a Colt Limited Edition Silver Dragon 1911 .45 caliber pistol. The gun was chrome with a Dragon etched into the slide. The wood grips were textured to resemble scales. Colt made only two hundred of them, each one owned by a Dragon. Badass, right?

Kevin was waiting at the end of the one-way driveway in front of the hotel. He was leaning up against a flat black Ducati 1098 sport bike that sported fire engine red rims. The kid had good taste in fast. He was out of uniform, wearing jeans tucked into black motorcycle racing boots and a white T-shirt.

"How you doing?" I asked.

"What was that guy?" he said, his stare intense.

"Not sure who he is but I'm..."

"I didn't ask who, I asked what," he said, cutting me off.

Shit. If I called Alamander out as a Dragon, then he might figure out that I was one too. I didn't want him knowing about me, but I still wanted to give him some answers. Pickle.

"You don't think he was human?"

"No sir," he said firmly, agitation in his voice. "I was trained to kill, Mr. Ddraik. The way I hit him should have snapped his neck in at least two places. Done it before."

He lowered his head a little at the admission before looking me in the eye again.

"I..." I started, but he cut me off.

"Then you lit him up with some sorta flamethrower!"

"He..."

"Then he fucking disappeared!" he almost shouted.

"Lower your voice and calm down," I said, putting the steel of command in my voice.

He wasn't confused or uncertain now, he was angry. I knew I wasn't the one he was angry at, I was just a convenient target. He stepped into my face to keep his voice down but lost none of his anger.

"Was he a... a vampire?" he hissed quietly at me.

I blinked at him, surprised the word had come out of his mouth.

"Was he?"

"Do vampires exist?" I asked, raising an inquisitive eyebrow at him. I wanted a better grasp of where this was coming from.

"I've seen one!" he said it with such conviction that I knew he was telling the truth. The semi-hysterical look in his eyes said the knowledge had been tearing him up.

"No, he wasn't a vampire," I said calmly, "And you're right, he wasn't human either."

He took a step back, exhaled a deep shuddering breath, and visibly relaxed a little, as if some huge weight had been lifted off of him. His eyes watered up and he blinked furiously to keep the tears from falling. He leaned against his motorcycle and folded his arms tightly across his chest.

"I knew it! I goddamned knew I wasn't crazy," he said softly, mostly to himself. He looked at me after a few seconds. "Are you? Human, I mean."

"We're not talking about me now."

I owed the kid a debt of gratitude twice over. That didn't mean I trusted him, but I was obligated to help him and it looked like he could use some. I didn't know how long he'd been carrying around knowledge of vampires, but it clearly had him walking on a narrow ledge of sanity that he'd been trying hard not to fall off of. He desperately needed to talk about it with someone who believed him, and I could alleviate some of my debt to him by being that person. I had to admit, I was curious.

"You saw a vampire?"

He nodded, lips pressed together tightly. A tremor wracked his body as he remembered it.

"Bloody scary motherfuckers."

"Pretty sure that's the understatement of all time."

"Tell me about it."

He rubbed his eyes, took a deep breath, and started talking. The words poured out in a flood.

"We opened the door, and the vampire attacked us. It ripped my CO's head off and tore the squad to pieces! It was drinking blood from his neck when it…"

"Whoa, slow down, soldier," I interrupted. "What door, where? Start from the beginning."

"Sorry. It's hard," he took a few slow breaths and then started again with more focus. "We were in the Afghan mountains above some tiny desert town in the middle of less than nowhere. It was supposed to be a hiding place for terrorist fighters, according to our bullshit intelligence. We found a maze of caves, but they were empty. Like no one had set foot in 'em for years, empty. We were about to call it a bust and bug out when we found the door."

"What kind of door?"

"Way in the back of the last cave. Looked like a bunker door, heavy steel set into the bare rock wall. It had symbols carved all over it. None we'd ever seen in country before, so we couldn't read 'em. No kinda lock on it that we could find. My CO decides to blow it open. The air that came outta this room…"

He shivered, wiped his eyes again, then continued.

"It smelled like death on fire, all rot and decay. It was so bad most of us puked our guts as soon as it hit us. The CO took four guys in and the rest of us held guard. They were in there about two minutes when we heard screams and gunfire. Mostly screams. Then they stopped."

He came to a choking halt, his bloodshot eyes were haunted.

"Take your time," I said.

"The silence was scarier than the screams and shooting. Before any of us got our wits straight enough to move, the CO's head got tossed through the door. The thing, the vampire, followed after it. It was holding his body and sucking on his neck."

His stare was a million miles away, looking into nothing, but he continued in a raspy voice.

"Christ, the stink of it was horrible. It was nothing but decaying skin and bones, covered in rags. It didn't even look like it should've been able to stand. Its face was covered in the blood gushing from the CO's neck and I saw its fangs. Not just two but a whole mouthful. It threw the CO's body at me like he was a rag doll, but it hit me like a horse kick. I went down and lost my gun. The guys shot it and it went down, and then got back up. When it attacked them, it moved so fast. Like, like…"

Words failed him. He just shook his head for a few seconds until he found his voice again.

"Nothing human moves that fast. It ripped the rest of the squad apart with its bare hands even though they kept shooting it. I'd gotten the CO's body off me and was trying to get to my gun when it turned to me and screeched. That sound… I froze. I didn't even realize I'd drawn my combat knife."

Kevin was trembling, and if he realized he had tears running down his cheeks he didn't care anymore.

"The fucking thing leapt at me, and all I could do was raise the knife up to my chest. It impaled itself on the blade, right through its heart. Completely blind luck. It fucking died right on top of me while I was looking into its eyes. They were all white. Just like the guy down in the garage."

No wonder he thought Alamander was a vampire.

"You were the only one still alive?" I asked.

"One of my buddies made it. The thing had torn him up pretty good but not critically. I patched him up and we sat there for hours trying to figure out what to do. We knew no one would believe us. We were staring right at the thing, and we didn't even believe it."

"What did you do?"

"We used some C4, blew the caves. Then made up a story about them being booby-trapped with explosives. Said we were positioned outside as lookouts and that's how we survived. The squad was too deep inside to recover. The story played, and we were both so fucked up from the experience that we were discharged and sent home with PTSD."

"How's your friend doing?" I asked.

"Committed suicide three months after we got discharged," he said quietly.

"Sorry," I said.

I could see the questions forming in his eyes and I raised a hand to cut him off.

"I know you want to know about me and what you saw in the garage. You have my word I'll give you answers, just not now. I've got to get to work finding Annalisa. Just know that I believe you, you're not crazy, and you're going to be ok."

He wiped his cheeks and then thrust out his hand. I shook it.

"Thank you, sir."

"Thank you for the save. Again. Go home and get some rest," I said.

I watched Kevin put on his helmet and rumble away on his bike as I waited for my car. I felt for the kid. I've lost a lot of friends in combat over my long lifetime. It sucks. A lot. It's why I mostly work alone these days. Which reminded me that I hadn't heard from Tat. I was getting worried about her, but with no way to reach her, worry was all I could do at the moment. Right now I had to go see a wizard about a hair.

CHAPTER ELEVEN

A valet pulled my car into the drive. A new Jaguar F-Type S model. V8, British racing, green with a dark tan interior, lowered over gloss black rims. Fast and sexy.

It roared like a big cat as I steered it at highly illegal speeds through the streets of downtown. I was heading toward the art lofts district just east of Chinatown, which wasn't far and didn't really warrant Formula 1 velocity, but I wanted to see how good my tail in the grey sedan was. It had jumped on my six when I left the hotel. They weren't very good, it took me all of five minutes to lose them.

Alamander's words kept slithering into my thoughts like a hive of poisonous snakes. I forced them into the background. Finding Annalisa had to be my sole focus. Alamander was a major part of that equation for sure, but I couldn't let his claims distract me. No matter how enticing they might be.

I pulled into the parking lot of the Brewery Artist Lofts. The old Pabst Blue Ribbon brewery was turned into low rent artist lofts in 1982, and you had to be an artist to live there. Duncan was a hell of a woodcarver, in addition to being a wizard. Yep, a wizard named Duncan.

I opened my glove box and pulled out a clicker, opening the garage door to his parking space. He didn't have a car, and since I subsidized his supplies and tools when he needed them, I got parking privileges. The garage would have had plenty of room, but every space that wasn't reserved for my car was packed with wood and wood crafting supplies. It always felt like I was parking inside a Home Depot. He used his shop to craft powerful rune-warded doors for select clients.

I squeezed out of the car and shimmied along the side of it over to the door into the house. Keys for that I don't have. I have a lot of respect for a person's home and privacy. A man's lair is his castle, and Dragons are big on lairs. Besides, Duncan put the same security runes and wards on his own doors that he put on his clients'. If I tried to force my way in, they'd probably explode on me. Or worse. I did the polite thing and knocked.

There was a moment of silence, and then a deep, formal voice droned, "May I help you?"

"Open up," I said.

"Who's calling?" came the voice again.

"Open the door, Greg, or I will pull off your tail and feed it to you." I was in no mood for his shenanigans.

The voice uttered a few words in an archaic tongue I didn't understand. A line of runes flashed into luminous white light on the surface of the door, running down the middle of it from top to bottom, then disappeared just as quickly. The door swung open.

"Feed me my tail? That's a little harsh don't ya think?" Greg said, all the false base and formality gone from his voice.

He floated in front of me, an impish grin on his face. Literally. Greg's an imp. No, it's not his real name, but you try saying Greggoylarmayanoush all the time. Best believe you'd shorten it. He was about two and a half feet tall with skin that was varying shades of purple, and looked like it had the texture of smooth wood. His nose was flat and wide, his ears were long and pointed, and his deep purple eyes were abnormally large for his small head. He fluttered about four feet off the ground, little bat wings on his back flapping furiously to hold him aloft. He wore a blue LA Dodgers cap backwards on his head and matching blue shorts.

"Better than your head," I said, "Where's Duncan?"

"Bedroom. Sleeping one off."

"Shit. Just perfect," I grumbled, barging past him.

I strode into the loft. The garage led directly into the woodshop, a mass of work tables, racks, tool cabinets, and wood-working accessories. A light coating of sawdust covered the floor. I went through the sliding door that separated the workshop from the large, open floorplan living space, and powered toward his bedroom door on the far side of the room.

I pushed open the bedroom's sliding barn door to behold the sartorial splendor of Duncan Zachariah Weaver. He was passed out on his bed, surrounded by Penthouse magazines and empty beer cans. Wearing only a pair of long red boxer shorts with yellow smiley faces all over them, and white gym socks, one of which was dangling halfway off his foot. I mentioned sartorial, right?

I sighed. Sometimes it was hard to believe this was the guy who had fought by my side over a dozen times, and made my awesome flamethrower ring.

"He had a go of it last night," Greg said, fluttering up next to me.

I noticed that a large dollop of shaving cream had been sprayed in Duncan's open palm. Greg saw what I was looking at and shrugged at me innocently.

"Can't resist, can you?" I said.

"It's my nature," he replied, grinning.

Which was true. Imps are the merry pranksters of the Fae. They do it to get attention and, weirdly, as a way to attract friendship. They just don't know when to stop. I glanced at the heavy silver bands that adorned his wrists and ankles.

"Could get painful for you if he wakes up in a humorless mood," I said.

"It'll be so worth it though," his grin bloomed into a Cheshire cat smile.

"Your funeral," I shrugged and kicked the bed.

"Duncan, wake up," I said loudly. He stirred slightly and grumbled but otherwise didn't move. I grabbed the bed by the footboard and lifted it two feet off the ground.

"Duncan!" I shouted as I dropped it.

The bed slammed to the ground and he half shrieked as he woke with a start, looking around wild-eyed.

"Whuzzat? Earthquake!" he slowly focused on me, "Red?"

"I need your help. Right now," I said.

"My help?" he said disorientedly, "Why? What for? What time is…"

I kicked the bed again.

"Focus!"

He rubbed both hands across his face and smeared the shaving cream all over half of it. There was a thump beside me. I looked down to see Greg rolling on his back in uncontrollable hysterics, his little wings beating on the floor.

"Not helping," I growled at him.

"Sorry," he managed to squeak out through his laughter.

Duncan sprang to the end of the bed and grasped the footboard, the clean half of his face flushed crimson red with anger.

"You little bastard!" he yelled at the laughing imp.

Greg sucked in a breath to try and stop laughing. He was only half-successful, and little squeaks continued to escape through his pursed lips.

"I'll skin you to your bones, you…" was as far as he got. His shaving cream-covered hand slipped off the footboard and he tumbled ass-over-head onto the floor.

Greg exploded in laughter, flipping over onto his belly and pounding the floor wildly with his hands and feet.

"Oh my God this is priceless! I'm dying over here!" he howled through the laughs.

I was caught between frustration and wanting to join him. Had to admit, it was kinda funny.

Duncan was on his back, right next to Greg. With a glare he raised a hand and shaped his fingers into an arcane sign. His hand lit up in a yellow glow.

There was a sound like a giant bug zapper, and Greg's bands lit up with a bright yellow flash. His whole body went rigid, and he yowled in pain. Smoke wafted off the bands, or maybe from his skin, I wasn't sure. They weren't actual bands, or silver for that matter. They were the physical manifestation of the binding spell that Duncan had placed on Greg when he summoned him.

"Still think you're funny, ya little fuck?" snapped Duncan.

"Best. Prank. Ever." Greg whimpered, his body twitching.

Duncan was about to zap him again, but I hoisted him off the ground by his outstretched hand and the back of his neck before he could.

"You can throw him in the fireplace later if you want, but right now I need your help," I shook him slightly as I spoke, redirecting his focus to me.

"All right, all right, leggo!" he fumed. "Put me down! I got a bad enough headache as it is without you shaking me like a damn bobblehead!"

I put him down, and he promptly thumped Greg in the side with his foot, though not hard enough to hurt him.

"Go get me a beer and some aspirin, dumbass," he said to the prone imp.

Greg shook his whole body, like a dog shaking off water, and then his little wings flapped him into the air.

"Sure, boss," he said. He was giggling under his breath as he flew away.

This was their normal relationship, as twisted as that sounds. Duncan would never really hurt Greg, he needed him too much, and Greg couldn't hurt Duncan. Annoy, pester, harass, and infuriate, absolutely. When he'd bound Greg, in typical drunk Duncan style, he'd screwed it up a little. He failed to completely bind Greg's prankish nature, leaving him with limited free will. Greg could mess with Duncan whenever he was passed out or asleep, if he didn't specifically order the imp not to. The pranks were harmless but could get really messy sometimes. Shaving cream-covered face being a perfect example.

Duncan was short, five foot six tops. He had the ruddy complexion and bulbous nose of a heavy drinker, with deep wrinkles surrounding his eyes. He was stocky and broad-shouldered, with the remnants of muscle that once probably made up a good physique. It had pretty much all drifted down to his sizable gut at this point. He was hairy all over, except his head which was shiny bald. It must have all gone to his beard, which was long enough for him to have separated it into three thick braids.

He grabbed a T-shirt off the floor and wiped his face clean with it, then tossed it back where he'd found it.

"Love your boxers," I said.

"Shut up," he replied as he shuffled to a large double armoire and opened it. "Is this gonna be heavy lifting?"

"No, nothing too strenuous."

"Thank God," he huffed.

He pulled out a pair of black, wide-legged yoga pants and yanked them on, followed by an emerald green silk robe. He started to take shape as an actual wizard, though a kooky one to be sure. He opened the other armoire door, revealing four staves hooked to the inside of it in U-clamps. Each one was a different length, and all were made of different woods.

"What am I doing?"

"Tracking spell."

"You got something good for me to work with?" he said, rubbing roughly at his eyes.

"A hair, the follicle is still intact."

He nodded and pulled a blonde oak staff out of its clamp. It was about five feet tall and had a solid silver owl statuette sitting atop the head of it, its eyes inlaid with large purple crystals.

He reached back into the armoire and grabbed a black cowboy hat off a low shelf. It had several long, black feathers sticking out of the hatband. He plopped it on his head. Now he looked like he should have been holding an electric guitar instead of a wizard's staff. Wizyrd Skynrd anyone? It was his trademark hat, but I always gave him shit about it. He caught my look.

"Shut up," he grumbled and stalked out of the bedroom. It was impressive that someone so short could stalk. I followed him back into the living area.

The room was a testament to his craftsmanship skills. He had built two second-level mini-lofts within the space, having plenty of room to work with twenty-foot ceilings. One served as a library and the other held a handmade bar and pool table. The center of the room was dominated by a semi-circular couch of dark brown leather, with a large square coffee table sitting inside the curve of it.

He aimed the staff at the square table and muttered something under his breath. The eyes on the owl glowed, and a soft purple light enveloped the table, and it lifted gently into the air. He moved the staff to the left, and the table floated in the direction of his movement. He tried to lower it gently to the ground, but it slammed down with a hard thump.

"Fucking hell!" he winced, slapping a hand to the side of his head. "Greg, where the fuck are you, ya damn worthless lump!" he bellowed.

"I could've lifted that for you," I said. I was met with a glare and held up my hands defensively. "Never mind."

Greg flapped out of the kitchen with a tray in his hands. A bottle of Red Stripe beer and two aspirin sat on it.

"Right here, boss. Don't get your balls in a knot."

Duncan snatched the beer and aspirin off the tray, popped them into his mouth, and washed them down with most of the beer in one long gulp.

"Seriously?" I said, staring at him.

"Hair of the dog," he grumbled, "Speaking of, gimme," he held out an open palm.

I pulled the handkerchief out of my inside jacket pocket and unfolded it. He plucked the hair off it and walked into the space the table had been occupying.

There were two large rings of iron laid into the floor, shaped into concentric circles. Each ring was about two inches wide and covered with elaborate runes. Inside those was another inlaid double circle, one gold, one copper. Finally there was an inlaid circle of various gemstones. It was one mother of a summoning circle.

He knelt inside and placed the hair in the very center of the ring.

"You got sunglasses on you?" he asked.

I fished in another pocket, pulled them out, and tossed them to him. He placed them just above the hair.

"Grab me a nail out of the workshop, dumbass," he barked at Greg.

The imp zoomed out and returned a few seconds later with a dull grey nail.

Dunc placed it between the hair and glasses, then stood with a grunt and stepped outside of the circles. Taking a deep breath, he raised his staff and brought the end of it down into contact with the copper ring. There was a flash of light, and a ring of copper-colored energy rose upward from the circle all the way to the ceiling. The gemstones began to glow.

He closed his eyes and quietly recited an incantation, almost singing it. At the end of the incantation, he exhaled deeply. Purple energy wafted out of his mouth and into the ring. As soon as it entered the ring the energy was immediately sucked down into the hair, glasses, and nail. He removed the staff from contact with the floor. There was another spark of light, and the ring of energy dissolved into thin air.

I'm always kind of in awe of people who are adept with magic, and watching them use it can be transfixing. As long as they're not trying to kill me with it, that is. I mean, he just exhaled purple energy, how cool is that?

Duncan bent over and picked up the glasses and nail then sat down heavily on the couch. He rubbed at his temple with his free hand.

"I need another beer."

"Gotcha covered, boss," said Greg, zipping into the kitchen.

He handed me the nail and glasses. They tingled in my palm.

"Put the nail on any flat surface, and it will lead you right to the owner of that hair. Just follow the way it's pointing. The sunglasses will show them in a corona of purple light. Makes the mark easy to see if they're in a crowd."

"Nice touch," I said with an approving nod.

Greg returned and handed Dunc another Red Stripe.

"You're not totally worthless, numbnuts," he grumbled, grabbing the bottle. He took a long pull then nodded at Greg with a smile.

"I need one more thing," I said.

"And I need a nap!" he snapped.

"It's not magic. I need some deep background research on my client, Annalisa VanSusstern."

"The superrich broad?"

I nodded.

"Why can't you do it yourself?" he grumbled, "She's your client."

"She's been kidnapped. I'm using your spell to track the people who took her. I don't have time to do research right now."

"Remind me never to hire you as a bodyguard," he said snarkily.

"If you hadn't all those years ago, you'd be dead now," I said, quickly losing my patience.

Despite his sixty-ish appearance, Duncan was actually a hundred and fifty-two years old. Wizards are very long-lived by human standards, and I'd known him for over two-thirds of his life. It's why I trusted him.

"Always gotta hold that over my head, don't you?" he griped.

"Only when you're being a pain in my ass."

I yanked the cowboy hat off his head and tossed it up into the library loft, "Now you have to go into the library to get your hat, research while you're up there."

"Very mature," he said, glaring at me.

Greg flew off after the hat.

"Annalisa was kidnapped by a White Dragon, who was working *with* Vanatori. They threw me off a forty-story building to get to her. The crazy son of a bitch thinks she's the key that will somehow allow him to undo the magic of the Test."

"Crazy is right," he scoffed, "That's impossible."

"I hope to god you're right, but crazy or not, he absolutely thinks he can do it. Imagine what would happen if all Half-kin became Full Bloods, at the same time?"

He scowled, giving it real thought. Greg flapped back over with the hat and plopped it crookedly on Dunc's head. His expression darkened as he straightened it.

"That wouldn't be good."

"Understatement. Oh yeah, also, a Blue Elf kidnapped Drop and Shrill. He's using them as leverage to blackmail me into giving him Annalisa, when I get her back."

"Jesus. Sorry, Red."

He knew how much the little buggers meant to me.

"He told me she's not human."

"A Darkling's not a trustworthy source of information."

"Normally no, but White Dragon kidnapping and all."

"What's the deal with this broad?"

"That's what I need you to research, there's clearly more to her than I knew."

"I gue… wait, you got tossed off a forty-story building?"

"Yeah. It was buttloads of fun."

"How did you… never mind. Was that her hair?"

"No."

"Why didn't you just bring me some of hers? I coulda' tracked her directly."

"This isn't my first rodeo, Dunc. She brushes her hair once a week and wears it in a long braid at all times. The follicles in her brush were all too old to be any good, and housekeeping at the hotel is meticulous. There wasn't a usable hair of hers anywhere."

"Blood?" he asked.

"Dammit, Dunc, I thought she was human."

When dealing with supernatural clients it's common practice for me to get a sample of their blood, for just this kind of situation. With humans, asking for a blood sample is a great way to lose a client.

"All right, all right. What are her parents' names?"

"Carlyle VanSusstern, Norwegian, and Kali Dagher, Indian."

"Feather or dot?"

Being politically correct was not Dunc's strong suit.

"India, Indian."

"Anything else you can tell me that might be pertinent?"

"It's her fiftieth birthday in three days."

"That could mean something," he said, scratching his head. "There's something else in three days, can't remember what though."

He was talking mostly to himself as he stood and headed towards the library.

"Greg, bring me some coffee and make some pancakes and bacon. I'll be in touch when I've got something, lizard," he waved a hand absently in my direction as he went up the steps.

"Do not let him touch a drop of alcohol until he's done with this," I said discreetly to Greg.

"Do my best chief. I won't have any choice if he orders me to get him some," he shrugged.

"Do what you can. Water it down, it'll make a good joke."

Greg giggled.

"Ohhh, I like this plan. Gimme knucs!"

We bumped fists, and I headed to the garage, the tingling nail in my hand and the sunglasses on my face.

CHAPTER TWELVE

The nail was sitting in the cup holder in the center console. Its circumference was just slightly larger than the nail's length, so it was free to spin without sliding all over the place. It was currently pointing in the opposite direction I was traveling, which didn't matter to me at the moment.

The nail was a backup. I was playing the lead I had gotten at the hotel first, and heading to Sword & Shield Security.

Sure, I could track the one Vanatori the nail would lead me to, but my gut told me S&S was the Vanatori's cover. Going directly there and taking a chance on cornering the whole gang would yield better results, if I was right. If my gut was wrong, then I could use the nail to chase down the smoker and beat answers out of him.

Traffic bottlenecked as freeways merged, giving me time to think and start trying to put pieces together. I focused on the letters Annalisa had received. I'd left them in an envelope at the

87

hotel's front desk and told the Feds they could pick them up there.

They were made old-school style. Letters cut and pasted from dozens of different magazines and glued on plain white paper that could've been bought at a million different locations. They might have taken more time to make and more planning to deliver, but they were way better in terms of being untraceable. Computers leave digital footprints, handwriting can be identified.

They'd been given to her in public locations. Two at restaurants where waiters had delivered them by hand. One at an office building, as she was exiting after a meeting. A security guard had handed it to her. The waiters and the guard had all given different descriptions of the men who asked them to deliver the letters.

The point of the hand delivery was abundantly clear. It said you're vulnerable. I can get to you anywhere.

That's when I'd been called in. My recommendation had come from a White Elf prince I'd worked for in the past. I saved his life twice. Annalisa didn't know that. She knew him as the head of a huge venture capital hedge fund she did business with. He told her I was a man very capable of dealing with things unknown. She'd had a serious relationship with him in her past, which is why she trusted his word about me so absolutely.

The messages were short, confusing, and obscurely threatening:

> *'Life as you know it ends soon and you will be the cause.'*
> *'You will cause the death of worlds. It must be stopped.'*

*'All will die if your key turns the lock. Protect yourself, or only
your end will prevent it.'*
*'The end is coming. You cannot stop it if you remain asleep.
Awaken or worlds perish with you.'*
'Wake up or die you stupid bitch!'

That last one lacked the dark poetry of the others. It was just plain rude, really.

When I'd first seen them, it was easy to read them as death threats. Especially coming from the perspective of the scared woman who had given them to me. I remember her hand shaking as she handed them over. But not one of the damn things said anything about killing her.

*'All will die if your key turns the lock. Protect yourself, or only
your end will prevent it.'*

That note resonated loudly now, with the new information I had. It also gave credence to the claims that she wasn't human. Something that the person who wrote the notes apparently knew.

Here's the thing, if he'd wanted her dead why hadn't he just killed her? He obviously had no problem getting close to her. Alamander and Nerufane being the senders didn't make sense, they wouldn't have warned her when they had plans to kidnap her, and neither wanted her dead, or so they claimed.

In actuality, all leaving the notes had done was drive her to hire me, and having me around is counterproductive to trying to kill someone. What if that had been the goal? What if the note sender had known she was in danger from a supernatural threat and wanted to protect her? Hoping that she'd hire someone like me to do the job.

It was a big fucking 'what if.' With enough holes in it to look like Swiss cheese. Why didn't he just warn her himself? How could he know about the threat when she didn't? How could he know she'd have access to someone like me? More importantly, who the hell was he, and what were his motivations for protecting her? And why be so damn cryptic about it? It was Swiss cheese that smelled like rotten Limburger mixed with old fish, yet my intuition wouldn't let it go.

I put my intuition into the back seat as I pulled off the freeway. I wound quickly through some back streets into an industrial part of Burbank then stopped against a curb about two blocks away from the Sword & Shield building. It was situated at the end of a dead-end street in a row of old squat commercial buildings. All brick and mortar, none more than three stories tall.

S&S was two buildings. The front building was one story, the larger back building was two. The second story was an addition that looked like a prefab bolt-together job. A metal barn-shaped structure taking up about half the roof space.

I counted five security cameras on the front building. One above the front doors, two on each corner, one facing the street, and one facing the back of the building. They had their angles well covered, leaving my approach options limited if I wanted to keep the element of surprise.

They were separated from their closest neighbor by a decent-sized parking lot and an empty building with boarded windows and doors. I drove into the parking lot of the closest neighbor, a wholesale pool supply place, and parked in a spot at the back of the building next to three large garbage dumpsters that were pressed up against the wall.

I unleashed a small swarm of flies as I jumped up onto the lid of one of the dumpsters. The heavy plastic made a nice springboard, and I pushed off of it hard, launching myself up to the second-story roof of the pool supply building. Without hesitating I sprinted for the far side, and with a hard plant on the ledge I easily sailed across the twenty feet or so to the empty building's rooftop. Gravel crunched under my feet and dust flew as I landed.

The next jump wouldn't be so easy. It required clearing forty feet of parking lot to make the roof of S&S. Coming up short would send me crashing straight into a brick wall. Not appealing.

The shed only took up about half the roof, so I had plenty of room to land. Piece of cake. If cake were a forty feet leap onto a building full of Dragon killing psychos.

I secured the sword cane to my belt as I studied my target. The shed addition to the roof was about fifteen feet tall and maybe forty feet long, with a row of windows that ran along the side that faced me. A camera was mounted above the door into the shed, but I wouldn't be in its field of view until I was already on the roof. Those windows were a different story. Anyone looking out would see me coming. *If it's easy, it's not fun.*

I palmed my knife, tightened my grip on the sword cane, bounced up and down on the balls of my feet a few times, and launched myself forward. I was high in the air, at the zenith of my leap, when two men holding crossbows charged out of the shed onto the roof.

Bugger me.

There isn't fuck all for cover in midair. My best chance of a defensive structure would have been a random bird flying in front of me. Preferably an albatross, or a condor. A pterodactyl would have been nice. None of them appeared. Stupid birds.

The first man fired. His aim was as wild as the look in his eyes, he didn't even come close to hitting me. The second guy, his bald head gleaming in the sun, did much better. His bolt pierced my calf. The battle-adrenaline running through my veins dulled the pain to a distant searing sting.

I hurled my knife at the first guy and my aim was much better than his. The serrated blade buried itself hilt-deep into his thigh. Blood sprayed. He screamed, revealing a mouth full of gold teeth, and collapsed onto his back as his leg gave out.

I crashed onto the roof at the same time. The shock of the crossbow bolt had thrown off my balance, and my landing was far south of controlled. I slammed onto the rough surface practically face first, skin ripped and tore from temple to chin as I slid across it. Ignoring the pain, I got my hands and feet underneath me and scrambled behind a small air-conditioning unit.

I recognized both men from the group of assholes who had thrown me off the balcony at the hotel. All their faces had burned into my memory like a white-hot brand.

I swiped a hand across my face to clear the blood from my eye, drew my gun from the shoulder holster, and popped up, ready to fire. Baldy had grabbed Gold Teeth under the arms and was just dragging through the door of the shed. Despite my burning desire to drill them both right between the eyes, I thought better about firing outside in broad daylight, probably why they'd used crossbows instead of guns. Before he kicked the door closed Baldy looked at me, his jaw was clenched with the effort of dragging his friend, but his eyes were calm.

I grabbed the bolt, clenched my teeth, and yanked it out of my calf. It came free with an unpleasant tearing sound. It was barbed. Jesus on a stick that hurt, even with the battle-adrenaline flowing.

I drew my sword from its sheath and charged toward the door. I barely slowed my momentum as I launched a side kick at it with my good leg. The door cracked in two and snapped off its hinges.

Baldy had gotten halfway across the room with Gold Teeth. A substantial trail of blood flowed from his leg, and his face was awash with pain. Baldy still looked calm as he dragged his friend backwards. Had to give it to him, he was a cool customer.

My heightened senses took in the room instantly. Metal working machines, a portable forge, and work tables took up most of the floor space. Racks of weapons, swords, axes, and maces lined the walls, along with several upright gun lockers.

They were heading towards an open trapdoor directly behind them. Before I could move a man popped up into view through the door, a patch covering one of his eyes. The memory hit me like the blow to the face had, he was the son of a bitch who'd broken my nose. His eyes went wide when he saw me. Well, eye.

The battle-adrenaline screaming through my veins, I charged forward grinning like an insane clown. Gold Teeth looked back over his shoulder and saw Eye Patch in the trapdoor.

"Help us, Jimmy!" he screamed.

"Gimme the gun!" Jimmy shouted down to someone below.

I ignored Baldy and Gold Teeth, leaping over them toward the trapdoor, snarling as I flew. When I really put the Dragon into my snarl it sounds something like a cross between a wolf and a velociraptor. Jimmy was so startled that he almost fell out of the trapdoor, grabbing onto the edge to keep himself up.

I landed and dropped to one knee right in front of him, bringing our faces very close. My grin lost none of its insanity, but my glare was cold.

"I'll be down for you in a minute, Jimmy. Be patient."

I smacked him in the face with the butt of my gun. He fell and crashed into two men beneath him.

I smacked the metal bar that was holding the trapdoor open. It slammed shut with a bang. I turned and picked up a heavy wood worktable, probably about two hundred pounds, and upended it on top of the door. From below, a volley of bullets thundered into it.

I caught movement out of the corner of my eye. I turned and twisted as a thin metallic spear whistled past my side and stuck in the wall behind me. Baldy faced me holding two spearguns. He dropped the spent one, keeping the other trained on me as he dashed toward the gun lockers against the wall.

He'd left Gold Teeth in the middle of the room. I ran towards him as Baldy fired the second spear. I batted it out of the air with my blade. He dropped the speargun and started fumbling at the gun locker.

I got to Gold Teeth and yanked him up. He was losing consciousness, probably due to blood loss and shock, but he came to with a start and a terrified scream as I lifted him. I flung him at Baldy.

He'd gotten as far as opening the door to the locker but dove for cover as his friend sailed towards him. I missed, but I heard Gold Teeth's bones break as he bounced off the gun locker and hit the floor with a fleshy thud.

Baldy had circled back toward the door that led onto the roof. He wasn't trying to run even though he hadn't gotten to the guns. He'd armed himself with a large mace and shield, and stood his ground. He was a beefy dude, almost my height and probably about two-thirty.

"Throwing me off a building didn't work. You think you're gonna kill me with that?" I said, smiling coldly at him.

He scoffed, clearly not sharing Gold Teeth's fear of me. Let's see if I can instill it in him.

I whipped the blade through the leg of a metal work table, severing it completely with an accompanying blast of sparks. I waved the blade at him.

"Think how easily this will go through that shield, into skin and bone. Tell me what I want to know and I'll let you keep your legs and your life," I cocked my head thoughtfully. "Well, at least your life."

"We've killed your kind, you're nothin' special," He took a few steps forward raising the mace. "Our ancestors killed the winged monsters that spawned you."

I gut laughed out loud. I couldn't help myself.

His face twisted with rage. "What the fuck are you laughing at?" he demanded.

"Your ignorance."

Dragon Hunters killed Half-kin, not Full Bloods. The difference between the two is astronomical. They added the historical tales of wings and fire-breathing to give themselves the supernatural version of street cred. No Full Blood Dragon has *ever* been slain by a mortal hand, except in works of fiction and movies.

This schmuck seriously believed those stories were true.

"Liar!"

"You've got balls, but they're where your brains should be," I said, still laughing.

A powerful wizard, very different from a normal mortal, was the only thing to give a Full Blood pause in terms of the human realm. Merlin killed several if the stories are true.

"Tell me where Annalisa is, or I'm gonna kill you, all of you, and burn this building to the ground."

"We're not afraid to die for the cause, beast. The wizard protected us against you!"

"Wizard?" *Wait, what?*

In response, he charged at me. Steel in his spine, tapioca for brains. Still, there was a confidence in his eyes that I couldn't quite figure out. As he got close his shirt fell open, revealing a pendant around his neck. A greyish-looking stone dangling from a thick silver chain. It glowed with a pale blue light that was getting brighter with every step he took toward me.

How the fuck did he get a Scalestone?

I suddenly felt as if I'd been dunked into the deep end of a swimming pool. I was overcome with that slow, low gravity feel you get when you're at the bottom of the deep end and then try to walk or run. You just end up going nowhere fast. Simultaneously I was struck with the very powerful urge to yawn.

The mace came arcing down at my head. Instead of fighting the low gravity feeling I moved with it bending down into a crouch. The swing whistled past my ear and the mace cracked into the floor. If dick nuts thought some low gravity and sleepy feels was going to give him an advantage I was about to show him how wrong he was.

The force of his swing threw him off balance, putting him in a perfect position for my counterstrike. I whipped my knee up over his lowered arm and slammed it into his nose. Baldy shrieked as bone shattered and blood sprayed. The blue glow from the pendant winked out, the swimmy feeling disappearing along with it.

My leg was above his arm, and I brought it down, along with the full weight of my body, directly onto his elbow. Snap, crackle, pop. He crumpled to the floor with a gurgling scream.

"You don't mind if I take a look at this, do you?" I said, yanking the chain off his neck.

"Gaugghh!" he replied.

The Scalestone was set onto a heavy silver pendant, grey in color and shot through with streaks of white and blue. It had been cut into an oval with rough edges. The stone and pendant were covered in tiny etched runes. The blue glow had faded to a fuzzy dot of light, pulsing ever so faintly from its center. It wasn't an actual stone, it was part of a petrified scale from a Full Blood. They were rare as hell and uniquely good at being enchanted for all kinds of things anti-Dragon because of the Dragon DNA in them. They could be imbued with all kinds of capabilities for defense, protection, and tracking.

"A wizard gave this to you?" I asked, pressing my foot into his mangled elbow.

He screamed from the pain, unable to speak. I kept up the pressure so his buddies downstairs got a long earful. *Yours is coming soon, assholes.* I eased off the pressure and brought the tip of my sword to his eye.

"Wizard..." I repeated. "Is his name Alamander?"

He sucked wind for several seconds before hissing in a cracking voice, "Yessss!"

It confirmed my suspicions that he'd somehow disguised his true nature from the Hunters.

"You guys are in for one hell of a rude awakening," I chuckled.

I grabbed Baldy and dragged him across the room to where Gold Teeth lay unconscious, his wound still bleeding from the knife buried in it.

Under Gold Teeth's shirt I found an identical chain holding another Scalestone, this one cut in a rough diamond shape. If these two had them, the rest of the Hunters might as well.

My thoughts snapped back to the night before when I'd gotten bushwhacked in our hotel suite. Walking down the hall toward the room everything had been so peaceful and calm. As I'd opened the door I was in the middle of a yawn, abnormal to say the least. It takes a lot to make me tired, even under extreme circumstances. Watching over Annalisa at a high-powered business dinner was the exact opposite of extreme.

The memories came back in a rush, clear as day now. There'd been no sounds, no smells. How had I missed that? I should have heard sounds of the elevator moving, water running, TVs on in other rooms. I should have been smelling food from the two room service trays we passed, the sweet traces of perfumes lingering in the air, the stink of cleaners and polishes used in the hallway, and the bodies of the men lying in wait in the room, especially the smoker. Sure as hell I should have sensed Alamander. My Dragondar should have lit up like a Christmas tree before I got two steps down the hall. I'd sensed nothing, and walked into the room with a big stupid yawn coming out of my face.

The Scalestones. Alamander, or someone, had enchanted the damn things to block Dragon senses. I'd been magically bamboozled.

I rubbed Baldy's shiny head. "That's a load off my mind," I said to him. He didn't notice because he'd passed out.

As much as I wanted to use this information to sooth my bruised ego the truth remained the same, I hadn't been good enough when it mattered, and Annalisa had been kidnapped. I didn't feel like a completely incompetent clod now, but Scalestones or not, I'd still failed her.

"Let's go see your friends," I said, bitterly as I lifted Baldy and tossed him across my shoulder. I yanked my knife out of Gold Teeth's leg. Blood gushed freely from the wound. He'd bleed out soon, blood debt paid in full.

There were at least three Hunters below, maybe more. It had gone from screaming agony to dead silence up here. That had to be playing hell with their minds. I still had a lot of whoop-ass left in my can, and I was ready to dump it all over their heads. I headed downstairs.

That's where things got FUBAR.

CHAPTER THIRTEEN

I jumped down from the roof on the side of the building facing the railroad tracks, so no one would see me, then I walked through the front door holding Baldy in front of me as a human shield.

We entered a small waiting room, plainly decorated with a cheap black leather couch and magazine-covered coffee table. There was a counter with two computer monitors and a couple of chairs behind it. The walls were adorned with posters promoting various security products. One of them, I quickly noted, featured a smoking hot, bikini-clad red head holding a Taser. Solid marketing.

A door behind the counter, with a camera mounted above it, led deeper into the building. Painted above the door in off-white, just slightly darker than the white of the walls, was a Templar Cross. The Vanatori considered themselves knights, and the cross was a symbol of protection.

I stepped close to the door and focused my senses. Whispered voices filtered in from behind it, but I couldn't make out what they were saying. There were no smells. The stink of sweat, deodorant, tobacco, food, gun powder... nothing. So there had to be at least one other Scalestone at work. I consciously checked my mental state. I wasn't feeling calm or peaceful. More violent and vengeful. That was good.

These guys had already proven they were dangerous, but when Hunters go after a Half-kin it's usually with weeks or months of planning, to give themselves an advantage. I had caught them with their pants down, and my bet was they weren't prepared for a full-frontal assault.

I drew my gun and kicked the door off its hinges. It fell to the floor with a thud. At the far end of a hallway stood another of the men who owed me blood debt, the Vanatori crest tattoo I'd seen on his neck at the hotel, standing out like a beacon. He was aiming an AR15 assault rifle at me. A glow emanated from beneath his button-down denim shirt.

"You better be a real good shot," I said calmly, gazing at him from behind Baldy's head.

"Conroy's still alive!" he yelled at someone behind him.

"How much longer remains to be seen." I wrapped my hand around Baldy's throat.

"Don't you fucking touch him," he snarled.

"You in charge?"

He said nothing as a bead of sweat trickled down his forehead. He wasn't.

"I didn't think so."

I walked towards him and retreated down the hallway, keeping the AR trained on us. As he backed through the doorway at the end of the hall, his eyes darted to the left for a split second and then back to me. Always a dead giveaway, the eyes. Most people can't control them unless they've trained themselves to and it takes years of practice.

I blinked my secondary lens into place. A heat signature bloomed into view on the other side of the cheap drywall doorway. A man was pressed up against the wall just inside of it. By the position of his arms and the cold spots on his hands he was obviously holding a gun.

"Is he your boss?"

"Who? What did you mean…"

My hand snapped up and I fired. The .45 round went through the drywall like it was wet paper. A spray of heat exploded from the hiding man's knee and he toppled to the floor howling in pain, practically landing on Neck Tat's feet. I blinked my infrared lens back up.

"I mean him," I said.

"Holy Christ! Mark!" Neck Tat yelled.

He stopped in his tracks, indecision running riot across his face. Should he help his friend, keep me covered, start shooting? I gave him no time to think about it as I quickened my stride towards the doorway. In a panic, he stumbled backwards, leaving Mark to his fate.

Mark's left knee had been blown apart by my shot, and the floor was splattered with his blood. He was writhing on the ground screaming, which got louder when he looked up and saw me. Bloody hell, dude, man up. I kicked him in the head, knocking him out, mostly just to shut him up. Mostly. The hunting rifle he'd been holding lay on the floor beside him. I stomped on the barrel, flatting it.

I pressed forward into a large room, a legit security company workspace. Tables with cameras and computers on them in various states of repair, storage spaces along the walls, several desks. Jimmy stood at the far end of the room, Neck Tat beside.

Shifting Baldy in my grip a little, I put my boot on the edge of a worktable and shoved with all my strength, launching it into the table behind it. They crashed together and toppled over, sending computers, cameras, and desktop paraphernalia flying everywhere. Jimmy ducked as a monitor flew over his head and exploded into pieces against the wall behind him.

"If you don't tell me what I want to know I will tear this place apart. Starting with his head from his neck," I shook Baldy for emphasis, my hand still clamped firmly on his throat.

"And if we do you'll just leave peacefully? Forget all about that blood debt you're here to collect," Jimmy said. His voice dripped with sarcasm.

An angry red knot had swollen on his forehead, where I'd pistol-whipped him. I should have hit him in his good eye. There was now a Scalestone around his neck, dangling on top of his grey T-shirt. A Glock 9mm rested in one hand, the other was behind his back. He stood with the confidence of a leader.

"Blood debt can wait until I have more time to enjoy it," I said, showing my incisors with a cold smile.

"Why do I find myself disinclined to believe that," he said, returning the smile.

"You've been living on borrowed time since you failed to kill me. I'm offering you a little more of it. A chance to run in exchange for the information I want."

"You think we're that stupid?" Neck Tat said, a tremor in his voice.

"Yes."

You can't give me an opening that easy and expect me not to take it. I mean, seriously.

"And what is it you want to know?" Jimmy asked.

"Alamander and Annalisa. Where are they?"

"We don't betray our allies."

"Your ally *is* your enemy."

"What the hell does that mean?" Neck Tat demanded.

"It means shut up. I'm not talking to you."

"We don't make deals with your kind, abomination," Jimmy said.

"You already have, you moron. Alamander is a Dragon."

Neck Tat's eyes went wide in shock, and his head whipped towards Jimmy.

"I'm supposed to believe that, coming from you?" Jimmy said.

"That's exactly why you should believe it," I said, "I know my kind when I'm around them."

Jimmy's eyes narrowed. "Impossible," he tapped his Scalestone. "This would have told us."

The stone was black with big swaths of copper running through it. There was a red gemstone in the center of it, pulsing steadily. The backing was different than the others, it was set onto a large silver Templar Cross.

All Hunters used supernatural means to search for Dragons. If you were human it was basically the only way to sniff us out. Jimmy's stone was probably handed down through generations of this particular group.

"He has access to magic that's powerful enough to counter your stone. It's why you dumbasses actually thought he was a wizard. He gave you these Scalestones, didn't he?"

I had the stones from Baldy and Gold Teeth wrapped around my wrist by their chains.

"If he could make these, you think he couldn't beat a detection spell on yours?"

"That's bullshit!" Neck Tat spat, the fear in his voice replaced by anger.

Jimmy didn't look so convinced. Like any good leader he was willing to consider other possibilities and didn't blind himself to seeing only his side of an equation. He was no fool.

"Why?" he asked, "What would be in it for him? Why not just take you out and grab the girl himself?"

"To hedge his bets against me, probably. If you hadn't noticed, I'm kinda hard to kill."

He frowned, and I could practically hear the gears grinding in his head.

"He wanted Annalisa, and dangling me in front of your noses as a reward for your help was something you obviously couldn't resist. Being served a Dragon was enough of a prize to keep you from seriously questioning why he wanted her."

"Jim, do not listen to this thing," Neck Tat said.

"Didn't I tell you to shut up?"

I didn't so much as glance at him as I said it. It probably exacerbated an already tense situation, but I was angry and almost out of patience. Plus, he had a neck tattoo. Neck tattoos are stupid.

His face flushed crimson, and he took a step toward me, raising the AR. Jimmy stuck out a commanding hand and waved him back.

"Easy brother, it will have its due in time."

"You and your little band of meatheads delivered Annalisa right into the hands of a Dragon who not only intends to do her harm, but played you like fools."

Vanatori kill Dragons because they truly believe they're protecting people from them, and they have thousands of years of history and tradition behind them reinforcing that belief and legacy. They'd done just the opposite in this situation.

Jimmy's frown turned into a flat line as he regarded me.

"What are you proposing, beast?"

I was honestly a little surprised that he was even considering my offer, but I didn't let it show.

"You tell me how to find Alamander, I let you live longer than the next ten minutes."

"Gee, thanks. You're not a convincing negotiator."

I shrugged. "You shouldn't have tried to kill me."

"We just shouldn't have failed," Neck Tat said.

Jimmy nodded in agreement. "Even if I decided to take your offer, I couldn't just tell you Alamander's location."

"Why is that?"

"He always contacts us, not the other way around."

"You never questioned why he wanted it that way?"

"Of course I did," he said with a shrug.

"And?"

"And that's all you need to know about it," his voice dripped with condescension.

I showed him my teeth, "Then you're useless to me. Guess I'll collect that debt after all."

I threw Baldy at Neck Tat. He had to drop flat on the floor to avoid being hit. Baldy's unconscious body crashed into the tables I'd kicked over. More of his bones broke.

I charged forward, raising my gun. Before I could fire Jimmy revealed the hand he'd had behind his back, in it was Tat's small unconscious body. He put the Glock to her head.

Dammit! I slid to a stop.

"Back!" Jimmy shouted at me.

I took several steps back, aiming my gun at the prone Neck Tat.

"I will disintegrate his head if you so much as breathe on her wrong," I growled.

He pointed the Glock upwards and draped Tat's limp body across the barrel.

"You'll stay where you are and behave, animal. Or I'll disintegrate *all* of her."

That should have set me off like a bomb. Instead, I was overcome by the calm feeling that he wasn't going to hurt her. Common sense and my own eyes told me that wasn't right, and my combat brain screamed at me to attack, but it was distant and muted, as if it were coming through a ten-foot wall of mud.

I heard the unmistakable racking of a shotgun from behind me. Oh, bloody hell. There was another Scalestone at work. I had time to turn my head and see the man in the doorway before he fired. Son of a...

The shotgun roared and agony ripped across my back as heavy buckshot tore into me. I was hurled forward and smashed face-first into the ground. Everything went black in a wash of pain.

#

I came to pinned to the floor on my back. Tall pieces of metal re-bar driven through both my hands, blood pooling beneath them. I could feel my body pushing out the buckshot pellets from my lower back, where they had managed to penetrate through the armor of my jacket. My legs were free. My nose was broken. Again.

Jimmy was nearby, a sledgehammer leaning against his leg. He was talking heatedly with the man who had put all the buckshot in my back.

They hadn't noticed I was awake, so I used their distraction to assess my situation as best I could. They had moved several desks and tables away from the wall to clear the space where they'd impaled me. The rebar seemed to be driven pretty deeply into the concrete floor through my palms, but I felt it wobble a little as I tugged against it. I scanned my hands. Oh, look at that, I was still wearing my ring.

I glanced above my head to see Tat duct-taped to the wall behind me. They had used three long pieces to stick her to it. It looked like she was held in place by a big silver asterisk. She was straining mightily, but the tape was too strong for her. There was no quit in the girl though, she had a warrior's heart.

She saw that I was awake, and as our eyes made contact, I waggled my ring finger at her. She gave me a grim nod of understanding in return.

Baldy, Gold Teeth, and Mark were laid out together on the floor across the room, being tended to by Neck Tat.

I turned my focus back to Jimmy and Don. That's right, Don. Short, fat, over sixty, hotel freaking security guard, Don. The same damn guy that had helped drag me out of the pool to save my life. The old bastard had obviously nullified the debt of gratitude I'd owed him.

"You can't trust him," Don said, jabbing a finger at Jimmy.

"I can't discount him, either. If he's telling the truth, then we've been in league with a Dragon and handed an innocent woman over to him. One he intends to hurt!" Jimmy said.

"Why would you even believe this animal? Keeping it alive is a mistake, kill it now. We'll deal with Alamander the next time he shows up."

Fortunately for me, Jimmy was still thinking like a leader.

"He told me about Alamander when he thought he had the advantage. If he's lying, then why?" "We're not killing him until we get more information and I figure out what the hell's going on."

"Hi, Don," I said through a very dry throat. "This is disappointing. I thought we were friends."

Don turned his gaze to me and fingered his shotgun, which lay on the table he leaned against, along with my sword cane and gun.

Seeing him connected some dots about what happened at the hotel. Like how the Hunters knew the camera layout and security systems so well, and which cameras to target. It also explained why Sword & Shield was called in as a backup contractor.

"Happy to disappoint you," he said angrily, a red flush rising in his face.

"How are they?" Jimmy called over to Neck Tat.

He was still playing medic for his three downed friends. As badly as I'd hurt them they were going to need a hospital soon.

"Not good, brother, we've gotta get Mark and Elijah to a hospital, they've lost a ton of blood."

I assumed that Elijah was Gold Teeth.

"Shit," Jimmy said.

"How did you catch her?" I said to Jimmy, nodding my head in Tat's direction.

"Alamander got her. She got too close to us after we left the hotel. I knew she would be a good piece of insurance in case you found us."

Damned if he wasn't right about that. Tat's far more than just in my care, she's my best friend. Seeing her helpless form had stopped me dead in my tracks.

Jimmy picked up the sledgehammer and walked over to me. He kicked my legs apart, stepped in between them, lined up the head of the hammer directly in line with my balls, then turned into a golfer's stance and gripped the handle firmly with two hands. I didn't like where this was going.

Don laughed out loud. I shot him an evil glare.

"What does he want with the woman?" Jimmy said, bringing my eyes back to him.

"He thinks she's the key to his plan."

"What plan?"

"Here comes a huge fucking lie," Don spat.

I swiveled my head toward him.

"His plan, Don, is to use Annalisa to eliminate the Test. If he can do it, it would make it possible for all Half-kin to transform into Full Bloods. No more killing each other to get there. Imagine if all of us were suddenly able to become the full-blown monsters you fear and hate so much. What's your world gonna look like then?" Asshole! I didn't add.

I was talking a lot to distract them from what I was doing with my ring. Also, out of fear of having my balls smashed, honestly.

Incindis was not just a flame-throwing weapon of molten destruction, I could be subtle with it if I wanted. I'd aimed the ring at Tat and begun pulsing intense waves of heat at her. I couldn't afford to look at her to see what was happening, I just kept it up and hoped it wouldn't be too much for her to take.

Don seemed more willing to keep quiet and listen after what I'd said.

"Jimmy, you need to hurry up with this shit!" Neck Tat shouted. "These guys aren't doing so hot."

Jimmy looked over at his men, concern and indecision playing across his face.

"You believe it's possible?" he said, looking back at me.

I was trying to keep them off-balance by spitting information at them that they would have to process. The more I could do to break their focus on me the better. My balls agreed enthusiastically.

"I don't know yet, but my gut tells me yes. I don't intend to give him the opportunity to try."

"Gonna be kinda hard for you to stop him when you're dead," Don said.

"Are you going to stop him if I don't? You handed her to him. The key he needed. Are you prepared to live with that? Knowing you helped a Dragon bring about the end of civilization as you know it?" I was responding to Don, but my eyes were locked on Jimmy's.

"Is this where you ask us to let you go so you can save the world?" Don snorted.

"Yes," I said, "If you're smart."

He was so stunned I'd said it, all he could do was gape at me.

"Where's he's keeping her?" I said to Jimmy.

Jimmy ground his teeth and furrowed his brow, thinking hard.

"Don't you fucking say a word, Jim!" Don commanded. Or tried to, at least.

"In the city, somewhere downtown," Jimmy said, "I don't know specifically, but I could probably find out."

"Goddammit!" Neck Tat shouted.

All three of us looked over at him. Gold Teeth had gone into convulsions.

"Either we get him to the doc now or he'll die!" Neck Tat yelled.

Jimmy didn't hesitate, his indecision evaporating. "Don, help get them into my truck!"

Hissing a curse Don sprinted over to the other men, leaving Jimmy alone with me.

That's when Tat moved. The adhesive part of duct tape doesn't react well to heat. It melts and loses its ability to stick to anything. She exploded off the wall in a burst of glowing orange faerie dust, screaming in a high-pitched battle cry. She streaked across the short distance and slammed into Jimmy's face full force. I heard his nose break. The sledgehammer fell from his hands as he staggered backwards, tripped over a computer monitor, and toppled over.

I clenched both fists awkwardly around the rebar and pulled with all my strength, tucking both feet underneath me as

I did it. My vision blurred as I hissed through clenched teeth and a ridiculous amount of pain. The rebar popped out of the ground.

"Fuck!" Don yelled as he saw what was happening.

Jimmy rolled away from me and scuttled backwards. His face was covered in blood pouring from his nose, but he wasn't letting it slow him down as he tried to draw his gun from its hip holster and move at the same time. I half dove, half sprawled at him, swatting at his leg with the rebar still stuck through my right palm. It smacked hard against his ankle with a satisfying crack and he went sprawling again.

Tat had caromed off Jimmy's face, and now she piledrove into Neck Tat's ear. His equilibrium got totally discombobulated and fell over, bringing Mark down with him. He'd been left holding him alone because Don had sprinted back to the table where he'd left his shotgun.

With a snarl, I pounced on Jimmy, just as Don got to his shotgun.

"Blood debt is forever," I growled in his ear, "You won't see me coming."

I stood and threw him at Don in one continuous motion. Stars exploded in my vision as my rebar-stuck hands screamed in pain and protest. I hadn't intended to hit Don, I was zero for two with thrown bodies today, after all. Jimmy landed short, but to my pleasant surprised he slid the rest of the way and knocked Don off his feet like a human bowling ball.

It bought us the precious seconds we needed to bolt. "Tat, exit!" I yelled as I turned, swallowed my pride, and ran for the front door. She zoomed in close, above my shoulder.

I know, I said Dragons never run when we fight, but that only fully applies when we fight each other. It didn't make it sting any less though. I yanked the rebar from my hands as I ran, my vision going blurry around the edges from the exertion and pain. If it wasn't for the battle-adrenaline surging through my system I didn't even know how much longer I'd be able to stand.

No bullets or footsteps chased us as we ran through the hallway into the reception area. I slammed through the front door into bright sunshine, and practically straight into the arms of Agents Buck and Hooper.

Hooray.

CHAPTER FOURTEEN

I looked like I'd just been mauled by a starving bear. Covered in wounds and blood, with my clothes torn to shreds. Hooper took one look at me and drew his gun, though he didn't quite aim it at me, just in my general direction. I was unarmed, my Wakizashi and Colt left behind as parting gifts to the Vanatori.

Their car was parked in front of the S&S building about ten feet away from me. Hooper was standing by the open passenger door, using it for partial cover. Buck was walking around the car and had stopped directly in front of it. She didn't draw, just coolly placed one hand behind her back.

Tat had instinctively ducked behind my back. I didn't know if they had seen her. I felt her climb underneath the tatters of my shirt and press herself against my back. What the hell were they doing here?

With my momentum stopped I could feel my knees wanting to buckle. I was keeping myself up through sheer force of will.

"Umm… hi?" I said.

Hooper took in my bloody splendor and chuckled.

"You look like you got run over by an elephant stampede, Mr. Ddraik. You looked better after you fell off the hotel balcony."

I honestly wasn't sure if I was in a better or worse place than I was thirty seconds ago.

"Perhaps we should call you an ambulance," Buck said.

"No thanks, I'm fine," my shaking legs disagreed with me. "I'd love to talk but I'm in a hurry, I got a hot lead. As a matter of fact, you should come with me to follow it."

I took a couple of steps. I had to get away from the building. If the Vanatori came out with guns blazing I would be dead center in the middle of a cross fire.

Hooper aimed at me.

"You should probably stop right there. By probably, I mean don't move."

"Is all of that blood yours?" Buck asked.

Her free hand gestured to indicate the mess that was me.

"Your current condition gives us probable cause to detain you until we ascertain the nature of the situation here," she continued.

The hand behind her back reappeared holding a 9mm Beretta.

I don't know how they found me, and I didn't have the time or mental wherewithal to even think about it. I did know that if they went inside S&S I was going to be arrested on all kinds of charges. Even without being charged they could jam me up for at least seventy-two hours if they really wanted to. I had no time to be stuck in a cell.

Unarmed and barely able to stand, I was going to have to fight. I couldn't let them stop me from searching for Annalisa. I desperately dug for adrenaline reserves, knowing my life depended on it.

"There's nothing in there worth wasting your time on. Follow me to my car and I'll take you to what I've found."

I started forward. I was going to try and get close to Hooper, my instincts told me he was the weaker of the two.

Hooper stepped away from the car door and onto the sidewalk, taking a few steps backwards to keep distance between us, as if he'd read my thoughts. His gun aimed squarely at my chest.

"You're not very good at listening," he said, "Stop. Now!"

Buck aimed at my head.

"His kind never is," she said.

My kind? Before I had a chance to think about what she meant by that, everything in my field of vision went hazy, like a thin gauze had been draped over my head.

"What the hell?" Hooper said, his eyes darting around wildly. "Where did he go?" His expression changed to surprise and confusion.

He couldn't see me? Buck's eyes narrowed and she inhaled sharply.

"He's not gone," she said.

The gauzy effect was actually a few feet in front of me, not directly over my eyes. I started to reach my hand out towards it.

"Put your hand down you dumb lizard!" snapped Duncan in a rough whisper from behind me. "You'll pierce the veil."

His hand grabbed the tatters of my shirt and yanked me backwards. I looked over my shoulder to see him glowering up at me.

"Dunc?" I had the same look on my face that I had just seen on Hooper's. "What are you..."

"Hold onto your lunch, Red."

Oh bugger...

There was the feeling of a huge sucking of air, then everything twisted violently inward growing tighter, and tighter, and tighter. Like a tornado winding in on itself. My stomach lurched and heaved as if it was being folded, then refolded into some perverse origami shape. My eyeballs felt like they were being squeezed out of my skull as my vision blurred across the color spectrum in a chaotic blast of fractal patterns. Then there was nothing.

CHAPTER FIFTEEN

Everything unwound with a gut-wrenching snap. Nothingness became time, space, and matter again. My vision swam in triplicate as my head spun wildly. I fell onto all fours and puked my guts out.

I hate teleporting spells.

I heard ragged breathing beside me. It took a second for my eyes to focus on him even though he was only two feet away from me. Duncan was down on one knee, breath coming in gulping pants, his face red and sweaty.

"That really sucked," he said.

"Understatement," I agreed, taking slow, steadying breaths of my own.

"You are one heavy fucker to carry over that kind of distance. That's damn sure a record for me."

As my vision cleared, I saw that I was half-sprawled on the living room floor of my home. Jesus, he had just teleported us thirty-five-odd miles from Burbank to Santa Clarita.

The cavernous ceiling loomed overhead like an old friend, open and crisscrossed with big, stained oak support beams. An immediate sense of warmth and security washed over me.

For a Dragon, the place we choose to call home is very, very important. It's where we keep our stuff, and I don't mean our treasure. We use banks and hedge funds for that these days. We store our personal histories in our homes. The most important things in them are valued more for memory than monetary worth. They are our sanctuaries. The place we feel most safe and at peace. When you live your life constantly looking over your shoulder for the knife that might be coming at your back, that means a lot.

A smile touched my lips. I hadn't been home in a while. Being by Annalisa's side was pretty much a twenty-four-seven job, and I hadn't had time to think about how much I'd missed it. Then I saw that I'd just tossed my cookies all over an expensive Persian rug.

"Bloody hell," I said, "This cost me seventy-five K, Dunc."

"It's not my fault you spend too much money on stupid shit," he huffed, "You're welcome, by the way."

"Be not an ass," Tat said to me.

She was hovering close to my shoulder. I hadn't even felt her slither out from under my shirt. She was a hot mess. Her skin was tinged red, from the heat bath I had given her, and covered in large patches of hardened resin from the now-cooled adhesive of the duct tape. Her long hair was wild, sticky, and plastered to her neck and back. She'd somehow lost her bikini top, but she didn't seem to care. Faeries aren't known for their modesty.

"He just pulled our fat from the flame," she said, landing on my shoulder.

"I had it under control," I said, lurching to my feet.

"Right," he said, looking at me skeptically. "I'll just send you back into the middle of the people pointing guns at your ass then?"

I wobbled and grabbed onto Duncan's shoulder for balance.

"Totally under control. But, thanks... a lot."

I picked up his cowboy hat, which had fallen onto the floor, and placed it gently on his head.

"Who were they?" he asked.

"FBI."

"How'd you piss them off?"

"It's a talent," I said, letting go of his shoulder as I steadied. "They think I might have something to do with Annalisa's kidnapping."

"While she's in your care?" he scoffed as he heaved himself to his feet. "They obviously don't know dick about Dragons."

"Not like I can tell them that."

"Facts," he agreed.

The Feds showing up at S&S raised the question, how had they found me? They might have been better at tailing me than I gave them credit for. Then again, they had seemed as surprised to see me as I had them, so maybe they'd followed the same trail back to S&S that I had, after they'd talked more with hotel security. Either way, I knew not to underestimate them again.

"That's not even the bad news," I said.

"Judging by the way you look I'm not surprised. Some shit go down inside that building you were running out of?"

"There might be a dead Vanatori or two in there."

I was on the hook for whatever Hooper and Buck found in there. The Feds didn't know about Dragons, Vanatori, or the supernatural world. They would just see a destroyed room full of injured and dying men, with me making a hasty, blood-covered exit from it. The Hunters could make up any story they wanted about what happened, and paint themselves as innocent victims. I wouldn't be surprised if there was already an APB out for my arrest. Bloody hell, this was the last thing I needed.

"Feds have found 'em by now. You're kinda fucked," Duncan said, echoing my thoughts.

"The mage has a point," Tat agreed.

"Thank you both for stating the obvious," I grumbled.

I smiled at Tat despite my sour mood and pain-wracked body.

"I'm glad you're all right, little one. I was getting worried. Looks like I had good reason."

"You as well," she said, "I thought your balls were done for."

"Not with you having my back."

"You speak true," she said with a cocky little smile as she floated off my shoulder, "Methinks I'm a fiery mess. I'll take my leave. I would shower, then slumber for a time."

She flew off toward her room, upstairs. I'd converted a large closet into a bedroom, for her it was practically a house within a house. She used the sink in her bathroom as a shower. I watched her go, grateful as always that she was by my side.

"Balls?" Duncan asked.

"Guy with a sledgehammer. They're fine," I said, waving a hand dismissively. "How did you find me?"

"I tracked Incindis."

Though we rarely used it, the ring could act as a homing beacon if he wanted to find me, or if I needed to call him to where I was.

"Oh, right."

It should've been obvious, but I wasn't thinking clearly. A busted nose, forty-story fall, high-powered electric shock, fight with Alamander, crossbow bolt, shotgun blast, semi-crucifixion to the floor, and teleporting had taken their toll. Go figure.

"Good thing you had it on," he said.

"You have no idea."

I gave him the condensed version of what had happened at Sword & Shield as we headed to the kitchen. I was ravenous, I needed food and water.

"Goddamn," he said, as he sprawled into the large wall banquet.

My kitchen was a chef's wet dream. Dual island stoves, a quad-stacked oven, a giant Sub-Zero refrigerator, Italian granite counters, and Brazilian redwood cabinetry. Cooking was a passion, when I had time to indulge it. In another life, when I was much, much younger, I'd been a chef for royalty in the Netherlands. What? I wasn't only about fighting and sex. Just mostly.

From the walk-in pantry, I grabbed several large bags of chips and a gallon jug of water, dropping them on the table in front of Duncan. I opened a bag and started inhaling chips as I went to the fridge and rummaged for more substantial food.

"You're in a pile of some very deep shit, Red," Duncan said.

"What else is new."

"No. Not like this," his tone was so serious that I stopped digging in the fridge and turned to look at him. His eyes, routinely bloodshot, were clear and focused. I studied him, sniffing as I did.

"You're sober."

"Stone cold. Staying that way."

That was bad, as ironic as it sounds.

"Wow, this *is* some serious shit."

"Cats and dogs will be fucking, next thing you know," he scoffed. "I don't much like the idea of the Earth being overrun by Dragons. No offense."

"None taken. I'm not thrilled by it either. Stay sober. I can't be babysitting your ass when the shit hits."

"Don't worry about me. But when we put this mess behind us, you're buying."

"Deal."

I returned to the table with a bag of apples and a large block of cheese. I wasn't going for gourmet, I just needed fuel and energy. I sat, practically melting into the kidskin leather of the banquet. God, I loved my house.

"What did you find out?"

"Your girl is a djinn."

"As in genie? Like Robin Williams in Aladdin?"

"Yeah, all that power but none of the funny."

I scowled. That didn't make any sense. "Why wouldn't she tell me that, seems kinda damned important?"

"She doesn't know it."

"How is that possible?"

"What do you know about the djinn?"

"Dad told me about encountering one once," I said.

"Fight or fuck?" he asked, genuinely curious.

"One, then the other. He said he had to best her to bed her. Probably wasn't much of a fight for him," I said cockily, as I practically ate a whole apple in two bites.

"Think again. The djinn that can make the transition between realms are extremely powerful. On the order of a Full Blood, for perspective."

My jaw might have dropped if my mouth wasn't full of food. There are few supernatural things on Earth that are as powerful as a Full Blood. Thankfully. It makes my line of work a lot easier.

"Did pops tell you anything else?"

I opened the jug of water and took a long pull from it, digging into my memory bank as I gulped. I was a little short on funds where the djinn were concerned.

"They're creatures of fire and smoke. Live in their own realm. Powerful magic wielders. They keep to themselves."

He stared at me, waiting for more.

"They grant wishes?" I said, shrugging.

"If you haven't fought it or fucked it, you're just clueless sometimes, ain't cha?" he said, shaking his head.

"Could you just get to the point?" I growled.

I was having a hard time focusing, which is what I needed to retain what Dunc was telling me.

"They have a caste society based on royalty, and aristocracy. There are three major houses of djinn, but there used to be four. A long time ago there was a massive war between the houses, the most powerful was decimated by the other three. The only royalty that survived, a prince and princess, legitimate heirs to the throne of the entire Djinn Realm, were forced to flee."

"They fled here?"

He nodded.

"Your dad may have been one of the last to have actually seen a djinn on Earth. They don't just keep to themselves, they're xenophobes. They almost never leave their realm, *especially* not to come here."

"Why the change? What stopped them?"

"That's where the stories you're familiar with come into play. Some wizards, long before my time, discovered that with the right kind of very powerful magic, djinn could be captured, bound, and placed in almost eternal servitude."

"Genie in the bottle," I said.

"It kinda turned them off from coming to Earth. By that point they'd already had an entire religion built around them by the Hindus, and convinced the Arabians they were akin to angels. Even with that, I guess they figured the downside wasn't worth the risk anymore, just for the fun of meddling in human affairs."

"How'd you figure all this out?"

"A lot of text and records research, some divination magic, and I contacted a couple of ether spirits that owe me favors and have their ears to the ground," he said with a bit of chest puffiness.

"There are spirits that owe you favors. Seriously?"

"I can be a badass wizard when I want to be, lizard," he snapped. "There was a time…" a pained expression washed across his face and he clamped his mouth shut.

It was true. Before he fell into the bottle, Dunc had been a force to be reckoned with, magically speaking. He rarely talked about what drove him to drinking, whatever had happened was too painful for him. Now was no different. He shook his head and waved a hand dismissively.

"Never mind. It was the mother's name, Kali, it rang a bell, gave me a thread to follow."

"Unravel the thread for me."

"On paper, Kali Dagher is the only daughter of wealthy Indian parents. The family stretches back dozens of generations. Her father, VanSusstern, is descended from Norwegian royalty. On paper."

"Something's wrong with the paper?"

He nodded. "The deeper I dug into the family histories the more they fell apart. Names that went nowhere, marriages that didn't exist, missing birth and death certificates. What was consistent was the name, Kali, always in the mother's line."

"What's special about the name?"

"In the Hindu pantheon Kali is the wife, or consort, of Shiva."

I almost choked up the big gulp of water I was taking.

"Shiva the Destroyer?"

"Same dude," he affirmed, "That's just one of his aspects. He's also known as the Transformer and the patron God of Yoga. The Destroyer and yoga. The fucking irony, right."

"You're telling me that Annalisa's father is Shiva and her mother is Kali?"

"In a nutshell, yep."

"Two of the most powerful gods in the Hindu religion?"

"Djinn who were deified by humans. They're not literal gods, they're archetypal interpretations of things people couldn't understand at the time. A lot of the old gods, Greek, Norse, Egyptian, Chinese, you name it, are based on people trying to humanize beings they had no way of explaining or comprehending. Their real names probably aren't even Shiva and Kali."

"Back to my prior question, how can she not know what she is?"

"This is mostly conjecture, but near as I can figure, when her parents' house lost the war, they ran to the one place they knew other djinn would never follow them."

"Earth," I said. "If you don't want to be found, go to a place your enemies fear to tread."

"Probably faked their own deaths every generation or so and continued the dynasty as their own children, or cousins, or something. The lines only get wonky if you dig into them the way I did, so no one was likely to notice. Especially not with their wealth."

That was very true. Over my lifetime I'd become a master at covering my own history and creating new identities. Being rich helped immensely with that, and my wealth was nowhere near Annalisa's. That kind of money makes it possible to keep almost anything secret.

"They replaced their djinn empire for a human one and eventually had a daughter. It's more conjecture, but my guess is they wrapped Annalisa in enough spells to hide her true nature, from herself or anyone who might come looking, and to put a clamp down on her natural born power. For all intents and purposes, she's human."

"Why?" I asked.

Duncan shrugged again. "All my conjecturing in the world wouldn't do you any good there. You'd have to ask her parents that."

"And they're dead."

"Which raises more questions, like…"

I waved a hand violently at him.

"Later," I said, rubbing at my temples. My head was pounding like a bass drum.

Djinn weren't immortal, but like Full Bloods they were extremely long-lived and hard to kill. Their dying in a plane crash seemed suspect, to say the least. But I hadn't been hired to investigate her parents' deaths, and unless it became relevant to finding Annalisa, I wasn't going to start. No need to complicate things any more than they already were.

"The job now is figuring out where Alamander's got her, and what he's planning to do with her."

"I wish I knew the answer to your first question, because the second one I'm pretty sure about. You said her birthday is in three days?"

"Saturday."

"Saturday at midnight, the planets align *and* the Material Plane will be in alignment with Djinn and Wyrm. It's been millennia since that happened."

"Holy shit," I breathed.

Alignments of any kind create straight lines of accessible power. For users of magic those lines are enormously powerful if they know how to tap into them. Metaphysically speaking, a cosmic alignment, in conjunction with three realms lining up, was power off the goddamn charts. A 50.0 on the magical Richter scale.

"My bet is, he's going to tap the energy from the alignment to undo the spells around Annalisa and let the genie out of the bottle," Duncan said.

"Then put her right back in. Literally," I replied. "He'll have a bound djinn, and he's going to use her to try and undo the magic that binds Half-kin to the Test. Somehow."

I scowled as I fought to put the information together and find some sort of answer, but the bass drum in my head had become a roaring V8 with straight pipes. Mentally, it felt like I was swimming in molasses.

"Something's missing. Alamander can't unbind the Test with just a djinn alone."

"No, he'll need elven magic as well," Duncan replied.

My brain was crawling along at such a slow speed that I hadn't remembered it. That's how out of it I was. It was Dragon 101.

When the Test was created, the elder Dragons didn't trust just their own magic to bind it. Fearing that one Order might put in a back door to free their line from the binding. Unlike most other races of the supernatural, Dragons don't have hierarchy, or caste. We never have. There are no houses, clans, politics, or laws. Just fierce independence.

For quite possibly the only time in recorded Dragon history they admitted to needing help from others, and enlisted the djinn and elves to help create the spells that bound all future Dragons to the Test. Both races were happy to assist. Apparently a lot of people weren't happy about unchecked Dragon hordes.

"Reds, that's some good news at least." Of all the elf houses, the Reds were the most honorable and the least involved in the affairs of others.

"Yes and no," Duncan said, "You can't apply your current knowledge of the Reds to the way they were back then. They weren't crazy like the Blues, but they were power-hungry and very anti-human."

"For example?"

"You've heard of Atlantis?"

I looked at him like he was an idiot. I had a roaring headache, not a lobotomy.

"Duh," I said, brimming with annoyed sarcasm.

Atlantis had been the most technologically advanced human tribe to ever exist on the planet. They'd even begun to incorporate magic into their tech.

"The Reds sank it and killed the entire population because they didn't like humans getting too powerful with magic," Duncan said.

"Christ. Yeah, that doesn't sound at all like the Reds I've dealt with." They had mostly been female. And usually naked. Geo-supernatural politics hadn't been a big topic of conversation.

I finished the cheese and began devouring another apple. It wasn't helping with my headache, but at least I wasn't starving anymore.

"They aren't like that today for the most part, but there are some."

I let that go for now.

"So, Alamander's plan is dead in the water without Red Elf magic," I said.

"Yep, but if he *can* pull this off..."

The tremor of fear that ran through his voice surprised me. His staff was laid across the table, and he'd had his hands resting on it while he'd been talking. His knuckles had gone white from the grip he now had on it.

"You're gonna pop your knuckles, Dunc."

He looked down at his hands and eased his grip. He hadn't realized what he'd been doing.

"It's worse than just unbinding the Test. Much worse."

"What's worse than a planet full of unchecked Dragons?"

"An army of enthralled ones."

A cold chill ran down my spine. Accompanied by a complete revulsion to the thought of being bound or controlled by someone.

"That's not possible," I snapped.

"Isn't it? Alamander will be a Full Blood, with a royal djinn under his absolute control, plus an unknown source of Red Elf power in his pocket. What if he can harness all that power to turn them into an army under his control?"

"It can't happen to Full Bloods." Could it?

"We're talking a cosmic level of power here. It's very possible if he, or whoever he's working with, knows what they're doing. It won't work on the older more experienced Half-kin like you, who've trained to protect their minds.

"But the young ones..." I interjected. There were hundreds of them. Oh my damn.

I remembered what Alamander had said to me in the hotel garage: *Imagine the worlds, the entire realms we could bring under our heel and control.*

"Bloody fuck all," I said, sagely.

It was all too much to process, and my mind and body were too wrecked to attempt it at the moment. I had tried hard to turn the V8 in my head into a V6, but it wasn't working.

"I need to sleep."

"At a time like this?" he said, incredulously.

I stood. It hurt. My legs didn't buckle, but they felt like rubber. As fast a healer as I was, Wolverine I wasn't. I'd taken such a beating that I barely felt any tingling, which accompanied my usual rapid regeneration. My body felt like it was on the verge of shutting down, and I needed to stop moving, stop thinking, and heal.

"Are you out of your lizard skull? We've got to find this woman!"

He didn't know all I'd been through in the last eight hours. I held out my hand to him, palm down. It trembled noticeably. His eyes went a little wide.

"That's not good," he said.

"I'm half a walking corpse, Dunc. I'm good for nothing and no one if I can't fight when the time comes. I need to be at a hundred percent to handle Alamander when I find him. I need six hours of hard sleep to get there. See what you can find out about the Reds, if they're involved in this, while I'm out."

"I'll find what I can," he said with a nod, setting his jaw.

I put a hand on his shoulder as I headed upstairs.

"Thanks, glad you're with me."

CHAPTER SIXTEEN

I laid down on my oversized bed, sinking blissfully into the thick memory foam mattress. I stared at the large fireplace across the room as flames danced slowly within it. The curtains were drawn over the floor-to-ceiling glass windows. Aside from the firelight and low crackling of the wood, the room was dark and quiet.

On the mantle of the fireplace rested a row of gold coins, propped up and laid out side by side along the length of it. They were almost as old as me. I focused on them as I slowed my breathing and drew in the heat from the fire, feeling it cover me like a heavy blanket.

My eyes closed, as if they were drawn down by lead weights. I sank deep into the darkness of my mind. Dragon coma, I called it. A hyper-deep, meditative sleep state that would double or triple my healing abilities. It was also only safe to do here in my home, or a similarly secure environment, because it left me vulnerable. Very little short of a bomb going off would wake me up when I was in it.

I dreamed. As I so often did, of my father.

It was my twenty-first birthday, and he had come to our little Scottish village of L'ay Lochmoore where my mother and I lived, as he had since I turned eighteen. He was here to give me a gift and teach me a lesson to go along with it. The lesson usually came in the form of a painful and embarrassingly fast beatdown. My birthdays weren't the only times I saw him, but they were the only times I received gifts. I just got the beatdowns on his regular visits, although he liked to call it 'training.'

He slid off the beautiful, eighteen-hand, dapple-grey stallion he was riding and strode into our little yard. I emerged from the house to greet him. Seeing him always caused a swirl of emotions in me, not all pleasant. Whenever I saw him I was conflicted by the need to earn his respect and approval, along with the burning desire to kick his ass.

He looked magnificent. Black riding breeches were tucked into gleaming black riding boots. A grey silk shirt clung to his powerful frame, covered by the most intricately filigreed, black leather jerkin I'd ever seen. A long green, grey, and black brocade-patterned greatcoat covered that. Immaculately tailored, it draped elegantly almost to the ground. A beautiful black silk scarf was wrapped around his neck. The ivory handle of a long sword peaked out from under the coat. In his right hand he held a blackwood walking staff. It wasn't the dress of a Scottish or English nobleman. It was a style wholly his own and more regal than either.

In a word, he was imperious. His face was handsome chiseled good looks with short, obsidian black hair. Combined with his olive complexion he looked like a Roman general, or emperor. If you'd taken away his finery and left him standing there naked, he would have looked just as powerful. Everything about him radiated it. Controlled, refined, immense, and ready to be unleashed in a whiplash second. To say I wanted to be him would be a monumental understatement. Bloody hell, just look at him.

He reached out a hand and presented me with a fine black leather bag.

"Happy birthday, Randall."

It was heavy and jingled with the weight of many gold coins. My eyes lit up.

"This is a fine and unexpected gift, father," I said, excitedly. Yes, I talked like that. It was a different time. Shut up.

He'd never given me money before, just weapons. It was more than enough to easily make us the wealthiest people in the village.

"They are not yet yours," he said, his voice conveying a touch of amusement. "You may keep five coins for every minute you last against me in combat."

I lasted forty seconds, tops. I ended up covered in my own blood, my hand dangling on my right arm with a broken wrist, face down in the mud. It was infuriating... and glorious, but mostly infuriating. My father, his foot planted on the back of my neck, forcing my bloody face into the mud, took pity on me as my mother spoke from the doorway of the house. She had been watching the whole time, even though she didn't enjoy seeing me get beaten.

"That's enough now, Roan. He's down," my mother said.

"Aye, Avingale. Sadly," my father replied.

I seethed as I flailed helplessly under the pressure of his boot on my neck. Which thankfully eased. He heaved me up out of the muck by my shirt, then counted five gold coins out of the bag and placed them in my good hand.

"What you earn in life is far more valuable than anything you're just given. It matters. Remember that, boy."

I nodded then stomped toward the house, embarrassed and angry.

"Will you spend some time, Avingale?" he asked my mother as I walked past her.

"Aye, Roan, it would be a pleasure."

Honestly, I think he just used my birthday as an excuse to come see my mother, as they usually disappeared together for two or three days after I got my ass handed to me. What he said to me that day never left me though, and it would turn out to be one of the most valuable lessons he ever taught me.

As I entered the house everything became black as the dream faded.

My eyes blinked open. The fire had burned down to embers, and I could see rays of moonlight peeking through the cracks in the curtains. The clock on my nightstand said 1:11 am.

I stood and stretched. Everything felt good, body and mind. I walked to the mantel and picked up one of the gold coins. A small smile touched my lips as I rubbed it between my fingers. They were one of my most treasured possessions, because of what they represented. 'What you earn in life is far more valuable than anything you're just given,' my father had said, and he'd never been more right. No matter how tempting Alamander's offer was, becoming a Full Blood meant nothing if I didn't earn it myself. My resolve became a steel bar in my spine as I put the coin back in its place on the mantel. I would stop at nothing to save Annalisa, and the Test as well.

CHAPTER SEVENTEEN

Duncan returned not long after I woke up. I was in the kitchen eating a stack of peanut butter and jelly sandwiches when a sucking sound and a burst of light from the living room signaled his arrival. He entered the kitchen a moment later, Greg fluttering behind him. He was flushed, and his brow was sweaty, but he didn't look ready to keel over and have a heart attack, like he had when he'd teleported us here. The imp was obviously a much easier passenger to teleport than my heavy ass.

Greg was wearing a kids-sized yellow and purple Kobe Bryant jersey, and a purple Lakers ball cap was backwards on his head.

"I really need to teach you how to dress, Greg," I said.

"Kobe's the GOAT. Where's your LA pride?" he said.

"I'm a soccer fan. Arsenal," I said.

"Soccer?" he whined, his jaw dropping. "We can't be friends anymore."

"I'm heartbroken," I replied.

"I need someone rational to talk to," he said, fluttering out of the kitchen. "Where's Tat?"

"Well, that's one way to get rid of him," Duncan said, chuckling. "Turns out he's more annoying when I'm sober."

I picked up the plate of sandwiches. "Walk with me, Dunc."

We exited the kitchen directly into the sunroom, a large open space with a twenty-foot lofted ceiling. It was relatively empty except for an armoire against one of the walls with several crash pad mats leaning against it. I used it as a tumbling, stretching, and meditation space. The side walls were bare white, and the back wall contained a giant lithograph print of the cover of Frank Miller's Dark Knight graphic novel. I don't compare myself to the Bat all the time for nothing. The fourth wall, made of floor-to-ceiling glass panels, faced a large deck.

"Open 1506," I said in ancient Gaelic, my birth tongue.

The panels slid open at the sound of the command, completely opening the room to the outside deck. I used the dead language for all the voice-activated features of the house. It hasn't been spoken in hundreds of years and was never a written language. Use anything other than that on my voice systems, and you'll end up on the hurting end of a few nasty surprises.

We walked out onto the expansive Italian marble deck and stopped at the rail, looking down on the pool sparkling below, surrounded by a landscaped lawn. My lair was nestled on about three hundred acres in the foothills of Santa Clarita. Dropping beyond the lawn was a small valley, hidden by the night's darkness. In it, rows of avocado and orange trees gave way to increasingly taller birch and pines. The trees backed into the mountains of the U-shaped canyon my property was nestled in. In the daylight the view was spectacular. Right now in the darkness, it gave me the comforting feel of vast, secure size.

The last time I was out here, Shrill, Drop, Tat, and I were sharing a bottle of hundred-year-old scotch, smoking cigars, and eating a Fae stew that Tat had taught me how to make. The memory should've made me smile. Instead, my blood rose to a boil at the thought of Nerufane holding my friend hostage.

"Damned Darkling" I growled.

I flung the plate of sandwiches at the wall behind me.

"Your trigger's wound a little tight," Duncan said, giving me a calm side-eyed glance.

I huffed. "Maybe."

"Reign it in. The Darkling's the least of your problems," he said.

"Tell that to Drop and Shrill," I snapped. I'd have thrown another plate if I'd had one.

Duncan took a deep breath as if bracing himself, and faced me squarely.

"You're gonna need help on this one, lizard."

He was expecting an argument. I didn't give him one.

"Yep."

His jaw practically dropped open.

"Who the fuck are you, and what have you done with the big arrogant lizard?" he said, thumping me on the chest with his staff.

I cracked a small smile. Except for Tat it was rare for me to take anyone into the field. Most Half-kin did things alone because they believed they were good enough not to need anyone else. I wasn't any different. Getting information was one thing, but the physical work and combat? That was all mine. This time though...

"This is much deeper shit than I usually get myself into."

"And that's saying something," he agreed.

"Kinda like Montana," I said.

Montana involved four werewolf hitmen and a very difficult Unicorn princess.

"This makes Montana look like a Sunday picnic, and you know how much I hate werewolves."

He was right. Saving Annalisa had become the tip of a much larger, infinitely more dangerous iceberg. A cosmic-scale iceberg. I smiled in spite of the situation.

"What the fuck are you smiling about, lizard?"

"It's my kinda fight."

"Don't be an idiot. This is no one's kinda fight."

I couldn't remember ever seeing him so focused or grim. I could understand the grim part. He knew what one Full Blood was capable of, let alone an enthralled horde.

"You learn anything about the Reds?"

"Maybe," he said with a shrug and a sigh, "It's thin though."

I made a continue motion with my hand. "Every bit helps."

"Like I said, they're not trying to destroy humanity anymore. For the most part."

"Explain, for the most part."

"There's a faction that's always wanted to reclaim their top spot on the planet. Some of them are here in LA."

There was a large contingent of Red Elves in LA, but unless you knew it, you'd never know it. It was easy for them to disguise themselves and blend in with humankind.

"Chulunn-Bat's house," I said.

He was an Earl. The highest-ranking Red noble from the West Coast to the Rockies. You couldn't be part of the supernatural world in LA and not know of him.

"Not his directly, he's a good dude. A smaller house under his authority."

"Which one?"

"House Ziwix."

I hit the railing with a closed fist.

"Right. The baroness. Figures."

"You know her?"

The baroness Orsa Rike was the iron-fisted ruler of House Ziwix.

"Not personally, but I've got ancient history with her brother-in-law, Pharyn-Cull."

"She's a bitch on wheels, apparently," Duncan said.

"Makes sense if you know Pharyn, he's a walking Machiavellian nightmare."

A hundred or so years ago I'd done some work for him, indirectly. That's when I'd learned about Orsa. She wasn't a baroness then.

"She and Ziwix are part of the faction that want to return elves to the top of the supernatural food chain," Duncan said.

"Sounds like the kind that Alamander might want to talk to. It gives us a place to start. Give me a few minutes to grab some gear," I said.

I hustled down to my armory. Yep, I got an armory.

"Open 1500," I said in Gaelic.

The door unlocked and I entered. One side of the room was my smith shop. A bellows, small furnace, and anvil were positioned in one corner, an electric hammer and metal bending machines were in the other. In the middle of the room was a station for bullet making. A long row of tall security cabinets lined another wall. The other half of the room was divided into a two-lane gun range.

I keyed in the security code of the gun locker. The insides of the doors were lined with handguns. The locker itself was filled with shotguns, rifles, and machine-guns from every maker around the world. I opened the locker next to it. It was the same repository of potential carnage and death-dealing, only in bladed form.

"Hello, lovelies."

From the blade locker I withdrew a much bigger sword cane than my lost Wakizashi. At almost five feet tall it was more of a staff. It contained a Japanese Odachi, which roughly translated into 'big, big sword.' It was. The blade itself was over four and a half feet long, with the grip adding another foot. I felt it pulsing through its heavy wooden sheath, the runes and magic Duncan had enchanted it with giving it a living vibration.

I pulled out a pair of Rondel daggers. English-made close-combat knives from 1450 AD. Each blade was exactly a foot long and sitting inside an ornately decorated scabbard. The pommel of each blade had a bull's eye etched into the metal. The symbol was the physical representation of an enchantment. It allowed me to throw the blades with extreme accuracy about three times farther than should have been physically possible, even with my strength. I strapped a blade onto each hip of the heavy leather belt I wore.

Last, I slid a Ka-Bar combat knife into the sheath in my boot.

From the gun locker I pulled two Desert Eagle pistols off the door, jet-black with custom blood-red grips. Each went into a holster of the double-shoulder rig I was wearing.

Lastly, I grabbed an AA-12 combat shotgun. Arguably the world's deadliest short-range gun. Fully automatic and with almost no recoil, it was devastating in close combat. The thirty-two-round drum-style magazine was loaded with Frag-12 explosive ammunition.

I retrieved a tactical ammunition bag from the bottom of the locker and stuffed three extra drum magazines for the AA-12 and six extra clips for the Desert Eagles into it.

I locked the room and made a stop in my bedroom for one last piece of gear. From my closet I grabbed a long, dark grey leather coat. It fell to just below my knees. It was fitted and flowing but just loose enough to hide any weapons I put on underneath it. The lining of the jacket was blood red. On the back, in the same blood red color stitching as the liner, was the Japanese kanji for 'protection.'

I'd had Duncan work the coat over with a layer of spells that were the magical equivalent of Kevlar. I looked at myself appreciatively in the mirror. The grey and red made for a nice contrast against my black T-shirt, jeans, and combat boots. Stylish and functional.

I met Duncan back on the deck. He was alone. I looked around suspiciously, Greg is never good unsupervised for too long.

"Where's Greg?" I asked.

"Probably trying to put the moves on Tat. Hang on."

The crystal at the top of his staff began to pulse with white light. A few seconds passed, and Greg was dragged unceremoniously onto the deck by his glowing bands, his arms and legs stretched out in front of him. He had an annoyed look on his face. As the light from Duncan's staff diminished so did the glow in Greg's bands.

"All you had to do was yell, boss," he said, folding his arms across his chest in a huff. "It's embarrassing getting dragged out here like this!"

Looking at Greg, it hit me like a wrecking ball. Nerufane's jewelry.

"Nerufane is bound," I blurted.

"What?" Duncan and Greg said in unison.

"He's bound. Someone is pulling his strings."

I was sure that those obnoxious diamond bracelets around his wrists and neck were accompanied by a matching pair around his ankles that I hadn't been able to see.

"He's trying to get Annalisa for someone else, not himself."

"That someone is a potential powerhouse then," Duncan said with a scowl. "Binding a Darkling is hard. They're like Half-kin, they'd rather be dead than enslaved."

It was a weakness to exploit, and it gave me something to bargain with, if...

"Can you break that kind of binding?" I asked.

"With enough time and prep, sure."

Offering Nerufane his freedom in exchange for my friends would almost certainly make him forget all about wanting Annalisa. One bridge at a time though. Finding Annalisa was still my first priority.

"Let's go have a chat with the Reds," I said.

"Why don't cha just kick a hornet's nest then put it on as a hat," Duncan replied.

"Not Ziwix. Chulunn-Bat."

Running head-first into Ziwix might have been my normal tactic, but that approach hadn't yielded much at Sword & Shield, unless you counted nearly ending up dead as a result. I was changing tactics. Flanking Ziwix, by going to Chulunn-Bat for information about them, seemed a smarter one.

"That's… wise," he said, raising an eyebrow at me.

Wisdom wasn't always my strong suit.

"It's a day full of surprises, isn't it?" I replied with a grin.

That's when the motion sensor alarm went off.

CHAPTER EIGHTEEN

It was an inner proximity alarm. Whoever it was, they were at the house. That shouldn't have been possible.

Every hair on my body must have stood up at once, as much in collective shock as from battle-adrenaline flooding my veins. I charged from the deck toward the front door, the Odachi in one hand and the AA-12 in the other. Duncan and Greg were close on my heels. As we got close Tat zoomed over my shoulder, angry sparks popping off the orange glow that surrounded her, matching the fierce blaze in her eyes. She was naked, as she frequently was around the house.

"Who would dare!" she snarled.

Faeries aren't used to having homes. Not in the traditional sense, and Tat had gotten a little domesticated after living with me for so long. Having her own room and the run of the house made her as protective of it as I was.

We entered the foyer. On the wall next to the front doors was a sixty-inch touchscreen monitor. It displayed fifty separate images from security cameras scattered around the house and grounds, covering every conceivable angle of approach.

With a touch on the screen I expanded the view of the front door camera. A man stood there. An average-looking Joe in his early thirties. Wearing faded jeans, a pair of dirty red Converse Chuck Taylors, a white T-shirt with a black hoodie over it, and a black ball cap on his head. His hands were tucked into his pants pockets, and he shifted nervously back and forth from foot to foot.

"How has the villain come so close to our doors?" Tat said.

"Bloody good question," I said, my voice a cold growl.

Even if you knew where it was, you can't just wander onto my property. Hell, just finding the entrance gate is hard if you don't know where to look for it. A gate he should never have gotten past without my knowing about it. Opening it without the code activates an alarm at the house. If you somehow bypass the code system, or force it open, or try to jump it, it sets off a ward powerful enough to kill. The camera angle on the gate showed that it was still closed, and we hadn't heard the ward go off, so there was no way he should be standing there. Yet there he stood.

I zoomed in on his face. Why did he look so damned familiar? Then it hit me. He was Annalisa's former driver. His name was Karl Bay. He had a clientele of rich business types, and he worked for Annalisa whenever she was in the States. When I took the job, I'd taken over all her driving duties, and he'd been let go for the duration of my employment.

I tapped through a series of cameras, from the driveway out to the front gate. Parked on the road just outside the gate was the grey sedan that I'd seen following me from the hospital and hotel. I'll be damned, it hadn't been the Feds like I'd thought.

He was clearly no ordinary Joe. Not with the ability to find my house and get this close to it without setting off any alarms or wards. He'd wanted to set off the front door alert. My initial surprise boiled over into white-hot anger. You do *not* just show up at a Dragon's lair without permission.

"Tat, you and Greg go around back and fly in behind him. Stay high and quiet."

"Aye," she said, "The intruder will rue his mistake."

"Dunc, I'm gonna want Big Greg," I said.

Greg smiled viciously. "Sweet!"

They flew off through the house, headed toward the deck.

I tapped a digital button on the monitor, activating a microphone.

"I've been known to kill uninvited guests," I said.

My voice came from speakers hidden in the archway above the front door. Bay stopped his shifting and jumped a little.

"I deeply apologize for the intrusion, I mean no disrespect," he said to the front door, not knowing where else to direct his words. He pulled his cap off his head deferentially.

"I'm feeling way past disrespected. Murderous, is more appropriate."

He had dark tan skin, but his face blanched noticeably when he heard that.

"I'm here to help you find Annalisa," he said quickly.

He'd just managed to put a pause on his possible impending murder. If he knew she was missing, then he might know something that could actually prove useful.

"Take ten steps backwards, and keep your hands where I can see them."

"As you wish," he said, backing away with his hands above his head.

"Throw Greg at him when I give the word," I said to Duncan.

"You got it," he responded with a nod.

I slung the Odachi across my back, raised the shotgun, and walked outside. Duncan moved with me, stopping on the porch as I continued down the front steps.

The closer I got to him, the angrier I became. My home is my sanctuary, safe place, lair, castle, Batcave, and fortress of solitude, all rolled into one. His being here was a violation of the most intimate order. As if he'd murdered my mother right in front of me.

Bay took one look at my face, saw the utter rage burning at him from my eyes, and started backing up as if pushed by the force of my anger.

"I understand how egregious this violation is, Master Ddraik," he said quickly.

"No," I said, "I really don't think you do."

"In service to Annalisa, I could think of no other course to take."

Interesting word choice. He was putting himself squarely in the servant class and it was completely natural for him. He was a man used to servitude, far beyond being Annalisa's driver.

He was still backing away from me.

"Stop moving," I growled at him.

"I understand your anger but please believe me, I am here to help you," he said, taking another step back. I don't think he realized he did it. "I have no wish to die."

"Epically bad choice coming here, then. Do you know where Annalisa is?"

"At the moment, no," he answered.

"Then what possibly makes you think you can help me?"

"I have means," he said quickly, "If we can find a way to work together, I believe..."

Means? If? Work together? Fuck this.

"Dunc," I said over my shoulder.

"Greg, sic 'em!" Duncan said, his voice ringing with a magic-infused echo.

"Banzai!" came a bellowing cry from above.

Greg dropped from the darkness. What hit the ground directly behind Bay was Big Greg, an imp in his true form. Roughly the size and shape of a silverback gorilla. His wings had grown into giant batwings, and his arms were almost longer than his body and ended in razor-taloned fists the size of canned hams. His mouth unhinged impossibly wide, like a snake's, and he roared. Froth and spittle sprayed from his lips.

Bay turned, took one look at Greg, shouted in fear, and fell over. He started scuttling backwards toward me like an epileptic crab, barely able to keep his hands and feet underneath himself because he was trying to move so fast. Greg stomped slowly towards him, slamming his huge fists into the ground and roaring ferociously. Bay bumped into me, and I put the barrel of the AA-12 firmly against his forehead.

"Maybe I'll let him eat you," I said.

Greg clacked his long sharp teeth together and drooled a lot.

Bay shook his head, his expression changing from fear to frustration. "Pull the trigger or serve me as a meal, it makes no difference. If you choose either course, then I cannot help you."

Dammit. Every burning emotion I had wanted me to shoot this guy's face off, but that could cost me valuable information about Annalisa if he actually had any. I took a calming breath. I could shoot his face off later if he turned out to be full of shit.

"That's enough, Greg."

The imp stopped mid-growl and started laughing hysterically. He sat down on his butt with a thump and wrapped his arms around himself in unrestrained giggling glee.

"Oh, sweet Jesus! Did you see the look on his face? He probably pissed himself. Dude, did you piss yourself?" he rolled over onto his back, shaking with laughter.

I glanced over my shoulder at Dunc, then nodded towards Greg.

"Shaddup, you moron," Duncan barked.

There was a flash of purple from his staff, and Greg shrank back to his bound size. He clamped his hands over his mouth to stifle his hysterics.

Tat zipped down and positioned herself between Bay's legs and cocked a foot back, ostensibly to kick him in the nuts if he tried anything funny. I didn't know how effective it would be, but I liked her style.

I glared down at him, "Who are you?"

"I am…"

"Say Karl Bay, and I'm letting her kick you in the nuts. Repeatedly."

Tat smiled wickedly.

"I cannot answer that question. Please ask another," he said with a pained expression and frustration in his voice.

"What?"

That caught me off guard and surprisingly cooled my anger a bit. He'd knowingly walked into an immensely dangerous situation for himself, then immediately started deflecting my questions, while claiming he was here to help? No sane person would do that unless they had no choice, or an ace up their sleeve, and he looked very out of aces.

"Why not?"

"I cannot," his eyes were pleading, "Please, ask another,"

"All right. You don't know where Annalisa is. Do you know how to find her?"

"I cannot answer that question either," he said, his frustration even more pronounced.

I had a thought. He might look human, but I'd bet my left nut he wasn't. Not with the ability to get this close to my house without setting off wards and alarms.

"What are you?"

He shook his head and said quietly, almost sadly "I cannot answer that. You must ask a different question."

"Tell me why you're here," I said, as I pressed the barrel into his head a little harder. It was a statement, not a question.

"Well stated, Master Ddraik," he said, his expression relaxing a little, "To protect Annalisa. The letters she received, I sent them."

"Prove it."

He rattled each one of them off, line for line. As her driver he hadn't been privy to what they'd said, so it gave his claim credibility.

"What was your purpose in sending her the letters?"

"It was an act of desperation. I was trying to keep her safe. I was in service to her parents and vowed to them I would."

Now that was telling. Humans weren't into making vows, except at weddings, and those didn't mean much going by the number of married women I'd slept with. They do, however, mean a great deal to beings of the supernatural kind. If you make a vow and it's sealed with magic, breaking it can result in anything from a mild case of warts to a bad case of death. Magically bound vows were a great way to force people to keep secrets. It didn't take much to figure it after that.

"You're like Annalisa."

His eyes went wide in surprise, and he smiled, "I didn't know you were aware of that."

"I'm full of surprises. So, are you?"

"Am I what, Master Ddraik?" He looked at me expectantly, like I was a contestant on a game show, and he was rooting for me. I wanted to punch him.

"Are you djinn?" I asked.

There was a pulse of light around his body, visible for only a split second, and it felt like something covering him broke. Like invisible shackles had been released and fallen off.

"Well asked, Master Dragon," he said.

"Damn," Duncan said, awe in his voice. "He had a geas on him, Red. So good I couldn't detect a whiff of it."

Duncan had walked around us and was standing opposite me, trapping the djinn in a cross fire if he tried anything funny. Tat was still in her nut-kick position, ready to strike.

"Give him some space, little one," I said to Tat, tapping my shoulder.

She flew to it as the djinn stood. He looked nervously at Greg, who sat uselessly on the ground turning his head back and forth between Duncan and me, like he was watching a tennis match.

"What's your name?" I asked him.

"I am In-Ra Dosham, Master of Servants to the late Lord and Lady Dahllaside. Rulers of Great House Dahllaside, keepers of the Sacred Light of the Black Rift, and rightful heirs to the Imperial Golden Throne of Djinn. Parents of the woman you know as Annalisa VanSusstern," he bowed at the waist.

I hadn't heard a title like that since I'd read Tolkien. I swear, I spend one really, *really* drunk night on a bar stool next to the guy babbling my snockered head off, and he gets all the credit for creating the centuries-seminal work of fantasy literature, and I never got dime one from it. Screw Tolkien... and the Orc he rode in on.

"Show me the real you," I said.

He nodded and entwined his fingers together in an arcane shape. The exterior illusion melted off him in layers, like ice in a desert sun.

The djinn who stood before me looked to be in his 70s, by human terms. His deeply lined face was long and slightly gaunt, accentuating sharp cheekbones and a hawkish nose. In contrast, his body was still fit, lean, and wiry. His skin was reddish black, which contrasted his bright yellow eyes that had vertical cat eye pupils.

He had a thick beard which tapered to a point, and his long jet-black hair was draped down his back in a braided ponytail, held in place at the top of his head by a shiny gold cuff. His upper half was bare, and a long skirt-like garment made of heavy white material and held up by a thick brown leather belt covered his lower half. Brown leather boots covered his feet. Around his neck was a thick gold necklace with a hefty blood-red stone dangling from it.

"Have I convinced you of my sincerity to help?" he asked.

I was convinced he was sincere about being a djinn. I was still miles away from trusting him.

"How long have you been with Annalisa?"

"Since the day she was born, in one guise or another. When the Great House Dahllaside was massacred, my masters fled the Realm of Djinn, taking me with them. I was the only one they trusted. I have been her caretaker since her birth, and her protector since her parents' deaths."

"Protector how?"

I am vow-bound to protect Annalisa with my life. The same vow commands me to never reveal to her what she truly is. Or reveal to anyone what I am, if it could in some way serve to inform her of her true nature."

I nodded in understanding. "I already know what she is."

"So I break no vow by revealing myself to you. It was her parents' wish that she live her life in the safety provided by being human."

Like being human is such a safe thing. "The letters. What were you trying to accomplish by sending them?" I asked.

"My hope was that someone like you would be hired to protect her."

Booyah! I'd been right about that. I mentally patted myself on the back.

"I began to feel the constant stirring of magical energies around her, as if there were something seeking her out. In all our time here that had never happened before, and I was faced with the painful realization that I could do little to directly protect her from a supernatural threat without revealing myself. As the energies grew closer and stronger, I sent the letters."

"Why didn't you come directly to me after she was taken?"

"Do you think I did not try?" he said forcefully. "Every time I tried, something prevented me. The federal agents at the hospital. The White Dragon at the hotel. Intervening at Sword & Shield Security would have been suicide."

He'd been staying close, had to give him that.

"You proved most challenging to find after you disappeared from there. It took me until now to find you again."

"How exactly did you pull that off?" If the security of my home was compromised in any way by more than just him, I'd never feel safe here again.

"If I may?" he asked, pointing toward a small pouch hanging from his belt. He started moving his hand slowly toward it.

On my shoulder, Tat's glow bloomed to full wattage in alarm. I actually had to squint.

"Stay your hand, trespasser!"

"Stand down, Tat. We're playing nice for the moment."

She powered down but continued, glaring daggers at In-Ra.

Using two fingers, he removed several reddish-brown hairs clumped together with dried blood from the pouch. My hair and blood.

"I retrieved them from the Sword & Shield Security building. A tracking spell led me here."

I'd probably left enough DNA at S&S for an army of people to track me, if they had the magical know-how. I made a mental note to go back and burn the building down when I had the time.

"And getting to my front door without being detected, or setting off alarms?"

"I am djinn. Though a minor one of the servant class, I am not without abilities. Magics to avoid your wards, veils to hide from your cameras, glamours to disguise, are all within my grasp," he explained.

"So, you're here to help? That's all?"

"There is nothing else. To see Annalisa safe is my life's purpose."

"Got any ideas on how to track her?" I asked.

In-Ra lifted the red stone hanging from his necklace. "Would her blood be of service?" His lips turned up in a slight grin.

"Hell yes," said Duncan, stepping forward.

"Hold your piss, stubby," I said to Duncan. "If that's her blood, why haven't you already tracked her with it?"

"To what end? I don't have the strength to fight the White Dragon myself. Even if I did, I could not rescue Annalisa without revealing myself to her. Which I cannot do. It must be used by an intermediary."

Much as I hated to admit it, that made sense. I held out my hand.

"Give."

He slipped it off his neck and placed it in my palm.

Our visit to the Reds just got put on hold. The stone was a direct link to Annalisa and one I was going to take advantage of right now. I tossed it to Duncan. "We'll go back to your place and use it there," I said to him.

As soon as the stone left my grip I drew one of the Rondel daggers and put it to In-Ra's throat. He didn't even know I had moved my arm until he felt the blade, whisper close against his throat. His eyes went wide in surprise.

I didn't yell. I didn't even raise my voice.

"There are exactly seven people who know the location of my home. They all earned my trust over long periods of time and were invited here in my good graces. You are not one of them. The only reason I'm not slitting your throat where you stand is because of your vow to Annalisa, and that stone."

His lower lip trembled.

"You are now number eight. If anyone new should discover my home, I will immediately hold you responsible and you will owe me blood debt. You understand what that means?"

"That you won't rest until I'm dead by your hand."

"And I promise you it will not be quick or easy. I will make it hurt."

He swallowed. It was more of a gulp.

"Vow to me now, with the same fealty you gave to the masters of House Dahllaside, that you will never reveal the location of my house to another soul. Swear it by your life and on your blood."

"I vow it. By my life and on my blood, none shall ever learn the location of this sanctuary from me."

I nicked his throat with the blade. Nothing deep, just enough to draw blood and sting.

"By your blood," I said coldly.

I held his eyes for a moment longer then sheathed the blade. "Put your street clothes back on, you can't run around in public looking like that. Go get your car and pull it in here. I'm driving."

I turned on my heel and went to the front doors. I locked the house and sealed the wards then strode toward the garage. Duncan and Greg fell in behind me. From my shoulder, Tat whispered in my ear.

"Methinks you should have flayed the villain and been done with him."

I grunted. She may have been right.

CHAPTER NINETEEN

We were powering down the 5 freeway in my black Dodge Ram 3500 dually. Quad cab with a modified Cummins turbo diesel, kicking out 800 completely eco-unfriendly horses. The thing had so much torque it could pull a house off its foundation. It was lifted six inches and sitting on big off-road tires. The glass was bulletproof, and the engine compartment was armored.

Duncan and Greg sat in the back. In-Ra was next to me riding shotgun. Tat sat on the dashboard in front of him, her orange eyes boring holes through him. It didn't go unnoticed.

"Have I offended you in some way, little Fae?" he asked her.

"Aye!" she said, stabbing an accusing finger at his face. "You invaded our home."

"I ask your forgiveness."

She folded her arms across her chest and squinted her fiery eyes at him.

"Ask all ye like. I'm not feeling forgiving."

"I know my offense was egregious. I am deeply sorry for it."
She jabbed a finger at him.

"You've brought us opportunity to save one in our care, for that I'll tolerate you."

I grinned. Tat always took my responsibilities and fights as her own. One of the many things I respected about her.

"But I'll nae be taking my eyes off ye, trespasser!"

In-Ra looked at me helplessly.

"Don't look at me. I agree with her."

He looked back to Tat.

"Were the circumstances different, the situation not so dire, I would never have done such a thing."

Did he know how dire? What Alamander actually had planned? I wasn't inclined to tell him yet, but I was curious about how much he knew.

"Do you know why Alamander took Annalisa?" I asked.

"He will use the power of the alignment to break the spells on Annalisa and release her true form. Then he'll bind her. What he can do with that kind of power is unthinkable."

Tat humphed condescendingly. I'd filled her in on all the information Duncan had given me, she fully knew what was at stake. He looked at her then quickly back to me.

"There is more? Worse than that?"

"Much more. Much worse," I said, but didn't elucidate.

His concern was wholly focused on Annalisa, his vow to her, and her safety. The bigger stakes were still unknown to him.

I started to get heavy on the gas pedal. "Can you veil the truck?" I asked In-Ra. "I'm going to break some speed limits."

"I am not sure if I can cover something this size completely," he said, frowning.

"I got this," Duncan said from the back.

"Hold your staff, Dunc, I wanna see what he can do."

"Hold your staff..." Greg repeated with a burst of giggles.

Duncan grumbled under his breath and elbowed Greg. In-Ra interlocked the thumb and forefinger of both his hands together and raised them to the center of his chest, closing his eyes in concentration. After a moment he exhaled deeply.

"Hammer down," he said, and grinned slightly.

I planted the accelerator. Driving behind a veil has the advantage of allowing you to speed like you're in the Daytona 500 because no one can see you. The disadvantage is that no one can see you, and at 120 miles per hour in a vehicle with the handling characteristics of a giant brick, things can get exciting fast if you're not paying attention. At 2:45 am there was very little traffic on the road, but there was still one near miss when a car in front of us made a sudden change across three lanes with no blinker, forcing me to lock up the brakes for a few seconds.

"Fuck-damn-holy-hell!" Duncan shouted.

"Jesus H. Christ on a taco!" agreed Greg.

"Stop being weenies," I said, as I punched it again.

I hadn't really cared if In-Ra could totally veil the truck. What I wanted to learn was how much it would cost him in terms of effort. I had my senses focused on him the entire time, taking in everything about him. His scent as it changed through his exertions, the taste and feel of the magic coming off him, the flush of his skin, the sheen of sweat on his forehead, how his muscles twitched harder and more often the longer he kept up the spell. I cataloged it all. I wanted to know if he was a minor adept, as he'd said he was back at the house, or if there was more to his power than he was revealing. My senses were telling me he was straining. Not at his peak, but not far from it either, by the time we got back to Duncan's place about thirty minutes later.

We hustled inside, straight to the living room. I was about to start moving the couch when the tip of Duncan's staff flared with bright white light. With a fluid movement, he lifted the big couch into the air and floated it backwards about six feet then landed it gently on the ground. With the same ease, he lifted and moved the table to a far corner of the room, uncovering the rings in the floor.

"Apparently Master Yoda doesn't have a headache anymore," I said.

"Sober I am, so powerful magic can I wield," he said, grinning.

From a small bookshelf he grabbed a gold brazier, a silver metal plate, sage, and some charcoal.

"A blood tracking spell is a lot more accurate than what I did for you earlier, but it's also a hell of a lot more involved, so shut up and let me work," he said.

There are few better conduits than blood for magically tracking a person. The hair tracking spell had been kind of a GPS, leading me to a specific target over distance. A blood spell could be used to open a direct portal to the person you were trying to reach, if you knew how to create one. Duncan did.

That was also why I didn't want him to perform the spell at my house. Like any doorway, a portal went both ways. If someone followed us back through before we could close it, they would've literally been in my backyard. I wasn't about to allow Alamander, or anyone with him, possible access to my home when Duncan opened it. He understood and respected my reasons. His summoning circle could also supercharge the spell to vastly increase its reach and accuracy. Something not available at Casa Ddraik.

Duncan knelt on the floor in the center of the circle, placing his tools in front of him.

"Gimme the stone," he said to me, holding out an open palm.

I tossed him In-Ra's pendant, and he quickly popped the stone out of it.

He put the charcoal in the brazier, whispered a word, and it instantly glowed red hot. He lit the sage with it and waved it over the stone in his open palm, then around his head for a moment. Little trails of the sweet-smelling smoke drifted around his body as he put the sage aside and focused intently on the red stone in his palm, murmuring to himself. He paused with a slightly confused look on his face then he glanced over at In-Ra.

"Clever," he said, "What's the djinn word for 'release'?"

"Tukoush," In-Ra replied.

Duncan nodded and closed his fist around the stone. He repeated the word and squeezed until his knuckles turned white. There was a popping sound, and dark red blood began to run from his fist onto the plate and pool there. He opened his fingers, and the last of the blood drained off his hand as if it were pulled, leaving it completely clean. He started chanting rhythmically as he sprinkled charcoal into the blood. The mix coalesced and thickened, swirling into a spiral pattern.

I quickly checked all my guns, making sure they were cocked and loaded, safeties off.

In-Ra was several feet behind me, glamoured in a completely different form. A short, stocky man in his forties with salt and pepper hair and beard, wearing a rumpled suit. When I got back through the portal with Annalisa, it wouldn't make sense for Karl Bay to be standing there.

Greg and Tat hovered in the air between the djinn and me.

Duncan's chanting rose in volume. The blood spiral began to spin in a circle, and energy coursed through it. The wall of the sealed summoning circle become visible with a pale blue light, running floor to the ceiling. With a wave of his arm, he broke the circle.

All that energy was sucked into the blood and then bloomed upwards into a vertical, round, flat circle above it. Made from crackling red energy, it had a circumference of about six feet and was about the width of a dime, sitting about six inches off the floor. Duncan rocked backwards off his knees and onto his feet, snatching up his staff and quickly taking a couple of steps back.

"Got her!" he said.

A black pinpoint appeared in the center of the crackling red mass and started to expand rapidly outward as the portal opened, obliterating the red energy until it danced only around the edges of the flat black circle. The black slowly began to fade to grey. Images on the other side became visible as the grey turned to white, like a TV image coming slowly into focus.

"Get ready to move!" Duncan shouted.

I'd been ready. I had the AA-12 in one hand and a Desert Eagle in the other. The Odachi was slung across my back. Battle-adrenaline was screaming through my veins, and my teeth were clenched in a ferocious, unreleased snarl.

The white became clear, and I saw her. She was sitting in a high-backed chair, and it looked like she was holding a teacup to her lips. Tea? What the hell? She was looking at something but not the portal, so it hadn't opened on her side yet.

Every muscle coiled as I prepared to leap. I never got the chance.

Annalisa turned her face directly toward the portal, a quizzical look on it. Then the white snapped back to black and the whole portal crashed in on itself, collapsing back into an angry crackling ball of red energy.

"Shit!" Duncan shouted, "She's been..."

He didn't get a chance to finish as the ball of energy shot at him like an RPG. He whipped his staff in front of him as the ball exploded around him. The room lit up like lightning had struck.

I was pushed backwards about five feet and had to drop to my knees to avoid being blasted over. Tat and Greg got blown backwards into the wall, hitting it with loud thumps. In-Ra was knocked flat on his back. Duncan flew sideways, hit a section of the couch hard enough to rock it up into the air, and bounced over it, crashing into the floor.

He must have been able to absorb a lot of energy from the detonation because the lightshow was much bigger than the concussive force of the blast. I was on my hands and knees for almost a minute, waiting for the stars to clear out of my eyes and the ringing in my ears to subside. When they did, I stomped over to In-Ra, who was still on his back in a daze.

"What the fuck just happened?" I said, barely restraining the rage in my voice.

"I do not know." He was blinking his eyes rapidly, trying to clear his vision. Tears ran down his cheeks.

"You're gonna have to do a whole lot better than that," I said, towering over him.

"This was not my doing. I swear it by my blood vow to you."

"Red," Duncan said weakly, "It's not his fault."

He was on his side, propped up on one elbow. Greg fluttered quickly to his side and helped him to his feet. He leaned heavily on his charred staff for support.

"I gotcha, boss," Greg said.

"Thanks, dufus," Duncan replied.

"What the hell happened?" I growled.

"She was shielded from her side."

Greg helped him onto the couch where he collapsed in a sprawl.

"Counter magic. Strong stuff," he said, "As soon as the portal started to open on her side all the energy backlashed."

"And you didn't anticipate that? Prepare for it? Isn't that fucking magic 101?" I shouted, fuming.

She had been right there, not more than six feet away from me. One leap and I would have had her in my arms. This whole thing could have been over. I was pissed and taking it out on Duncan. He wasn't in the mood for taking it.

"Did you want to cast the spell, lizard?" he fired back at me, his face turning red with anger, "Oh wait, you don't know how!"

I'd struck a nerve. A big one. He shot to his feet and glared at me with steel in his eyes.

"Don't fucking tell me how to do magic until you can do it better than me, asshole! So basically never!"

I unconsciously took a couple of steps toward him, my fists balled. The stubborn old bastard stood his ground. We stared at each other for a long moment, the tension growing between us until I felt a cool, tiny hand on my face. Tat hovered there, lightly touching my cheek.

"Be calm, Anii," she said, using the faerie word for lover, "You should nae treat your friends so. Twas not his fault the effort failed, your rage is misplaced."

I drew a long breath and exhaled, consciously dialing back my anger.

"You're right. You ok, little one?"

"I am," she said, smiling back at me. "Worry not."

As usual, she was my voice of reason when I needed it. I relaxed my stance and took a step back.

"Sorry, Dunc. She was so close. I could have had her."

He shook his head at me, his glare fading as the corners of his mouth turned up in a tiny grin. "Fucking Dragons," he huffed.

"You need anything, boss?" Greg asked him.

"Ice and aspirin."

"Check," he said, and fluttered off quickly. Tat zipped after him.

"It wasn't a total loss, lizard. I got a general fix on her," Duncan said, slumping back down on the couch.

"Where?"

"Somewhere between Koreatown and downtown."

"Dammit, still a lot of real estate," I muttered. Still, it was better than nothing.

"Was Annalisa drinking... tea?" In-Ra asked

"Sure looked like it," I said.

I don't know what I'd expected, but I can tell you without a doubt, it wasn't seeing Annalisa calmly sipping from a teacup. Magically restrained in a casting circle, locked in a dungeon, tied to a bed, and sedated. Those scenarios I could picture. Not fucking tea. I took another deep breath, forcing the red cloud of anger out of my head so I could think clearly.

Alamander had been polite enough to approach me face to face and invite me to join him before he'd tried to kill me. Thinking about it now, there was a very strong feeling of old-world manners and charm about him, even in his speech patterns. He seemed to be holding on to more of the time he was born in than I did. I was very much about being part of the present, not the past. Not all Half-kin are like that. It made them more conspicuous when dealing with anyone but other Half-kin, or supernatural beings.

So there was logic to the idea of his treating her well and seeing to her comfort. Treating a female prisoner like a helpless damsel was more prevalent behavior than you might expect from many supernatural beings. If they knew said female was weaker than them or they weren't, you know, trying to eat her.

Greg flew back in carrying a cloth full of ice and a glass of water. Tat flew beside him, holding a bottle of aspirin. She handed the bottle to Duncan as Greg placed the ice gently on his head.

"Thanks," he said to them. He popped the cap, swallowed some aspirin right from the bottle, and then drained the water.

"What now?" he said, after he swallowed.

"The Red Elves," I said, scowling. "I need to have a talk with Chulunn-Bat."

CHAPTER TWENTY

"I'm gonna need the big stick, then," Duncan said, heaving himself off the couch and heading to his bedroom.

Tat landed on my shoulder, "I do like the Reds, they are so pretty."

Contrary to popular belief, not all elves are.

"We're not going to sightsee, Tat."

"I shall multitask," she said, flicking my ear.

"Why do we go to the Red Elves?" In-Ra asked. He was keeping a little distance from me after my outburst at him. Good, he should be scared of me.

"Because he said so," Tat barked, hooking her tiny thumb at me, "Tis all ye need to know."

As good as she was at cooling my jets when I got heated, she could hold a grudge like no one's business if she wanted to. Duncan emerged from his bedroom holding a new staff.

"Big stick," he said with pride.

I could see why he called it that. It was about five feet tall and made of shiny black wood. Its entire length was inlaid with metal bands of gold, spaced about two inches apart. At the top of the staff was a copper Phoenix which looked as if it were flying upward out of a ring of gold metal flames. The bottom of the staff was capped with a rune-covered iron spike.

"Compensating for something?" I asked.

"Says the guy with the giant dick on wheels parked outside?"

"Touché," I said, "Let's roll."

The five of us piled back into the rolling dick and headed toward Beverly Hills. It was a little past 4 am as I sped down the 101. The sky was just starting to lighten in the east as the sun crept toward the horizon.

Benedict Canyon is a long winding road that snakes upward from Sunset Boulevard into the lofted hills of Beverly, eventually ending at Mulholland Boulevard. Following its route, you'll pass gated drives and high wall, often covered by expansive tree lines. They block massive houses, sitting on huge tracts of land, from prying eyes. Barely a glimpse of a rooftop is visible behind these modern embattlements.

Such was the case of the gate I was stopped in front of. Chulunn-Bat ruled the entirety of the West Coast Red Elves from the unseen compound that lay beyond it.

Rousing him at this hour probably wouldn't go over well, but I wasn't overly concerned about it. I only had two full days left to save Annalisa and stop a catastrophe. If I had to interrupt a high elf's beauty rest so be it. He wouldn't be the first elf lord I'd pissed off.

Duncan had his arm out the passenger window, his fingers extended outward toward the gate.

"Magic's in the air. Kinda a dome over the whole property. Damn big one."

"Wards?" I asked.

"Doesn't feel so defensive. Probably a glamour, or shield of some sort, to protect it from view from the air."

I reached through the window and pressed a button on the call box.

A formal male voice responded almost immediately, "Hello. How may I help you?" Not a hint of sleepiness to it. Round the clock security, no surprise.

"My name is Randall Ddraik. I need to speak to Chulunn-Bat."

"At 4:45 in the morning, Mr. Ddraik? Do you have an appointment?"

"No."

"I'm very sorry, Mr. Ddraik, Chulunn-Bat does not see people without appointments."

"It's extremely important."

"I'm afraid I can't accommodate you. We'll be happy to receive you when you have an appointment."

Fortunately, I spoke elvish conversationally. "My name is Randall Eric Ddraik, Half-kin Red Dragon. I'm here to see Earl Chulunn-Bat of House Bat. It's a matter of great importance."

There was pause then he asked, "Are you alone, Mr. Ddraik?"

"I have four companions with me," I said.

Duncan guffawed out loud.

"Excuse me?" said the voice in the box.

I whipped my gaze to Duncan. "What'd I say?"

"The word you used for companion roughly translates to concubine or prostitute."

Greg burst into laughter. I growled under my breath. Ok, so my elvish was more, um... casual, than conversational.

"I'm with a wizard, a djinn, an air sprite, and a soon to be injured imp," I said, reverting back to English.

Greg tried his best to shut up.

"Hold, please," said the voice, with a bit of a chuckle in it this time.

We waited for about five minutes, then the gate began to swing open.

"Follow the drive and stay to the left when it forks. You will be met in the rotunda."

I pulled through the gate and headed down a sloping drive. It was lined with trees that had been perfectly cut to form a shaded canopy over the entire driveway. The road forked after fifty yards and I veered left. Down the drive to the right I could see what looked like one, or maybe two very large houses.

The rotunda was large enough to fit twenty cars comfortably but was currently populated with about a half dozen exotic sports cars and SUVs.

As a man who appreciates a good lair, I was impressed with Chulunn's spread. It was four stories of modern, swooping, curving glass and steel. If the Disney Concert Hall and a Frank Lloyd Wright house got it on and had a child, this place would be the result.

As I pulled to a stop my skin started vibrating in a most particular way. My muscles coiled and my jaw clenched. Duncan caught my expression.

"What's wrong?" he asked.

"There's another Dragon here," I said, "Dunc, you're with me. Be ready. The rest of you stay in the truck."

I got out and met Duncan on the passenger side. We faced the front doors together. I pushed my coat back over my hips, exposing the pommels of the Rondel daggers, keeping my fingers close to them.

The doors swung open and the Dragon emerged, four elf guards brandishing tactical rifles trailing close behind him. Even with all that firepower coming towards us, I relaxed a little. I knew him. His name was Cuda.

He was Steel-born, from the Metallic Order of Dragons. Seven feet tall and three hundred seventy-plus pounds of bulging, dense muscle. He looked like a comic book superhero come to life. The Honda I could bench press, make his a Cadillac. A '57 Coupe DeVille.

His skin was as dark black as chocolate and so smooth he looked like he'd been dipped in it. He was... brutish-looking, that was the best way to describe him. He had a short faux hawk of tightly curled black hair. Large white bone, circular earrings dangled from each lobe. He was wearing a white T-shirt, and I could practically hear the threads screaming for dear life, trying to hold the seams together. Baggy red sweatpants and black and white Air Jordans covered his legs and size eighteen feet. The pommels of two blades jutted up above his massive traps, strapped to his back in some kind of double rig I couldn't see.

Despite his size he walked with a languid, relaxed stride that suggested the ability to move fast. I'd seen him fight and knew it wasn't just a suggestion. He was as good as... almost as good as me.

"Randall, great to see you, mon!" His pearly white teeth beamed at me, all the brighter when contrasted against his dark skin.

He reached out with a huge hand and clasped me tight on the shoulder with it. Cuda was Caribbean and still spoke with the accent. At least when he wanted to.

"You too, near-kin," I looked him up and down and shook my head sadly, "We have got to talk about your style."

"It ain't my fashion sense I get hired for."

"Lucky, you'd never work if you did."

He chuckled, a deep rumbling sound.

"When did you go to work for House Bat?" I asked, nodding my head toward the elves behind him.

They had stopped about six feet back, three men and one woman. Their casual jeans and button-down shirts were counter-pointed by the aforementioned serious hardware in their hands and short swords strapped to their hips. None of them stood over five-seven, which was normal. Reds were the shortest of all the elf houses. They were tense, looking at me as if I were a bomb that might go off at any second.

"Bout three weeks ago," said Cuda.

"Chulunn needs your kind of protection? With his whole house behind him?"

He countered my question with one of his own as his hand got a little tighter on my shoulder.

"And you be showing up now, why?" he asked inquisitorially.

My eyes narrowed, and I tensed out of pure reflex. I glanced at his hand, then returned my gaze to meet his. I didn't like what that squeeze, or his tone implied.

"Curious coincidence, no?" he said, "I'll be needin' to know your reasons."

He winked at me and I understood. He was putting on a show for the elves behind him. He knew that if I was asking to come in the front door, not knocking it down, my immediate intentions were safe enough.

"I'm just here to talk, Cuda."

He removed his hand and nodded, "Thing's been getting tense within the Houses..."

"Cuda!" barked the female elf, cutting him off. "Chulunn-Bat will decide what information to share with him, not you!"

Cuda's smile became a flat line and his expression turned stone cold as he turned to face her.

"What's that you be sayin' now?" he said, his voice a low rumble.

His bulk had been blocking most of my view of them, and I peered around his massive back to take a good look at her. She was hot elf-candy. A midriff bearing a red T-shirt underneath her opened black dress shirt revealed four of what looked like an eight-pack stomach. She had on tight black leggings tucked into black knee-high combat boots. Her long strawberry blond hair was pulled back into a loose ponytail.

"House affairs are not yours to discuss with outsiders," she snapped.

She took a couple of steps forward her red eyes flashing with anger. Red Elves are so called because of their eye color. Deep, solid red with no discernable iris, slightly larger than a human's eyes, making them really stand out on their preposterously pretty faces.

"Don't get snappy at me, little bird, no matter your relations," Cuda said, "I work for Chulunn-Bat, not you."

I grinned. People hired Half-kin because you couldn't get better in terms of security and protection, but it came with some conditions and you accepted those if you hired us. A certain amount of bossiness was tolerated but only from the person paying the bills, not any of their lackeys. On past jobs I'd knocked a few heads together, literally, to remind those who'd forgotten that.

She didn't cow, maintaining her own cold gaze back at him. Tough, I liked her immediately. The three men behind her stepped up to stand by her side. They looked fit and lithe, like gymnasts ready to spring into a tumbling run. Also ready to pull the trigger immediately if she ordered it.

"Then take them to him," she said, icily.

Cuda looked back at me, flashing a big toothy grin, "Chulunn-Bat's niece, Kiava. She be havin' entitlement issues. C'mon, let's go see the boss man."

Cuda led, we followed, the elves brought up the rear. Fingers firmly on triggers.

The interior of the house was as modern and swoopy as the exterior, with contemporary minimalist furniture, big open spaces, high lofted ceilings, and flowing staircases. It was beautiful and cold.

"Not very hospitable," Duncan mumbled.

"But so pretty. And the ears!" Tat purred, from her perch on my shoulder.

Tat had a thing for ears, which was the Red's other discerning characteristic. They were six inches of pointy.

"You're gonna hurt my feelings," I chided her.

"Wouldst that I could, beast," she retorted playfully, flicking my ear. I think she flicked it, it may have been a bite. It's not like I can see my ears.

We arrived at an elevator deep in the house. All of us fit inside with room for a few more to spare. We went up to the third floor, and the doors opened onto a large conference room. As we exited the elves fanned out behind us, keeping their backs against the wall and their guns at the ready.

The whole room was painted red, from floor to ceiling. Two giant, red-tinted mirrors covered one wall. I felt like I was in a blood clot. A gleaming black marble conference table dominated the middle of the room, sitting on a glistening blackwood floor.

Chulunn-Bat dominated the far side of it, which was impressive for a guy who stood only five foot two. He carried himself like he was taller than Cuda, and he radiated the strength of someone who could command armies.

"Forgive my casual appearance," he said, "I was asleep and not expecting visitors at this hour."

He was wearing shiny red basketball shorts and a white tank top. His feet were bare. His short white hair really made his eyes and ears stand out.

"Forgive the late intrusion, but it couldn't be helped," I said, "What I need to discuss with you is urgent."

"You travel with an unusual group of companions, Mr. Ddraik."

"Yeah, they're fun at parties," I said.

"I can only imagine. Very well. Sit, talk," he gestured to a chair at the table closest to him.

We settled in around the table, except for Tat who stayed perched on my shoulder. Cuda had positioned himself behind Chulunn at a respectful but defensible distance.

I glanced at Duncan, and he gave me an almost imperceptible nod, smoothly shifting his staff so that it was angled at the elves by the elevator, readying himself for any possible threat behind us. He did it so casually he might as well have been scratching his nose.

"Do you know a White Dragon named Alamander?" I asked.

He cocked an eyebrow at me. "I am familiar with the name."

"Has he come to see you?"

"No. Others I know, but not me."

"Other elves, or other supernaturals?"

"Others of my House."

"Do you know what he talked to them about?"

I had all my senses focused on Chulunn-Bat. A person's body gives off all kinds of telltale signs when its owner starts lying. Increased heart rate, sweating, nervous twitches. When I'm tuned in, I'm kinda like a Half-kin lie detector.

"Why would I be inclined to share that information with you?"

Nothing, not a single tell of any kind. He was as calm as a windless day.

"Because the fate of the realms might depend on it." It was vague but still enough to keep his attention.

Chulunn glanced at Cuda.

"Randall is OK, boss. If he coming to you with his hands empty, you can trust his intentions," Cuda said. The bona fides of a Half-kin can carry a lot of weight.

"I don't know what he talked about, but I do know whom he spoke to," Chulunn said, looking back to me.

"Orsa Rike?"

He tapped his fingers on the table, and his brow furrowed at the mention of Orsa. I might have gotten a blip in his heart rate.

"Orsa. A thorny subject, one deeply in my side of late," he said with a frustrated sigh.

"I have reason to believe that thorn is gonna get a lot deeper in a very short time," I said, "I just need to be sure you're not in bed with her."

"That bitch is the last woman I would ever bed. I would rather be made a eunuch."

Jesus. I've never met a woman who pissed me off so much that I'd want to remove my junk over sleeping with her. That's just crazy talk.

"Did you wake me at this ridiculous hour, with your matter of great importance, just to speak riddles?" he said, fixing me with a red stare.

"I'm not trying to be obtuse, just cautious. I'd rather err on the side of not helping the world end," I said.

"World end?"

"Figuratively. It's probably just as bad though," I said.

"Still with the riddles?"

My limited knowledge of Chulunn said that he was a strong leader and an honorable man, his name literally translated into 'strong stone.' I had to risk that was true, and tell him at least some of what I knew. He wasn't going to give me information about his house affairs otherwise.

"Whatever House Ziwix is up to, and it is most assuredly something, they will get it done before we finish our conversation if you don't start being more forthcoming."

He extended his arm, exposing the arteries in his wrist.

"Would you like to add touch to your sensory scan, to help decide if you can trust me?"

He might have the appearance of a middle-aged man, but I knew he was well past the thousand-year mark. It's hard to get something past a thousand-year-old elf. Even one wearing basketball shorts.

If he wasn't involved with Ziwix I lost nothing by telling him what I knew, and I stood to gain a lot. On the other hand, if he was playing me to see how much I knew and if I was a threat, then things could go to hell real quick once I started talking. Especially if the elves behind us started pulling the triggers their fingers were so itchy on.

As if reading my mind Chulunn looked at the guards.

"Lower your weapons, you will not need them."

They obeyed without hesitation. I studied him for one measured beat and then took the risk.

"It's like this…" I said.

I told him everything about Alamander, Annalisa, and our theory about House Ziwix's involvement in the impending Dragongeddon. I told him about Nerufane kidnapping Drop and Shrill in order to blackmail me into giving him Annalisa, and the Darklings' unknown master. I left out the part about the Vanatori. They weren't relevant to the situation anymore. It had absolutely nothing to do with any kind of embarrassment or bruised pride about having to run out of Sword & Shield. Nothing at all.

Chulunn listened intently, the furrow in his brow deepening the more I explained. In-Ra's mouth was agape by the time I finished. This was all news to him as well.

"Alamander must be insane," In-Ra said.

"Aye, Orsa as well," Chulunn agreed. "They would have to be, to even consider attempting such a thing," Chulunn said. His look was distant for a moment, then he refocused on me. "What do you want from me?"

"To start, all the information you can give me on Orsa and House Ziwix."

As flat as his expression was, I might as well have been looking at a statue.

"What?" I said.

"Information such as that is not just freely given."

I blinked at him, "Seriously?"

"Contentious as our relationship is, our affairs are intertwined in many ways. I will not just give you…"

"For fuck's sake, I don't want bank account numbers and business holdings. I couldn't give two tits about that kind of information. I want to know why she thinks this way. Who else could she be working with? And what would make her want to attempt something this colossally stupid?"

"Dragons and their attitudes," he said with some annoyance, "Her mentality, all of House Ziwix in fact, is a holdover from a time long ago when elves were the dominant race on the planet and walked openly, above man. They are the only elves I know, of any clan, who desire a return to those days."

"The entire Red Clan would benefit if they pull this off," I said, "You'd have a lock on the top of the supernatural food chain. Your access to power would be staggering."

I wanted to know if Chulunn had given this real thought. I'd been tempted when Alamander asked me to join him, before I knew if what he was proposing was even possible. I knew how intoxicating the thought of power could be.

"We are not power mad conquerors. If Orsa and Alamander succeed in this madness, she would surely kill any who she thought were a threat to her. Which means all of House Bat for certain, and quite probably any other houses of the clan that did fall into step behind her. Orsa is a paranoid megalomaniac, she would never leave dissenters to her newfound power, alive."

He had a strong point, and a vested interest in helping me prevent their plan from succeeding. For the safety of not just his house, but a lot of the Red Clan.

"She can't be acting alone," Chulunn said.

"How do you mean?" I asked.

"She doesn't have the authority, the will, or quite frankly the intelligence to undertake something this monumental."

"Who would back her in a play like this?"

"Her brother-in-law, Pharyn Cull."

"Bloody hell. I was afraid of that." He'd just confirmed my suspicions.

Chulunn raised an eyebrow at me. "You know him?"

"We have history. Almost two hundred years ago. He's a piece of shit."

"That's putting it mildly. And somewhat unelegantly."

Amongst his own kind, Pharyn was called the Blue-Red. His reputation for backstabbing and manipulation rivaled that of a Darkling. He was just a baron when I dealt with him. He was a duke now and outranked Chulunn.

"Pharyn and Orsa share philosophies when it comes to humanity. He has long been her benefactor and the reason her thorn can poke so aggravatingly into my side. He uses her in his machinations to keep his hands clean, and protects her from the Conclave when she needs it."

The Red High Noble Conclave was the ruling aristocracy of the clan. It was comprised of the heads of all the family houses and ultimately commanded by the reigning king or queen. Chulunn sat on the Conclave, Orsa didn't. Ziwix was part of the larger House Bat, and that didn't grant her a seat at the big table.

"What's his beef with humans?" I asked.

"Pride. He would rather rule in the light of day than thrive in secret, or manipulate from behind the scenes as we do now at times. There's also the matter of a human killing a Red King centuries ago. The cause of the Atlantis incident. One of that king's sons eventually became the founder of House Cull. He's never forgotten or forgiven what he takes as a personal affront from humanity."

It sounded like Pharyn was taking blood debt to the extreme.

"How does this information serve you?" Chulunn asked.

"Know your enemy."

"Wouldn't you be better off finding the djinn herself?" he asked, tapping his fingers lightly on the table.

"Been trying. Duncan almost had her with a tracking spell but got stonewalled by some powerful counter magic. We only managed to narrow her location to somewhere between Koreatown and downtown."

His pulse noticeably quickened when I said downtown, and I could see the gears working in his head.

"What are you thinking?" I asked.

"The tower," he said.

"Tower?"

"The US Bank tower, downtown. It's owned by Orsa. She and a contingent of House Ziwix make their home on the top seven floors. It would be an ideal place to sequester your client."

That made sense. "Do you know a way we can get in undetected?"

"Possibly, but now that you have involved me, I cannot allow you to take such a direct approach. Things between houses cannot be handled…"

I cleared my throat loudly and narrowed my eyes at him.

"You don't allow me to do anything. I'm sharing information out of respect. This situation affects far more than the two of us. Working together is in both our interests, but I don't work for you."

Chulunn's eyes narrowed to blood-red slits, and I could feel the air around him begin to hum with power. I'd just stomped over the line of respect and pissed him off. I didn't care, he wasn't seeing the big picture.

"All due respect, Earl Bat, what's happening here is the prelude to a goddamned nightmare about to be made very real. It's a metric fuck-ton more serious than any etiquette, or political bullshit between your houses."

He stood up. His eyes barely reached mine even though I was sitting, and I still got the impression I was being towered over. The air that was humming around him began to press up against me like a big, vibrating hand. Then abruptly it stopped. Chulunn's expression went from anger to surprise then back to anger, only not at me.

"I said keep your weapons down!" he bellowed, looking over my shoulder at the guards behind us.

I heard the simultaneous racking of multiple gun slides.

"Duncan!" I yelled in warning as I jumped to my feet. He was already ahead of me, never having taken his eyes off the guards.

A beat ahead of them, he spun out of his chair and swept his staff through the air in an arc. A half dome of translucent purple energy flashed to life in front of us, reaching from floor to ceiling.

The elves fired in unison. The shield shrieked in a cacophony of echoing sounds as gunfire slammed into it and ricocheted away.

I spun to face the shooters, putting myself in front of Chulunn, Tat still on my shoulder. In-Ra was on his feet, his glamour gone and a long dagger in his hand.

"Dunc?" I said.

"Got this," he snapped.

I looked over my shoulder at Chulunn, his fists were balled, and his expression was equal parts fury and confusion. Cuda was at his side.

"Not your orders?" I shouted at Chulunn over the racket.

"By the red of my eyes, no!"

They took their eyes very seriously.

"Fuck-balls!" Duncan yelled.

I looked back toward the guards. Two of them had lowered their guns and drawn their swords. The blades swam with silvery energy and were pointed at Duncan's shield. In unison the energy unleashed, lashing into the shield like angry vipers, turning it white where they struck.

Duncan grunted and was pushed backwards about a foot. Filigreed cracks covered the shield, and purple sparks started flying off it where the bullets were hitting.

"Shield's gone after another hit like that!" Duncan yelled, "Do something, lizard!"

"Allow me, wizard," Chulunn said, his voice hard as a sledgehammer. He stepped around me and up to Duncan, placing his hands on the splintering shield. Red energy flowed out of his hands into it, turning it blue where the two colors touched. The whole thing solidified and thrummed with new power. His timing couldn't have been better, as two more silver snakes of energy whiplashed into it.

"Impressive," Chulunn said through clenched teeth. "Too impressive."

The shield was protecting us, but it was also preventing me from getting to our attackers. There had to be a way around that. I realized it was right in front of me.

"Cuda, the table!" I shouted over the din. He nodded in understanding. "Duncan, push the shield forward past the table!"

He lowered the head of his staff and drove it toward the shield, taking a couple of steps forward as he did. Sweat covered his forehead, and his face flushed bright red. Chulunn moved with him, his teeth bared in a fierce snarl as he matched Duncan's steps. The shield moved forward until the full length of the table was on our side of it.

I grabbed one end, Cuda grabbed the other. We lifted it by its thick stone legs and turned it sideways, holding it at shoulder height like a giant marble shield. It took up almost the entire width of the room.

The shield shrieked again as it was hit by more of the silver energy. All the elves hurling it now.

"For fuck's sake, this isn't as easy as it looks!" Duncan yelled.

"You wanna hold the table?" I shot back. "As soon as they hit it again, drop the shield."

I looked at Cuda. "Ready?"

I AM DRAGON

"Ya, mon!" he said grinning fiercely.

The table must have weighed more than two thousand five hundred pounds, and he looked like he might as well have been holding a pillow for all the effort he seemed to be exerting. Show off.

The shield screamed as it was hit again. Dunc and Chulunn let it fall the second after, and Cuda and I charged forward like a couple of unchained bull elephants. The elves only had about two seconds to realize what was happening, by then it was too late. There was nowhere they could have gone except back into the elevator, but its doors weren't open.

We slammed into them at a dead run, crushing them between the table and the wall. Bones snapped, there were some unappetizing squishing noises. The table broke into three pieces and the wall cracked as if an earthquake had hit it.

A second before impact I saw an elf come leaping up over the table. It was Kiava. She tucked into a summersault and landed on one knee with her sword pointing right at Chulunn. Its blade dripping with silver energy.

"Dielli'te ji Felthat damnos!" she hissed, in a voice not her own.

Before she could unleash the charge, she was pummeled by Greg and In-Ra. Greg landed on her head like the ugliest hat in history, his belly in her face, arms and legs wrapped around her skull. In-Ra hit her from behind, knocking all three of them to the floor. He used the hilt of his dagger to strip the sword from her hand and caught her wrist in a lock hold. The blade clattered across the floor, the energy dissipating harmlessly.

Seconds later I was next to the downed threesome. I was just about to yank her off the ground when she began writhing and screaming.

"Holy shit!" Greg yelled, releasing her and flapping into the air.

"By my blood!" In-Ra said in shock, yanking his hands off the thrashing girl as if she were red hot. Which, it turns out, she was.

We watched as she burst into flames. The look on her face was one of confusion and agony. She was as surprised as we were by what was happening. Her expression vanished as she was completely consumed by the fire. The heat was intense, and the others took a few steps back. Oddly, the flames were confined to her body, not burning the floor at all. I moved toward her and blinked my secondary eyelid into place. A white-hot center point of heat around her neck bloomed into view. I reached down to grab it, my natural Red Dragon immunity to fire protecting me. What I pulled back was a necklace, a patch of melting skin coming off with it. I would have felt bad about that, but she had just tried to kill us. My sympathies were limited. As soon as I'd removed the necklace the flames died down and went out, leaving a charred, stinking mess on the floor at my feet.

I blinked back the lid and looked at the necklace. A simple silver chain with a big white stone dangling from it. It couldn't have been ordinary silver or it would have melted to slag in so much heat.

"What the hell just happened?" I asked, looking at Chulunn.

He stepped to my side. There was a coldness radiating from him that prickled my skin. It was very hard to read emotions in those solid red eyes, even so I could tell his were a swirling mix of deep anger and deeper heartache. It was a long moment before he answered me.

"My niece was just murdered before my eyes. May I?" he asked, holding out his hand.

As I placed the necklace in his palm the elevator doors opened and about a dozen elves flooded into the room, leaping over the broken pieces of the table. They were armed to the teeth and trained their guns on everyone who wasn't Chulunn-Bat. He held up a staying hand, barely looking up from the necklace.

"Hold, brothers," he said in a commanding voice. "I am safe, these are friends, lower your weapons."

They did as instructed but stayed very sharp and focused on us.

"Did you hear her voice, boss mon?" Cuda said to Chulunn. "She's been squawking at me for three weeks now. That wasn't her voice speakin'."

"No," Chulunn said, "It was Orsa's."

We moved to the far end of the room, allowing the contingent of guards that had entered to search the bodies of the dead, and respectfully cover Kiava's remains.

"Why would she try and kill you?" I asked.

"Kiava was the daughter of my youngest brother. He married a woman of House Ziwix despite my strong advice against it. Two years after the marriage he was killed in a hunting accident in Africa," Chulunn said.

"Suspicious circumstances?" I asked.

"On the face of it, no. Merely a tragic accident. He was the only non-blood member of Ziwix on the expedition, so I was suspicious, though I could prove no wrongdoing."

"What was she doing here as one of your guards?"

"After the accident I took her and her mother into House Bat as a gesture of trust and goodwill toward Ziwix. Her mother went back to House Ziwix years ago, but Kiava stayed. She had access to both houses."

"You trusted her?"

His expression turned darker. "Not completely."

"Then why give her access?"

"Because I loved her," he said, looking at her covered body with a pained expression. "To maintain tradition and code. And because it was a useful way to convey false information to Ziwix when necessary."

"You allowed her to live in the heart of your house all these years, just to feed false information to House Ziwix?"

"Friends close..." he nodded, his voice grim. "Also to try and ascertain whether or not they were feeding any to me."

The man was shrewd. I had to admit it was a smart ploy, one that required the foresight and long-term thinking of a chess master. He stared at the necklace in his palm.

"And that?" I said to him.

"That's a Loci," said Duncan, "A damn strong one."

"Loci?"

"A conduit for focusing magical energy from a distance," Chulunn said, "I'm sure Orsa was using it to listen in on our conversation."

"It's not still on, is it?" I asked.

He shook his head.

"That means she knew we were here, and what we were talking about," I said. There goes the element of surprise, goddammit.

"It was used to take the minds of my guards, and to sub-stantially increase the power they wielded through their swords," Chulunn said.

"That takes an awful lot of power," Duncan said, sound-ing impressed. "Is Orsa a strong enough magic wielder to pull that off?"

"No," Chulunn said, "But Liwix is."

"What's a Liwix?" Greg asked, hovering by Duncan's side.

"Not what, who. She is a Magus-Sai."

Duncan whistled. "Not many of them left."

"Liwix the Ziwix!" Greg burst into a fit of giggles.

"Pipe down, dumbass," Duncan said, zapping him into silence with the binding bracelets.

"Enlighten me," I said to them.

"It was the Order of Magus-Sai who sank Atlantis," Duncan replied.

"Very good, wizard," Chulunn said, "After that incident, the High Conclave deemed the Order too powerful to exist independently. They were separated, and each house was given its own Magus-Sai. They were forbidden from passing their full training down to following generations. As they died off so too did the level of magic they were able to wield. There are few left today. Liwix is more than capable of what we witnessed."

"Kiava's mind may not have needed taking," I said skepti-cally. "Respectfully," I added.

"I may not have trusted her completely, but I loved her like my own daughter, and she loved me. Passing information is one thing. Subtlety, misdirection, subterfuge, these are the way in matters of House and politic. But she would never willfully try to kill me. This I know," he said, glaring at me, his red eyes practically smoldering.

He was angry, I could use that anger.

"Orsa tried to kill us to prevent our interference. She tried to kill *you*, using your own kin," I said, "Are you gonna keep following code and tradition and watch the world, and your House, burn because of it?"

He stared at the Loci in his hand, the anger never leaving his face.

"Felth'shi dher," he said in a grating voice.

I was pretty sure that was the elvish equivalent of 'fuck her.'

"Come," he said, "There is much to plan if we would assault the tower."

About damn time. Orsa had tried to kill him in his own house and then flambéed his niece in front of him. What more did you need to want to kick some righteous ass? As if preventing Dragongeddon wasn't enough cause.

"Have transportation meet us in the rotunda," Chulunn said to one of the guards as we entered the elevator.

"Yes, sire," he responded, then quickly spoke into a small walkie-talkie.

Two electric golf carts were waiting just outside the front doors, and we piled in along with several more elf guards. They took us quickly back down the driveway to where it forked. We made a left and veered down the sloping road we had passed on our way in.

Two houses loomed in front of us. A main house that was three stories and a large guest house that was two. They were built in the faux French Normandy style that was very prevalent in Beverly Hills mansions. Imposing, elegant, grey stone structures with lots of ornate trim and gilding. It was apparent from the vastly different architectures that the two large properties had been separate estates at one point. Chulunn had turned them into one massive compound.

Two red-skinned imps flittered around the grounds tending to the gardens, which were lush and immaculate.

"Hi, guys!" Greg yelled cheerily at them as we passed.

The imps ignored him and continued about their work, not even glancing up.

"Who put the sticks up their asses?" Greg asked loudly.

"Perhaps you should consider a tighter binding," Chulunn said to Duncan.

"What? Perhaps you should take a flying..." Greg was in the middle of saying when he got zapped into silence again.

"You might be right about that," Duncan agreed.

After Chulunn turned his gaze, Duncan winked at Greg, who stifled a smile and kept silent.

We stopped in front of the doors to the main house. On either side of it were ornate statues of elf warriors on horseback, carved from white marble. The eyes of the stone warriors and their mounts were filled with a swimming red liquid, making the eyes seem alive on the inanimate stone.

Tat whispered in my ear, "Yon statues are creepy."

"Follow," Chulunn said as he hopped off the cart.

As he led us past the statues their liquid eyes seemed to track us, and there was a faint momentary resistance in the air as we passed between them. I glanced at Duncan.

"Wards," he said matter of factly.

We entered an impressive foyer with a double grand staircase leading up to the second floor. We passed through a giant ballroom that could probably hold three hundred people with elbow room to spare, then outside to a stone path that went straight to the second house.

I hesitated to call it a guest house because it was big enough to give a good impression of a bed and breakfast, which should give you an idea of how enormous the main house was.

About a half dozen elves geared for combat, carrying light arms and small blades, were waiting for us outside the front door. Even though they knew we had just saved Chulunn's life they eyed us warily.

"He is not our enemy," Chulunn said, "You will not treat him as such."

That was all it took. They visibly relaxed, fists unclenched, hands came off the grips of guns, heartbeats slowed. A few even gave me a nod.

Warriors and soldiers have been my tribe for almost my entire life. Something I could recognize instantly was a commander who had the respect and loyalty of his troops. What I saw in the elves' eyes was complete trust, willingly given. Their leader had said I was ok, and that was enough for them. Chulunn had my respect. I have an affinity for those who can lead well. Especially while wearing basketball shorts.

He took us into the smaller mansion. The inside was not what I was expecting. The house had been gutted on the first two floors, and the cavernous space had been converted into a giant training room. A combination of a gym, an Olympic gymnastics arena, a Ninja Warrior obstacle course, and the Batcave. It was one of the most epic training spaces I've ever seen. I may have drooled a little.

Another two dozen elves waited inside. Chulunn walked to the center of the room, and we surrounded him in a loose ring.

"You've heard what has transpired. Orsa Rike murdered Kiava and tried to do the same to me, and our guests. A direct attack on our house," he held the Loci aloft as he spoke. "We are not going to let it stand, she will be held accountable for her actions."

Someone behind me grumbled "Felth'shi dher," under their breath.

"There is more at stake. She is involved in a plan that will prove catastrophic to life on this planet if she succeeds. We're going to stop her, laws and politics be damned."

Resounding cries of support and enthusiasm came from the encircling throng.

He pointed at me, "This is Randall Ddraik, Red-son Half-kin. He and his friends have come to us as allies. Together we are going to take the tower. Make yourselves ready, we strike tonight."

CHAPTER TWENTY-ONE

It took three hours to come up with a plan to assault the tower. It involved a helicopter, scaling elevator shafts, and a whole lot of chaos and misdirection.

Our go time wasn't until 10 pm. It would give Orsa time to fortify, she knew something had to be coming after her attack on us, but a nighttime raid was the only thing that would work strategically. To our advantage, it was a Saturday, and the building and surrounding areas would be nearly deserted at night. Downtown LA is not the same teeming social hub that Hollywood is, and the nightlife that does happen is limited to certain areas. The bank tower wasn't one of them.

Chulunn had the blueprints for the entire area. He might have been bound by politics and rules, but that hadn't stopped him from preparing for the day when he might have to go head-to-head with Orsa.

It was 10 in the morning when I left Chulunn's compound with Duncan. Greg, Tat, and In-Ra stayed there. We had plenty of time, and I didn't want to waste it just waiting around until nightfall. We headed back to the Saint Marque to contact Nerufane.

Going back to the hotel was a big risk. I'd seen nothing on the news about what happened at Sword & Shield, and my police sources told me there was no APB or warrant out for my arrest, but I was still operating on the assumption that the Feds were looking for me. So there was a good chance they had staked it out.

I didn't have a choice though. I'd left the crystal summoning rose locked in my weapons bag, in the closet of my bedroom, and it was my only means of contacting Nerufane. I wanted my friends back, and I had a plan to get them while eliminating Annalisa as the bargaining chip. I was going to make the Blue Elf an offer I was hoping he couldn't refuse.

As we got close to the hotel, I called Kevin on his cell phone.

"Hello," he answered.

"Kevin, it's Randall."

"Hi, Mr. Ddra… Randall. What can I do for you?"

"Has anyone been at the hotel looking for me?"

"No, sir," he said, sounding slightly confused. "But I was off yesterday. I could check with the other guys and see, if you want me to."

"Yeah, do that. I'm about ten minutes out and I'm in a bit of a bind. There's too much to explain, but I need to get into my room without anyone seeing me. Can you help me out?"

I wasn't certain I could completely trust the kid, but it wasn't like I had many options. I did know he was relying on me for answers he desperately wanted. That kind of desperation lends itself to a certain level of trust. I was counting on that. Kevin didn't hesitate.

"What do you need?"

Ten minutes later we were pulling into the parking garage. Kevin met us at the entrance. He'd talked to the valet and told them he was taking care of a VIP who didn't want to be disturbed. I'd put Duncan behind the wheel, and I was hunkered down in the back, out of sight. Kevin hopped in the passenger seat, giving me a surreptitious glance before looking at Duncan.

"Howdy," he said to Duncan. "I'm Kevin."

"Nice to meet you, kid, I'm…"

"No names," I interrupted.

"That serious, sir?" he asked, glancing back at me without turning his head.

"Yep," I said simply. "Safer for you that way."

Duncan huffed. "Call me Wiz," he said to Kevin.

"All right. Nice to meet you, Wiz."

He directed Duncan down to the lowest level of the garage, where I'd fought Alamander earlier. We parked close to the alcove that led to the computer room. From there he led us to a service elevator that took us up to my floor.

"Do me a favor," I said to Kevin as we got off. "Go down front and keep an eye out. Call me if you see anyone that looks out of the ordinary."

"Out of the ordinary, how?" he asked.

"Like cops or Feds."

He kept his expression pretty even, but I could see some concern.

"Roger that." He handed me a key card, "This'll allow you to access the service elevator when you're ready to leave."

"Thanks. I appreciate your help. We'll have that talk soon."

"I'm counting on it, sir," he said as the doors closed.

"That the kid that pulled you out of the pool?" Duncan asked as we hustled down the hallway.

"Yeah. He tackled Alamander as he was about to fry me, too."

"You owe him twice over? When's the last time that happened to you?"

I thought for a second, "Japan."

"The Yakuza thing?"

"Yep."

Long story. The condensed version: Yakuza, a ninja, very hot twin geishas, a Banshee, a terrified little girl, and a priceless sword.

We entered the suite, and I quickly retrieved the crystal rose from my weapons case and met Duncan back in the living room, where I placed the rose on the coffee table.

"Just watch and listen. I'll cue you in to talk," I said.

I spoke Nerufane's name then moved away from the table to give him some space when he showed up. I didn't want him to be on the defensive right off the bat, or to see me as more of a threat than I'm sure he already did.

The rose began to pulse with a red light, getting brighter with each beat. After five pulses or so it popped up into the air about six feet above the table and bloomed into a large, rose-shaped flash of light. There was an obnoxious peal of nasally laughter, and when the light subsided Nerufane stood in front of us on the coffee table.

I thought he couldn't possibly have topped his previous outfit. I was so wrong.

It was almost the same as the first one, except this time everything was shiny red patent leather. Trench coat, booty shorts, boots, the whole bit. The only thing missing was the top hat. His long blond hair was unbound and splayed down his back in a luxuriant wave. In one hand he held the ball of Eriel glass that held Drop, in his other was the rose, which he tucked behind his ear.

"Hello, Randall!" he trilled, his voice still annoying, his smile brilliant. It faded quickly when he didn't see what he was hoping for. "Oh pish. I don't see Annalisa. Is she glamoured as this fat old man?" he said, pointing at Duncan.

"I don't have her yet."

He glared at me and his tan skin darkened a shade. "Unfortunate."

"I have something better."

Nerufane directed his gaze to Duncan who was sitting in a corner. "Is this fat little toadstool supposed to be better?"

"Thrilled to meet you too, Darkling," Duncan said.

Nerufanes skin turned bluer, and he bared his teeth in a cold, tight smile. "Rude."

He dangled the glass ball above the hardwood of the coffee table, threatening to drop it.

"I think you should send him away. He is not part of our business."

"I think you should shut up and listen to what I have to say."

"*What* did you say to me?"

He wasn't expecting me to challenge him. He believed he had the advantage here, and in truth he probably did. I knew I was risking Drop's life, but I wanted to keep Nerufane off balance, which meant a little calculated risk was necessary.

"We probably don't have a lot of time before your master calls you home," I said with a sigh. "Let's not waste any of it."

He began spinning the glass ball around his finger by the chain.

"Blue Elves *do not* have masters!" he hissed.

"I guess that makes you the first of your kind to be bound. Sucks to be you," I said, casually sitting down on the couch across from him. I looked at Duncan. "What do you think?"

"I think he looks ridiculous."

"Bloody hell right he does. About the jewelry, I mean?" I said.

"Gaudy as hell. Strong-ass binding though."

Nerufane almost dropped the spinning ball but managed to catch it with his other hand. I had to fight the urge to leap for it. His eyes narrowed, and his skin fully darkened to its natural shade of blue. We definitely had him off balance.

"Who are you, toadstool?" he said, his voice now in its deep base register.

"Wizard. Call me toadstool again and I'll show ya just how powerful, bud."

He put both hands on the glass ball, and his forearm muscles flexed as he applied pressure to it.

"I do not want him here."

I could hear his heart racing, and he had started sweating, his forehead glistened with it. He smelled of fear, and Duncan was the cause. Interesting.

"Our deal is I get Annalisa back for you in exchange for my unharmed friends," I said, splaying my arms across the back of the couch and stretching out my legs languidly. "I brought him here because we can offer you a better deal."

"Our deal is nonnegotiable."

One thing I've learned in five hundred years, everything is negotiable. You just need to have the right kind of currency. I was betting my friends' lives that I did.

"What if he can break your binding and set you free?"

Nerufane released his death grip on the glass ball, stepped very carefully off the coffee table, and folded his arms across his chest. He arched one eyebrow sharply as the tiniest of smiles played across his lips.

"What if indeed," he cocked his head at Duncan, "Could you do this, toadst... wizard?"

The ability to offer freedom to a bound Darkling, priceless.

"Think so. Let's find out for sure," Duncan said.

He stood and started toward Nerufane. The elf clutched the glass ball firmly and stretched his arm out behind him, keeping it as far out of reach as possible.

"Have a care, darling, I'd hate for the little dew Drop to turn into a wisp of steam."

Duncan stopped about three feet away from the elf, "Extend your free arm over to me," he said.

Nerufane looked at Duncan warily, "Fricasseed, barbecued, boiled. Perhaps just raw."

"What?" Duncan said.

"Why, I'm just thinking of all the ways I can eat a drake," Nerufane giggled, his annoying voice back. He turned his gaze to me. "Should the fat little cupcake here try something foolish, I'll delight in making a culinary choice."

"He won't try anything. You have my word," I said.

"Satisfied?" Duncan said.

"Rarely, but I will take a Half-kin's word. You may proceed, cupcake."

"Your arm, gimme," Duncan groused.

Nerufane complied, but from the sound of his heart and the smell of him I could tell how tense he was.

Duncan stayed where he was and extended his staff out toward the bracelet.

"This might hurt, elf. Grin and bear it."

I swear there was a tinge of enjoyment in his tone.

Nerufane's bracelets and necklace exploded into scintillating waves of colors, running riot through the diamonds. The area of his boots around his ankles did the same, the light show muted by the patent leather covering the jewels that lay beneath.

The Phoenix statuette atop the Big Stick burst into real flames, which flowed with swiftly changing colors of their own. The air grew hotter and hummed with power.

As the Phoenix got close to the bracelet the colors of the two began to sync and the flames licked out to touch the diamonds. They flowed through purple, red, orange, yellow, and finally to a crystalline clear that matched the diamond's original color.

Like a striking viper the living Phoenix snapped its head forward, grabbed one diamond in its beak, and ripped it from the bracelet.

Nerufane hissed in pain and jerked his arm back.

"By the holy dark! Damnable wizard!"

Just like that the light show was over. The Phoenix was once again a solid statuette, in its inanimate beak was a single diamond. Duncan plucked it from the bird and held it up for the elf to see, a smug look on his face.

"Damnable maybe, but I can set you free," he said, his voice as smug as his expression.

A shriek of laughter burst from Nerufane's lips. It made me want to leap across the room and throttle him just to shut him up. I opted for restraint.

"Feels like our arrangement just got negotiable," I said.

"Deliciously so," he trilled, clapping his hands together. "I apologize for calling you a toadstool," he said with an exaggerated bow toward Duncan.

"Gee, thanks," Duncan replied.

"When do we start?" he asked excitedly.

"Slow your roll, Blue. This little test run was just to make sure I could do it. Your binding is deep, I'm gonna need to cast a full circle and then work through the layers. I'll need time to prepare and more tools than I have on me. It ain't gonna be easy on you," Duncan explained.

"It can be done. That is enough."

Nerufane was beside himself with giddiness. So much so that I thought it was a little strange. About the only true emotions Darklings ever show are anger and, well, anger. Getting an honest emotional reaction out of one is damned near impossible. It's what makes them such good manipulators. I didn't trust it.

"It's gonna cost you," I said.

"Well of course, Randall, freedom always comes at a price."

"Mine's steep."

"Name your terms," he said, still all smiles and lilting happiness.

"I want Drop back now."

He looked at the glass ball in his hand, then smirked.

"Done, but the puddle stays in the ball. I'll release him after I've been unbound." He placed the ball gently on the coffee table. "And?"

"You return Shrill as soon as your binding is broken."

"When I'm free, I shall gently place him into your loving hands. I'll even feed him nothing but filet mignon until then. Anything else?"

There was one big else.

"You give up claim to Annalisa."

"Done and done!

He'd just given me everything I wanted without putting up a fight. Not even an argument.

"You've got no problem with any of these conditions?"

"Taking Annalisa was not my idea. If I'm free, I have no want or need of her, your friends, or you." He took a few steps forward and leaned in close to me. "Don't take this too hard, darling, but you're of zero interest to me personally."

It was too easy. No way was I going to believe a Darkling didn't have something else up his sleeve. I kept pushing.

"One more thing," I said, "Who's your master?"

His whole face pinched inward as if he'd just bitten the mother of all lemons. He struggled to find his voice. Held up his wrists and shook the bracelets at me.

"I really *can't* say, darling."

I looked at Duncan. "Lemme guess, he's bound not to speak that information." He nodded in affirmation.

As if on cue his bracelets and necklace began to glow with orange light.

"Oh pish. It appears our time is done again, Randall," he plucked the rose from his hat and twirled it in his fingers. "Quickly now, when shall we exchange your friends' freedom for mine?"

"Tell your master I'll have Annalisa before midnight tomorrow, but I'll need your help to get her, so you'll need more time here when I call you."

He looked quickly to Duncan, "How long will you need, cupcake?"

"At least thirty minutes, but an hour to be safe."

Nerufane placed the rose on the coffee table next to Drop's prison, as the orange glow expanded around him.

"I shall do my best to convince him, though he can be stubborn to say the least."

The glow swallowed him and he disappeared. At least I knew his master was a 'he.' Unless that was a lie. Stupid elf.

I picked up the glass ball, raising it to my eyes.

"Hang in there, buddy, I'll get you out safe."

"Ya big softy," said Duncan.

I had to admit I was happy to have him back.

"Can you really break his binding in thirty minutes?"

"Yeah. It's mostly prep time, but there's a few things I need to get back at the house that can speed up the process."

"All right. Head downstairs and keep an eye out front. I'll get the truck and meet you in the driveway. I'll give you a five-minute lead, call me if you see anything."

After he left, I retrieved my weapons case from the closet, put the glass ball and rose safely inside it, and headed to the service elevator.

I emerged into the garage and headed to the truck. I gently placed the weapons case on the floor of the back seat, making sure it was wedged in firmly. I don't know what life was like for Drop inside the ball, but I didn't want to make his imprisonment any more traumatic than it probably already was by bouncing him all over the place while I drove.

I extracted myself from the back seat and closed the door. I would have thoroughly enjoyed beating the blue off Nerufane, but having Drop back and knowing that I wouldn't have to fight him for Shrill and Annalisa made things much easier. Taking on a gang of Red Elves with a Magus-Sai and Alamander fighting at their side was going to be hard enough.

I felt like I'd just had a win, and I let myself enjoy the feeling for a moment. It didn't last long.

The sound of heels on pavement coming toward me startled me slightly. I should have heard them long before they got down to this level of the garage.

Agent Buck walked out of the ramp and into view. She was wearing a black minidress with spaghetti straps. It clung to her body like liquid skin. Her five-inch black stiletto heels clicked softly as she stalked toward me with a feline, sensual grace. She looked spectacular.

"You disappeared on us at Sword & Shield Security, Mr. Ddraik," she said, the corners of her lips tugged up in a sensual smirk.

Somewhere in the deep lizard part of my brain alarm bells were ringing. They obviously couldn't see how short her dress was, so I ignored them. I couldn't seem to form any words to respond, as the carnal part of my mind lit up like the Vegas skyline at night.

"Nothing to say about that?" she asked.

You'd think that would have ratcheted the alarms up to eleven, but it didn't. It seemed like a valid question. She was an FBI agent in the middle of an investigation after all.

"Nope," I said, taking a few steps towards her. "They were closed when I got there." Ridiculously, it sounded like a plausible lie to my own ears. Did I mention how short her dress was?

One strap of said dress fell off a shoulder, and she licked her lips. I swear I felt heat pulsing off her body. My brain cranked the warning alarms up to twelve, but they fell on deaf ears because a different part of the same brain was wholly uninterested in hearing them. It was busy focusing on another part of my anatomy.

"I didn't come here to talk about them anyway," she said, "I didn't come to talk at all."

She tugged on her dress and it slid off her body effortlessly, as if she were coated in oil. It crumpled around her feet like a puddle of solid smoke. She was six feet of flawless, toned perfection. I watched her muscles move and flex with riveted attention as she took a few more languid steps towards me.

"Do you want to talk?" she asked, her voice husky.

I shook my head, almost drunkenly. "No."

"What do you want?"

"You," I said, my voice thick with lust.

"Then come take me," she breathed.

Everything, aside from her obvious good taste of course, was completely wrong with the situation. Yet the only thing I wanted was to do just that, take her in the longest, hardest way possible. Then make her beg me for more. I opened up my stupid mouth and said, "My pleasure. I've wanted you since I first saw you."

"Yes, Dragon, of course you have."

I heard her say the word but it didn't register. At least not fast enough.

"Wait, what did you say?" I said, struggling through the haze of lust. The alarms were finally starting to force through some clarity, when I heard Hooper.

"She said Dragon."

He'd somehow gotten close to me without my noticing. He was wearing all-black tactical gear, a heavy bulletproof vest, and a sleek black helmet. In his hand was an oversized Taser pistol.

My eyes recognized what I saw, but they just couldn't process it fast enough for me to move. It's like there was a heavy fog between comprehension and reaction, where normally the two are virtually simultaneous for me.

In what looked like slow motion, the Taser spikes launched at me, wires trailing out behind them. One hit me in the shoulder, the other in my chest, and electricity surged through me. I got lucky as my spell-protected coat absorbed most of the charge from the spike in my shoulder. It still dropped me to my knees as my leg muscles seized, but it wasn't the T-rex tail smash I'm sure it should have been. It hurt, but the pain served to wake me out of my stupor.

Battle-adrenaline surged through me in a flood, the fog lifted from my senses, and everything snapped back to clarity. I almost couldn't believe what I saw. Hooper was wearing the Scalestones around his neck. At least six that I could plainly see.

I launched myself at Hooper, wearing the crazed smile of a ten-year-old who's just ridden his favorite rollercoaster a dozen times in a row. The snarl that escaped my throat was hungry and not at all human-sounding. It wasn't the reaction he'd been expecting from me after taking the Taser hit.

He backpedaled fast as he went for the 9mm on his hip. As targets went, Buck was naked and farther away. Hooper was close, and he had weapons and the damn Scales. I had to take him out before he was able to use them again to overwhelm my adrenaline surge, or shoot me.

I chambered my right leg back to deliver a kick, purposely telegraphing it a little. He did what a well-trained fighter would do, he stepped forward into my kick, cutting the distance between us and shortening the arc my leg could travel to hit him, reducing my power. It also stopped him from going for his gun, which was my main objective.

He might have been well-trained, but that didn't count for much against me, he just couldn't read what was coming. I swung my arms around my body to the left, and the momentum spun me around as my left knee came up... you know what, never mind, the explanation would just be confusing. Trust me, it was badass.

I hit him with a spinning back kick from the left, not a side kick from my right. My foot slammed into his head, and the helmet cracked under the impact. He flew sideways and smashed to the ground in an unmoving sprawl.

I repeat, badass.

Everything sharpened into even greater clarity as the hypnotic and deadening effect of the Scales stopped completely, no longer having Hooper's will to power them. Good thing too, because it gave me a chance to spin toward Buck and brace myself. I was slammed into by something big, furry, and moving like greased lightning. I was driven backwards into the wall, the wind knocked out of me.

Before I could get a clean look at what hit me, I was ripped off the wall, swung around, and thrown across the garage. I skidded across the floor twenty feet before I came to a stop. I shook my head to clear it as I jumped to my feet, adrenaline still surging.

Buck was crouched down over Hooper. At least I think it was Buck. She'd packed on at least seventy pounds of muscle mass, and her body was covered in glossy, short black fur with muted black spots, like a Leopard's. She was much taller, or maybe longer was a better description. Her legs had transformed into something decidedly more feline, and her appendages looked more like paws, sporting big, very sharp claws. A long tail whipped around behind her.

Are you fucking kidding me? She's an Ailuranthrope? Short version, were-cat.

She had a long, clawed finger on Hooper's neck, checking his pulse. She looked up at me and bared her teeth in a snarl, revealing incisors that were long and sharp. Her face had the long, pronounced snout and flat nose of a cat, and her ears were tall and pointed. Her eyes had vertical irises. Not gonna lie, she'd lost all sex appeal.

What the hell was going on? Hooper was using Scalestones like a pro, and Buck was a fucking were-cat? None of this made sense. I held up my hands placatingly.

"Hold on there, kitten. Let's talk for a second."

It was apparently the wrong word choice. The growl that came from her throat as she charged at me was somewhere between a jaguar and a hyena. It definitely beat my snarl.

I pivoted to the side and spun as I drew the Rondel daggers, slashing at her with both blades. I felt fire across my leg as her claws scratched deep into it. She howled in pain as my blades ripped into her side. Damn she was fast.

I knew this fight wasn't a good idea. If they were Feds, as they said, I couldn't afford to let them take me, not with everything that was in motion for tonight. I couldn't kill them either for the same reason. The kind of heat that would bring I just didn't need. I had to end it and go ghost, fast.

Buck stopped on a dime, turned, and reared up on her hind legs, clawed hands rising above her to strike down at me. I drove up from a crouch, swinging my arms upward with every bit of force I could muster. I was holding the dagger pommels up, the end of each tipped with a thick disk of solid steel. They slammed into the underside of her jaw with a solid crack.

She reeled backwards, and I thought the fight was over, but then her long arms came down, claws clamping onto my shoulders. She pulled me down with her as she fell backwards and did something decidedly cat-like. Her rear legs tucked up tightly under her and then struck up at my stomach. My coat partially protected me, but the claws of one foot cut into my skin just below my chest and slashed all the way down my abdomen to my belt. My stomach ran slick with blood, but the battle-adrenaline flooding my system kept the pain at a distance. She kicked out with her legs and launched me over her head, sending me crashing onto my back.

I rolled over my back and came up onto my feet. Buck was crouched on all fours looking loopy and unfocused. I had really rung her bell with the jaw strike. She'd clawed and tossed me purely on instinct. I leapt, landing square on her back, and wrapped my arms around her thick neck, squeezing with everything I had. I dug the disk end of one of the pommels into her jugular. She reared up onto her hind legs, but they gave out, and she toppled over sideways. I landed with my feet beneath me, still squeezing. She spasmed once, twice, and then went slack. I held on for a few seconds longer just to be sure she was out. She remained still.

"Good kitty," I said, scratching her between the ears as I let her go.

Her unconscious body transformed back into human form. Her sex appeal came back with it... sort of. I stood up with a fierce smile on my face. What? It was a good fight. I didn't have time to enjoy it though, I had to move fast before any more agents came down here. I turned toward my truck just in time to see Hooper fire the taser. Both darts sank deep into my chest this time. There was an onslaught of pain, just like getting hit by a T-rex tail, then everything went black.

CHAPTER TWENTY-TWO

Pain shot through me, and I heard myself yell as my eyes snapped open. My breath came in ragged gasps.

Buck and Hooper stood in front of me, about ten feet away. The Taser darts were still in my chest, and Hooper was holding the gun, his finger on the trigger.

I gritted my teeth and stared at them, pushing the pain to a distant corner of my brain. I willed my breathing to slow and assessed my situation.

We were in the main room of the Sword & Shield Security building. The chair that I was strapped to was in almost the exact spot where I had been spiked to the floor. It was most likely a not-so-subtle way to drive home the point that they knew what happened here, and let me know how bent over the barrel they had me. At least I was less crucified and slightly more comfortable this time.

I was sitting in a chair, naked from the waist up and tied to it with some very thick metal cabling. It lashed my arms together tightly behind me, torquing my shoulders back and preventing me from getting any leverage to move them. The same cables bound my legs all the way up to my thighs.

The wounds that Buck had clawed into me were still fresh, four angry red slashes running down the length of my torso. They were mostly knitted back together and buzzing nicely. The blood had been cleaned off. That was nice of them.

My weapons were on a table behind them, including my ring, which was inside some kind of transparent crystalline box. My coat and shirt were in a crumpled pile next to them. Barbarians.

"Would it kill you people to use a hanger?" I said.

"Seriously? Your clothes? That's what you're worried about?" Hooper said, shaking his head in disbelief.

I smiled at Buck. "Any chance you still want to get naked, kitten?"

"None. And do not call me that again," she replied, her voice cold.

"You don't know what you're missing."

"Wasted time and crushing disappointment?" she replied, managing to look even colder.

"Ouch."

"I used low voltage to wake you up, buddy," Hooper said, waving the taser. "I'd be happy to turn it up to high if you wanna keep talking shit."

The Scalestones still hung around his neck, but I wasn't feeling any of their effects.

"Untie me and try it," I said.

"Don't think so."

"Yeah, that's what I thought. Pussy."

All bluster aside I was in a bad spot, and I knew it. I cut to the chase.

"I'm guessing you know what happened in here," I said.

"Oh yeah," said Hooper, "Right about now it sucks to be you."

"It never sucks to be me," I said. So maybe not all bluster aside. "Are you even FBI?"

"Very much so," Buck said.

"We're the supernatural division," Hooper said.

Bloody hell. I didn't know they had one of those.

"What do you want?" I asked.

"To put you away for murder," he said, "Our job is to keep guys like you in check."

"I didn't murder anyone."

"The man who died would probably disagree with you."

Dammit. My situation just got a whole lot worse.

"I was acting in self-defense, with nonlethal force, against many assailants. When you saw me, I was escaping for fear of my life. Removing myself from a deadly situation, so as not to cause more harm to myself or any of the lunatics attacking me. Nobody was dead when I left this building."

Dying maybe, but not dead.

"The whackadoodles did almost kill me, by the way. I'm fine though. Thanks for asking," I said.

"That's a very sound legal argument," Hooper said, looking at Buck.

"Indeed," she agreed with an expressionless nod, "It might matter if you were ever going to get any kind of a trial."

"There's no court for the supernatural, buddy. We deal with your kind as we see fit. Secret division, different rules." Hooper said.

Things weren't adding up. Hooper said they wanted to put me away for murder, now they were threatening to make me disappear, or just kill me. I had no doubt they could make both of those happen, but if that were the case why even threaten me with a murder charge? Why not just make me disappear and be done with it? They wanted, or needed something from me.

"Can we stop beating around the bush? What do you really want?"

They glanced at each other and then Buck spoke.

"We want you to tell us what you know about the White Half-kin, Alamander."

I wasn't expecting that. Buck read it on my face.

"Yes, we know who he is. We are trying to learn what he is attempting to do," she said.

She'd just given me a bargaining chip. A very small one but it was more than I had a second ago.

"What's in it for me?" I asked.

She hadn't expected that. Her expression actually changed a hair, no pun intended.

"You're in no position to negotiate," she said.

"I think I might be, kitten," I said, trying to rattle her.

She walked towards me.

"Uh-oh, now you've pissed her off," Hooper said.

She backhanded me full force, putting her weight into it. My head snapped around and I tasted blood in my mouth. Damn the woman could hit.

"Call me kitten again," she said, as her hands began to morph into those big clawed appendages of hers, "Please."

If I rattled her anymore I would get my face clawed off. Buck had been a serious and potentially lethal opponent, and I respected anyone who could fight as well as she did.

"Sorry, I won't use the word again."

She backed off a little, her claws reverting back to hands.

"Look, I'm not your enemy, and I'm not the bad guy here. Annalisa is in my care, and since you obviously know about my kind, you know what that means. What happened here, happened because I was trying to find her. These Vanatori were the ones at the hotel who took her... with Alamander's help."

They looked quickly at each other then back at me.

"Vanatori do not work with Dragons," Buck said.

"They didn't know. Alamander tricked them."

"You don't expect us to beli..." Hooper started.

"We don't have time for this!" I almost shouted. I didn't know how long I'd been out or what time it was, but every minute I spent here was a wasted one. "By my word, I swear I'm telling you the truth."

Buck regarded me for a moment. I had her attention at least.

"Explain your urgency," she said.

"Which is?"

I had to get out of here, and being cautious wasn't going to do anything but waste precious time. I broke out the only weapon I had access to at the moment, the truth.

I told them everything I knew about Alamander. Our fight in the hotel garage, his affiliation with the Vanatori and House Ziwix. His plan to unbind the Test and what it could mean if he accomplished it. The destruction, death, and chaos that would follow if he enthralled a horde of Full Bloods. They were quiet for a few seconds as it all sank in.

"No bullshit?" Hooper said.

"None."

Buck grabbed the taser wires and yanked the darts out of my chest. I was hoping that meant she believed me.

"I don't give up other Half-kin, even if they've tried to kill me. We handle our own, in our own way. What Alamander's attempting is bigger than just my kind. If he succeeds, it will catastrophically affect human and supernatural alike, and will engulf Earth *and* the realms. I've only got until tomorrow midnight to find and stop him, so you understand why I feel a little pressed."

I hadn't told them about Annalisa's role in the unfolding drama, what she was, and how she was integral to his plan. It didn't go unnoticed.

"What's VanSusstern's part in all this?" Hooper asked. "It's gotta be a big one."

"Annalisa is still my client and entitled to confidentiality, but she's the lynchpin Alamander needs to make his plan work. That's all I'm willing to tell you. For now."

I was walking a negotiating line. I didn't really have room to balance on, but she was in my care, and that was something I wouldn't compromise on, no matter how over the barrel I was bent.

"I'm trying to stop him and save her. Whether you want to believe it or not, we're not enemies," I reiterated.

They turned their backs to me and talked for a few moments. I couldn't hear them and I should have easily been able to. All sound had gone muted to me which meant Hooper had activated one of the Scalestones.

When they first came at me in the hospital, I'd dismissed them as run-of-the-mill Feds. That had proven to be a mistake. They'd played me like a fiddle in the garage. Buck's manipulation of my baser instincts, enhanced by Hooper's skillful use of the Scales, had left me wide open to their initial attack, which meant I could not take them lightly. Sound returned as they faced me.

"Let's say we believe what you've told us. If we let you go after Alamander, would you agree to deliver him to us alive?"

That was a curve ball I did not see coming, but I wasn't about to look a gift horse in the mouth.

"Yes," I said without hesitation.

"Despite the fact that he owes you blood debt?" she asked skeptically.

There was no denying they knew an awful lot about my kind.

"I'll kill him eventually, it doesn't have to be right now. Same goes for the Vanatori," I said, giving her a cold grin.

She thought for a beat then said, "Acceptable. You will capture Alamander and return him to us alive. Do we have terms and agreement?"

It was a question you only heard asked of one supernatural being to another. It was the formalizing of a bonding agreement, with clearly stated terms and conditions, enforced by the honor of the participants entering it.

"Yes. In exchange, you forget I was ever in this building with the Vanatori."

I was basically asking for a get out of jail free card, which was a risk considering the disadvantage they had me at, but I didn't want the Vanatori deaths hanging over my head. She looked at Hooper, who nodded.

"We have terms," she said, looking back to me.

"And agreement," I said.

She walked behind me and began unlocking the restraints.

"How did Alamander get on your radar in the first place?" I asked her as she worked.

"Through the Vanatori. They work for us," she replied.

"Say what?" I said, wisely.

"Unofficially. Think of them as confidential informants. We supply them, keep them protected from the law when they need it. They help us keep track of your kind in return," Buck said.

"Keep track of or kill?"

"When they find a Half-kin, we add them to our database to track and gather intelligence on," she said.

"We're not interested in killing you. You guys do a great job of that on your own," Hooper added.

"If they succeed in killing a Half-kin they've discovered, so be it. It's the way of things between you. They are on their own when they go up against one of you. We don't interfere unless there is collateral damage to civilians."

"Why do I feel like I just got played, in our terms?" I said.

"Because you did," Buck said.

"Ain't that a bitch?" Hooper chuckled, grinning broadly.

I glared at him. They weren't going to jam me up for what I'd done to the Vanatori in the first place, they just used the threat of it to get me to accept their terms. Hooper's glee in it pissed me off, but I begrudgingly respected the play.

"The Vanatori found Alamander?" I asked Hooper, glaring at him.

"No. He found them. We don't know how. They told us they'd met a wizard, who had information on a Dragon. Obviously, something we wanted to investigate. He gave them these," he tapped the Stones around his neck. "Then gave you up as a target for them, telling them that despite appearances, Annalisa was your captive not your employer, and he needed their help to free her from you."

"Wait a damned minute, you've known I was a Dragon since before you saw me at the hospital?"

Hooper's grin became a big condescending smile. "Surprise," he said, enjoying this way too much.

Bald little dickhead, I didn't say out loud. I might have mumbled it very quietly.

"We don't know how he beat their Scalestone and kept his Half-kin nature hidden from them, but we discovered it," Buck said.

"How?" I asked.

I felt the tension starting to ease on the restraints, but I still couldn't have gotten out of them.

"We sent in an agent to talk to him after the Vanatori received the Scalestones. Alamander killed him," she said. There was a clear note of anger in her voice and a rapid increase in her heartbeat.

"Sorry," I said, sincerely. I've lost team members over the years. It sucks every time.

"Our agent was a Half-kin," she said.

I blinked at her, completely gobsmacked. We might hire ourselves out to clients, or join a mercenary group, or an army somewhere, but taking a 9-to-5 payroll job? That just didn't happen.

"What kind?"

"Green," she said.

I was… double-gobbed? Twice-smacked?

"How did you pull that off?" I asked, somewhat incredulously.

Greens are the only type of my kind that could be described as solitary, preferring to live in mountains and forests, usually only coming to civilization to satisfy their carnal appetites. So employing one to help you keep tabs on other Half-kin, that by and large habituated in metropolitan areas, made literally no sense.

Buck noticeably paused in her work at the restraints, before resuming without answering my question.

"The Vanatori set up the meeting here. We know this building, have access to all their cameras, and had him wired for sound so we could observe the meeting in real time. We ordered the Vanatori to vacate during the meeting, making it safe for him to be here without them learning we have a Dragon on our team. They would find that unacceptable," she explained.

"That's putting it mildly," I said.

The cables around my legs came undone and dropped to the floor, but my arms and upper body were still securely bound. Locks continued to open.

"They recognized each other as Dragons immediately. It was no small surprise to either, but Alamander seemed very pleased. He spoke about a great change for Dragon-kind, one that he would soon make a reality. A paradigm shift he called it. He did not provide anywhere near the details he did to you," she said.

"He couldn't, he hadn't grabbed Annalisa yet. He's much more confident now that he has her," I said.

"He asked our agent to join him, which he rebuffed. Saying he might consider it when Alamander could provide him with more information."

He might have accepted Alamander's offer if he'd been given all the information I had. I know how much I'd been tempted by it. If I were being totally honest, the idea still pulled at my genetic heartstrings, though I would never follow that pull.

"How was he killed?" I asked.

"Without honor," Buck said, harshly. "Alamander struck by surprise when he was rebuffed. No challenge, no warning. Our agent was cut down by magic, his head was... he did not Roar."

That made me as angry as Buck sounded.

A Death Roar is sacred. The final release of a Half-kin's energy, happening involuntarily at the exact moment of death. Any Half-kin around when it happens absorbs a part of that energy, though it's most often a one-on-one exchange. When we fight and kill each other, the victor receives the Roar as the prize for a victory well won, and we honor receiving it. Even if we don't die in combat, which is rare, we still Roar, like I almost did when I was thrown off the hotel balcony. A Half-kin dying without releasing his Roar is a death without honor, or meaning.

"Bloody hell," I said, angrily. "You sure you don't want me to kill Alamander?"

"No," Buck snapped.

She pulled on something with a yank. My shoulders were torqued back hard, accompanied by a nice jolt of pain. I was pretty sure she did that intentionally.

"Stand up," she said.

As I did, all the cables went slack and dropped from my upper body to the floor, landing in a large pile at my feet.

"Impressive restraint system."

"It was designed for creatures much stronger than you," she said.

I moved to my pile of stuff. I picked up my shirt and made a bit of a show of shaking it out before putting it back on, while looking daggers at Hooper. Then I started reaffixing my weapons. He watched me, his hand resting firmly on the gun on his hip.

"Truce and agreement," I said, eyeing his hand.

"Call me paranoid," he said with a slight shrug.

My cell phone told me the time was a little after 5. I called Duncan.

"What the actual fuck!" he yelled as soon as he picked up. "What happened? Where are you?"

"I'm fine, dad, sorry I missed curfew. Don't worry, my virginity is still intact."

"Don't be a shithead! I saw you get taken. They somehow blocked Incindis, and I couldn't track you."

That explained the box Incindis was in.

"What the hell's going on?" he barked.

I quickly explained what had happened with the Feds.

"Jesus. How have they been keeping that division on such the down-low?" he said.

"Definitely a question to answer at another time. You at Chulunn's?" I asked.

"Yeah. He's been more than a little concerned with you going ghost, considering what he's putting on the line. Get your scaly ass back here."

"I'm on my way. Let Chulunn know I'm bringing the Feds."

"Seriously? You think that's a good idea?"

CHAPTER TWENTY-THREE

We walked out the back door of the S&S building, Hooper in front, me in the middle, Buck bringing up the rear, emerging into a parking lot. It was hemmed in by three concrete walls and a security access gate. Their car, a black Chevy Suburban, was parked sidelong to the door in the middle of the lot.

On instinct, I inhaled deeply as we exited and smelled him immediately, nervous sweat, mint gum, and spicy deodorant. Heartbeat hammering like a drum.

A shot rang out. Hooper spun slightly and fell to the ground as his leg went out from underneath him.

"Get clear, Mr. Ddraik!" Kevin shouted.

Bloody fucking hell.

I jumped over Hooper and crouched in front of him, using myself as a shield. Behind me, Buck drew her gun.

"Everybody stop!" I yelled.

Kevin was behind the hood of the Suburban, a Glock 9 millimeter in his hands. I glanced behind me to see Buck down on one knee, aiming back at him. Hooper, despite taking a hit to the leg, had drawn his gun and was trying to get a bead on Kevin, but I was blocking him. He was probably perfectly happy aiming at my back as a substitute.

"Kevin, you don't know what you're doing, soldier. Hold your fire." I shouted.

"You're safe, sir?" he asked.

"Affirmative," I replied, "Stay covered until I explain this."

I turned and faced them, still acting as a shield for Hooper. The fact that I just turned my back on a shooter seemed to calm them down, as both their racing heartbeats slowed.

"Yeah, so about this," I said.

"You know him?" Hooper said through clenched teeth. He wasn't bleeding much, so it was a glancing wound. I'm sure it still hurt like hell.

"His name's Kevin. He's the hotel security guard who pulled me from the pool. He also saw me fight Alamander in the parking garage."

"What the hell is he doing here?" Hooper said.

"I don't know. Holster your gun, I'll go find out."

"Fat fucking chance."

Couldn't say I blamed him for being pissed.

"Fine, but keep it aimed on me not him."

"Not a problem."

I glared at him, "I just jumped in front of you as a shield, would a little gratitude kill you?"

That shut him up. Jesus, what a dickhead.

"Yeah, you're welcome," I growled.

I stomped toward the SUV, fuming. Not at Hooper, but at Kevin. I'm a goddamn Dragon, I didn't need some kid following me around trying to save me every time he thought I was in trouble. I didn't make it to five hundred years old on luck and good looks. What the fuck was he even doing here?

"Stand down," I barked, not hiding my anger.

"He's trained on your back," Kevin said, keeping his eyes locked on Hooper.

"Because I told him to. He'll holster as soon as you do."

His eyes darted to me, then back to Hooper. "You sure?"

I snatched the gun out of his hand so fast it took him a second to realize it was gone.

"What. The fuck. Are you doing here?"

"I was getting off work when those two showed up. They drove into the garage in this SUV. A bunch of other guys in suits blocked off the entrance to the lower two levels. They flashed FBI badges."

That explained why no one came down there while we were fighting.

"I didn't trust it. Not with all the weirdness that's been surrounding you. I snuck down there just in time to see them loading you into this thing. I hopped on my bike and followed them here. Been waiting outside ever since."

"I don't need protecting," I said, emphasizing the point with a jab of my finger into his chest.

He stood his ground.

"I believe that, but if something happens to you, I don't get answers to questions that I desperately need answered. No disrespect, but this was more about me."

Christ, this kid. He was turning out to be one of the ballsiest humans I had ever met. My anger faded but didn't completely disappear.

"I wasn't sure if they were legit. I winged him on purpose."

"I'm sure that will make him feel much better," I threw a thumb over my shoulder in the direction of Hooper and Buck, "The problem is, they are legit. You just shot a federal agent."

He blanched. "Fuck me."

"That sums it up about right," I said, "I'm hoping we can work it out. Follow me over there. Probably best to keep your hands where they can see them."

Without hesitation he raised his hands to the top of his head and locked his fingers together. I led the way, just in case Hooper got an itchy trigger finger. It wasn't necessary. He'd already holstered his gun. He'd rolled up his pants leg to cover the wound and was pressing down on the roll of cloth to stop the blood flow. Buck stood lightly on the balls of her feet, her gun at her side and ready.

"Agents Hooper and Buck, this is Kevin. He's sorry he shot at you," I said.

"At?" Hooper said, incredulously. "You *shot* me. This blood isn't from a miss. Give me one reason not to arrest you for attempted murder."

"I apologize sir, I wasn't trying to kill you," Kevin said. "I watched you take Mr. Ddraik out of the garage when he was unconscious. I didn't know who you were, and I wanted to make sure he was all right."

Hooper lurched to his feet, hissing in pain as he did. "Why should I believe you?"

"If I'd wanted to kill you sir, you'd be dead."

I looked at him with a raised eyebrow. "Maybe you should let me do the talking, Kev."

He didn't.

"I'm an Army Ranger, master level sniper and marksman. Over sixty confirmed kills to my name. I hit what I aim at. I aimed at your leg, nothing more. You could probably arrest me for a few other things, but attempted murder wouldn't be one of them, sir."

The kid had a really big pair on him, that was for sure. Hooper's glare didn't falter as he asked a question I wasn't expecting.

"What Ranger unit?"

"173rd Airborne Brigade Combat Team. 2008 to 2012," Kevin said.

"Afghanistan?"

"Yes, sir."

"I knew some people on station there, back then," Hooper said.

It was the way he said it, the emotion in his voice and how his eyes got distant for just a moment. Call it soldier's intuition, but I knew there was much more to it than Hooper just knowing people there.

He took a limping step to Kevin, getting right in his face.

"You don't shoot a federal agent without ramification. Consider yourself under arrest for aggravated assault. Until I figure out what to do with you, you're coming with us."

I shot a look at Hooper. "That might not be the best idea right now, all things considered."

"Nobody's asking you," he said.

I took a deep breath and bit my tongue. Cut him a little slack, Randall, he just got shot.

He handed a pair of handcuffs to Kevin.

"Put them on and get in the back."

"Yes, sir," Kevin said.

He cuffed his hands in front of himself and clambered into the back of the SUV.

"Let's go," Hooper said, hauling himself into the passenger seat.

"This is a bad idea," I said to Buck.

"Like he said, nobody's asking you," she said, walking around to the driver's side.

Breathe, just breathe, I told myself as I got in.

CHAPTER TWENTY-FOUR

No one said much on the ride to Chulunn's compound. I didn't think anything nice would come out of my mouth, so I just kept it shut. Kevin, except for a few quick glances at me, just kept his head down. Hooper and Buck... honestly, at this point I don't know what they were thinking. I'd just hit them with a ton of information, gotten one of them shot, and asked them to get involved in an elaborate assault on a public building. They might have been a bit overwhelmed. Or just pissed at me.

At the compound gate we were directed down the driveway to the training house. Chulunn and several of his soldiers met us out front. They were now all outfitted in various forms of black tactical clothing and gear. Chulunn had a Kevlar vest on over a long sleeve black turtleneck, and a short sword hung from his hip. He looked a lot more like a leader than when he'd had on basketball shorts.

Kevin's jaw dropped when he saw the elves. He was too stunned to get any words to come out of his mouth.

"Yes, they're elves. No, you're not crazy. Just roll with it for now, I'll add it to the list of questions to answer," I said before I got out.

He nodded mutely before following me out of the car.

"Agent Buck," Chulunn said to her as we approached, "I would have preferred to be meeting again under different circumstances. I see you have a new partner."

"Agent Hooper, meet Earl Chulunn-Bat, Earl of House Bat," she said, in introduction.

"My pleasure, Earl Bat" he said, reaching down to shake Chulunn's hand.

"You know about their supernatural division?" I asked, surprised. I hadn't even considered that.

"This shouldn't surprise you, considering my station," Chulunn said, cocking his head at me. Not a hint of arrogance in his voice, just a matter-of-fact statement. He turned his attention back to the Feds.

Well, didn't I feel like an idiot.

"Why are you bringing a captive here?" Now there was annoyance in his voice.

"He shot me, while trying to help him," Hooper said, pointing at me.

"Help I didn't need," I interjected, also annoyed.

"We haven't decided what to do with him yet, and there was no time to take him somewhere else. We were hoping you'd let us warehouse him here until the night is over," Hooper said.

"Our apologies for the presumption. These are unusual circumstances," Buck said quickly.

"Very well. Take him upstairs and secure him in the library," Chulunn said to one of his soldiers.

The soldier took Kevin by the arm and started leading him away. He looked at me, looked at the elf, then back to me again, and a smile tugged at his mouth. As confused and maybe scared as he was this was probably helping Kevin.

"You brought them Randall, so how are the agents to help us?" Chulunn said.

I smiled, "Here's what I'm thinking."

It was 6:30 by the time I finished filling everyone in on my changes to the plan.

"You're out of your mind," Hooper said.

His leg wound had been treated with some salve from one of Chulunn's healers and then dressed. From the way he was moving around on it you would've never known he'd been shot.

"We need a perimeter, you can provide it. No one on the ground gets hurt," I said.

They exchanged glances. Buck actually frowned a little.

"You want me to bring you Alamander or not?" I said, staring hard at them.

"Can you control traffic and logistics on the ground?" Chulunn asked.

"We can... manage it," Buck said.

"Controlling it might be a stretch," added Hooper.

"That's enough," I said.

The chaos and misdirection I had added to the plan would keep the local authorities distracted from the tower.

"This will work," I said to Chulunn.

I hated having to share command and needing Chulunn's approval, but I didn't have much choice. Without his knowledge of the tower and manpower, the whole plan was dead in the water. I respected him though, so that made it easier at least.

He was silent for a beat as he thought, then nodded, "Acceptable."

Damn right.

Our assault was two-pronged. The ground team, led by Chulunn with Cuda, Duncan, Greg, In-Ra and a cadre of Chulunn's soldiers, left the compound early to make their way into the tower utilizing the inside knowledge we had from the blueprints.

My team took to the air at 10 pm. Chulunn had an Airbus H160 helicopter sitting on a helipad in his backyard. Sleek, fast, and able to carry up to twelve people. There were seven of us on board, myself, Tat, and five Red soldiers.

The chaos and misdirection started at 10:30.

Two elves staged a running gunfight on the streets by the LA Times building. While another two did the same between the Disney Concert Hall and Ahmanson Theatre buildings. Running and firing wildly on the streets, they were shooting blanks from AK-47 machine guns, and they were loud. It lasted for less than two minutes, then they all disappeared behind veils, gone before the echoes of their shooting had stopped.

In case you don't know downtown LA geography, let me explain.

The LA Times building is located almost next door to LAPD headquarters. Disney and the Ahmanson attract a huge civilian population on the weekends, and they're less than half a mile from the LA Times building. A wild street gunfight in those two places was going to draw a huge police response to the area, consuming a massive amount of their resources for a long period of time, all of it away from where we were going to be.

From our vantage point in the sky we saw the first cherries light up on police cars as their response started. The helicopter lurched forward from where we'd been hovering. I tightened the shoulder straps on my parachute, making sure it was firmly secured, then moved to the side door and slid it open. Tat hovered near my shoulder as the elves lined up behind me.

Hooper, Buck, and their team would cordon off a one square block area around the tower within what we knew was going to be a large police perimeter. They could effectively manipulate other law enforcement within their zone under the mandate of federal authority. Ideally, the cops would be too busy trying to figure out what the hell was going on to worry about it until we were done in the tower.

The helicopter banked up sharply then leveled off and came to a hover. Tat shot out the door ahead of me. Adrenaline surged through my system as I jumped. There were a few seconds of wind rushing past my ears as I counted to three and pulled my ripcord, then relative silence as my chute bloomed above me. I looked down and spotted the large helipad on top of the tower. Pulling on my toggles, I started a steep, fast spiral down toward it.

Even though Orsa knew we would be coming, she didn't know when or how. We wanted both teams to have the element of surprise but were utilizing the two-pronged strategy so at least one would.

The helipad rushed toward me. It made for an ideal landing surface. It also made us ideal targets if Orsa had guards stationed up there. If the ground team was doing their job it was possible that it would be clear, but not guaranteed.

My senses were focused on the helipad as I banked in to land, but peripherally I saw the flashing lights of police cars and firetrucks, accompanied by a cacophony of sirens, all moving away from the tower and toward LAPD headquarters and the concert hall. That part of the plan was working. So far so good.

I was about two hundred feet from the helipad when good turned bad.

A gang of elves came charging onto the roof armed with assault rifles. I drew one of my Desert Eagles and dropped the first two before they got to the stairway leading up onto the helipad. The rest of them dove for cover, and I lost sight of them.

I came flying in from the side of the helipad away from the stairs. They would have to come all the way up to the pad to have any kind of shot at me, and that would make them as exposed as I was. I holstered my gun.

"Tat, keep an eye on them. Distract them if you can," I barked at her.

She had been flying just off my shoulder the whole time. She darted downward, extinguishing her glow as she went. If she could buy us a precious few seconds of safety that was all we needed.

As I flew in to land, I pulled hard on both toggles, flaring my chute and slowing my forward momentum to almost nothing. I pulled the release clasps, and the whole chute and pack tore away from my back, and I dropped onto the landing pad. I dropped into a forward roll to stop my momentum. I drew both Desert Eagles in mid-roll and came up onto one knee, aiming at the stairs, ready to blow the face off any elf who might come up.

Fortunately, none did because I got clobbered from behind by one of the elves on my squad. He had misjudged his landing speed and barreled into me after cutting his chute, knocking me flat. I looked up in time to see him bounce across the pad, his rig still attached at one shoulder, and tumble over the edge onto the roof below. There was an eruption of gunfire, then silence. Fuck.

The rest of the elves, having landed safely, quickly tucked in around me in a semicircle, guns drawn and covering all the angles around us. The squad's commander was a perpetually scowling, gruff-voiced elf named Kritten. He was slightly taller than the others by about two inches and had a bright spot of blue in his left eye. He started heading toward the edge of the pad, where his comrade had gone over.

"Felth'shi thema, dura kaan!" he growled.

I wasn't quite sure how to translate that, but I got the gist of it enough to know he was furious. I lunged forward and got a hold of his tactical vest just before he was out of reach, and pulled him back.

"Focus now, avenge later," I said with hushed intensity.

He narrowed his eyes at me for a hot second, hurt and anger burning in them, but then he nodded. "Aye, but avenge him I will."

I was angry too, but being a good leader is always about keeping your emotions in check and your thinking clear.

"Fine, but let's be smart about it," I said.

Tat landed on my shoulder.

"The Ziwix Reds have encircled the landing pad beneath us," she said.

The edge of the helipad jutted out over its base by about three feet, giving the Ziwix below us plenty of space to hide and cover under. It was a sure bet that some of them were trained on the staircase and would light us up in a cross fire if we were stupid enough to try and go down it. They couldn't come up for the same reason, they'd be walking straight into a hail of bullets. That could make for a long standoff that we absolutely didn't have time for. We'd already lost the element of surprise and needed to get moving again, fast.

"Light 'em up," I said to her.

She nodded at me and zipped off my shoulder, her glow still off.

"She'll show us where they are. Line up on her marks, shoot on my word."

Tat flew out over the edge of the platform then flew back into its radius and flicked on her glow for a split second, marking the position of a Ziwix below, then she went dark again. I tapped one of the elves on the shoulder, and she moved out silently, dropping into a belly crawl as she neared the edge. Another elf crawled forward to the edge of the helipad at the next position she marked. Tat repeated the process six times.

I gave the go sign. I made a gun symbol with my thumb and index finger and pretended to shoot it, military sophistication at its finest. The elves silently tilted their guns over the edge of the helipad. They were shooting blind, but thanks to Tat they knew exactly where to aim. The screams from below were a testament to their accuracy.

I had positioned myself at the staircase, Tat had marked a Ziwix on either side of it, setting up the cross fire I'd predicted, then flown back to my shoulder. I drew the Rondel daggers.

"Flash 'em!" I said to Tat in a whisper.

She launched off my shoulder, zipping straight down the staircase. She stopped short and blasted her glow to full wattage. It was dark up here, especially under the helipad where the Ziwix were hiding. Tat going fool bloom with the elves staring right at her momentarily blinded them. A moment was all I needed.

I leapt off the helipad, and in midair I spun around so I was facing the wall the two Ziwix were crouched against. I fixed on both and hurled the daggers. I landed with the Desert Eagle already in my hand. One elf was crumpled on the ground, the blade through his heart. The other was still alive, the Rondel embedded hilt deep in his shoulder, right where it met his pectoral muscle. He was a tough little guy, hissing through gritted teeth and trying to draw a pistol on his hip.

I got to him before he could get the gun out. I grabbed his free arm and slammed it into the wall above his head. I put my other hand on the pommel of the dagger.

"Where is Annalisa?"

I pushed on the pommel and began making very small circles with it. He tried not to scream and lasted for about two seconds.

"T…t…two floors down… in Orsa's sitting room," he stuttered through the pain.

"How many more of you?"

"Over forty," he managed to choke out.

I stopped moving the blade. Chulunn's team had a few more than half that. With Cuda, plus the magical abilities of Duncan and Chulunn, it was enough to tip the scales, if they'd gotten the element of surprise. They were going to sneak up the private elevator shafts that only accessed the top floors of the tower, using magic to shield their approach. Still, forty was a lot.

I yanked the blade out of the elf's shoulder. Kritten shot him.

"Smart?" he growled, rhetorically.

"Enough," I nodded. He'd made good on his promise. I couldn't blame him, blood debt had to be paid.

"Let's move," I said to the elves who'd huddled up around me again. "Shoot, stab, or piss on anyone who's not one of ours!" With swords and guns drawn they were right on my heels as I kicked open the stairwell door.

I charged down the stairs and slammed through another door, emerging on the top floor. We were in a hallway, elevator banks about twenty feet to our left, a doorway leading into an open room to our right.

I could smell blood, gunpowder, sweat, adrenaline, and several odors I could only chalk up to magical energies, but they were all distant, drifting up from the floor below us. No one engaged us as we sprinted down the hall to the elevators. I grabbed the doors and wrenched them open. The elevator car was stopped several floors below.

"Kritten, take your men down the shaft to the floor below, that's where the fight is. I'll take the stairwell, Tat you're with me. We'll come at them from two directions."

Without word or hesitation Kritten leapt onto the elevator cable and started sliding down it. The other three followed behind him.

I ran back into the stairwell and down another two flights of stairs, the sounds of battle, gunfire, and metal striking metal growing louder as I descended. My Dragondar lit up. Alamander was close.

The scene I encountered when I burst from the stairwell was almost funny.

The room was a big half-circle-shaped space, decorated in an ultra-modern style, except all the furniture was elf-sized.

The kid-sized proportions weren't the funny part. The funny part was Cuda.

He was directly in front of me, several deep cuts on his body flowing blood, a ferocious grin on his face as he whirled and slashed with a blade in each hand. He was fighting four Ziwix Elves on his own, and his massive bulk made it look like he was fighting in the middle of a Barbie Dream House gone cuckoo. He was standing on a pile of small broken furniture, three elves were unconscious, or dead, at his feet.

The rest of the room wasn't so funny. Wounded and dead elves lay everywhere, blood and gore covered the floor and decor. I took in everything as I charged across the room, battle-adrenaline speeding up my perception to lightning quickness.

"Tat, help In-Ra!" I barked.

She had been flying just off my shoulder as always, and she shot forward toward the djinn. He was backed up against the floor-to-ceiling windows with four of Chulunn's soldiers beside him, facing down six Ziwix. Greg lay unconscious on the floor between In-Ra's feet, blue blood running from his slack-jawed mouth. With a saber in each hand, In-Ra was a whirlwind of speed, helping make up for his side's lack of numbers, but forcing him to stay on the defensive to protect Greg.

I ran past Cuda and slammed an elbow into the head of the last Ziwix he was dealing with, sending her sprawling to the floor. "Cuda, help me with Duncan!"

"Got to help Chulunn!" he shouted, sprinting off in the other direction.

Dammit! Duncan was near In-Ra and Greg but completely unable to help them. He had his staff planted on the floor in front of him, the Phoenix a riotous blaze of living flame breathing out a steady blast of golden energy. It had coalesced into a half dome shield about ten feet away from him, that he'd trapped more than a dozen Ziwix soldiers inside of. His brow was crimson red and beaded with sweat from the strain.

Inside the shield, the Ziwix were using their swords to furiously fling blasts of silvery energy at it, or slash into it. If they got out, it was over for Duncan, In-Ra, and Chulunn's soldiers. They would be overwhelmed by sheer numbers.

On the farthest side of the room Chulunn faced off against Orsa Rike. He held a gleaming short sword in each hand. Blood ran down his shoulder from a deep cut. Orsa, her long dark hair cascading wildly around her shoulders and down her back, held a sword with a curved double-edged blade that dripped with Chulunn's blood.

"Help the others, Cuda, I can handle this bitch alone!" Chulunn snarled.

"Brave of you to accept death without any help, old man," Orsa spat back.

They came together in a furious clashing of steel and then backed off, circling each other.

Cuda changed course back toward me, just as the elevator doors wrenched open and Kritten and his soldiers leapt out.

"Kritten, the dome!" I shouted, pointing as I ran toward it.

Without hesitating he and his men joined our charge.

"Bout fucking time you got here, lizard!" Duncan said through gritted teeth.

"Drop the shield!" I barked in response.

He did. Literally. The dome dropped downward into the floor as if it were being sucked through it, coating the Ziwix in its residual energy as it passed over them. Their movements slowed as if they'd been covered with lead coats. Dunc sank to his knees with it, spent from the effort.

Cuda and I plowed headlong into the Ziwix while Kritten and his elves came at their flank. We made short work of half of them before the energy wore off. Whatever Tat had done had been enough to give In-Ra and his elves breathing room. They had driven themselves forward off the wall and were turning the tide.

"Your girl!" Duncan shouted at me in a hoarse voice, pointing to a door in the middle of the room.

I could feel Alamander in the room behind it. I broke off from the fight and ran at it, crashing through the door like a mad gorilla. I got three steps inside and was stopped dead by an invisible force of energy slamming into me like a giant fist. I flew backwards and smashed into the wall behind me. It was several layers of heavy drywall and I cratered into it, then peeled out and crumpled onto the floor, leaving a full body imprint in the wall. I spat blood and shook my head to clear my blurry vision.

Across the room, Annalisa stood beside Alamander. She was still wearing the elegant black evening dress she'd had on the night she was taken, but her shoulders were draped in a red elven shawl that fell almost to the floor. He had a hand on her shoulder but didn't appear to be restraining her in any way.

In front of them stood an old elf. She looked it, which was rare, it took a lot of wear and tear to make an elf look old.

"Felth'shi, sarr lest!" she snarled, narrowing her eyes at me.

She had a head full of grey and white hair dangling down her back in long thick dreadlocks, with dozens of multicolored beads and crystals interwoven into the strands. She wore a red knee-length peasant dress and tall brown boots. A wooden staff was in her hand, a feathered dream catcher dangling from the top of it glowed with energy.

"Go felth'shi yourself, Liwix," I spat back at her as I stood, more wobbly than I expected. That giant invisible fist had hit me like, well, a giant invisible fist.

"Randall, stop this attack," Annalisa said.

I heard it immediately, her voice, something in her tone and cadence was wrong. I'd watched her bend corporate titans to her will just by speaking. Her voice was bereft of that power and confidence now, it sounded unnaturally hollow. I was sure she was under some kind of compulsion or enchantment.

"Annalisa, these people are not your friends, and your life is in serious danger. You need to come with me." I took a few steps towards her. Liwix leveled her staff at me in response.

"No," her voice was firm, the commanding voice she used with subordinates. "I'm staying of my own accord. I don't need you to rescue me. Stop the killing, take your people and go. I release you of your obligations to me."

Liwix's lips curled into a tight smile. It was a smile that said, 'You lose.'

"I have simply told her the truth of herself, near-kin," Alamander said.

The left side of his face had the somewhat glossy look of skin still healing from burn injuries. I had torched him in the garage. Good.

"He's told me what I am, shown me. I'm djinn."

Now I knew she was spellbound. Annalisa had an exceptional mind, but no one could be told there was a whole supernatural world that they didn't know existed, and that they were a super-powered djinn royal, and just be okay with it. Her strong mind would be rebelling against what she'd learned, not accepting it.

"I guarantee you he hasn't told you the whole truth," I said as I sidestepped, trying to get on their flank. Liwix tracked me with her staff, keeping herself firmly planted between us.

"Come Half-kin, give it another try," Liwix sneered.

Felth'shi... whatever.

"Randall, respect what I'm telling you. I need to learn what being djinn means, and understand who I really am," she said with seeming conviction and sincerity, wanting me to believe her.

I knew whatever bullshit Alamander had fed her wasn't anywhere close to the whole truth. She didn't understand that she would be enslaved and used, trapped in his control. Or what his plan for her was. I didn't have the time to try and convince her of the truth right now, I just had to save her, even if it was against her will. She'd thank me later.

Whipcrack fast the Desert Eagles were in my hands, and I unloaded them at Liwix and Alamander. The Magus-Sai moved as fast as I did, waving the staff across her body. The dream catcher expanded in front of her becoming a giant, glowing energy version of itself, stretching from floor to ceiling. The bullets exploded into bursts of green sparks as they struck the shield, filling the room with a deafening roar.

Alamander only moved to step in front of Annalisa, shielding her with his body. He clearly had a lot of trust in Liwix's power, which proved warranted, because not one bullet got past the dream catcher.

Before I could try anything else Orsa came flying through the doorway, tumbled across the floor, and stopped in a heap just past my feet. Wisps of smoke wafted off her body accompanied by a charred skin smell. Her clothes were burnt tatters. Chulunn followed her through the door, stalking in like a panther, his eyes glowing bright red.

"Yield, Orsa," he said, his voice low and hard. "Or die."

"Die," she panted.

I had to respect her fighting spirit.

In-Ra sprinted into the room, and Annalisa's eyes widened. Maybe it was seeing a djinn in person, but she reacted to the sight of him much more powerfully than anything I had said to her.

"My queen! Alamander misleads you! Si'salay salam kosh nam!" he shouted.

There was the tiniest flash of light around Annalisa, which fizzled out almost immediately. Annalisa looked like she had understood him perfectly though, and she stared at him with a dawning recognition that came from some deep, unconscious level.

"I know you. How...?" she said. Her gaze whipped to Alamander, her eyes filled with confusion and doubt. "How do I know him?"

"Go!" Orsa said weakly to Liwix.

"But my liege..." Liwix started to protest.

I don't know where she got the strength, but Orsa whipped her hand out, and a ball of green energy shot out of it. It struck In-Ra square in the chest and crumpled him to the floor in a heap.

"Now! Complete the plan!" Orsa hissed in a whisper.

Alamander grabbed Annalisa roughly, wrapping both arms around her, as Liwix stepped backwards close to them. A black disc opened underneath them, and they dropped into it, then the portal shrank in on itself and vanished. It was the same disappearing act he had used in the hotel garage.

I was in mid-charge at the dream catcher shield, and I had to skid to a stop to avoid slamming into the wall behind where they had just been.

"Goddammit!" I yelled.

Chulunn stepped to Orsa. She was out cold, having used all her reserves for the blast of energy she'd flung at In-Ra.

Cuda stepped into what was left of the doorframe. He was shirtless at this point. Despite all the fighting he'd been doing, his thick skin had already stopped bleeding from the cuts all over it. I knew from firsthand experience that his hide was tough enough to shrug off a .22 caliber bullet, so I wasn't surprised.

"Fightin's done, boss."

"Bring her," Chulunn said, pointing at Orsa's limp form.

Cuda picked her up and slung her over his shoulder like a rag doll, then followed Chulunn back into the other room. I helped In-Ra to his feet, he had a nasty burn on his chest, but he was proving to be tougher than he looked. I half carried him out behind them as he fought to get his feet back under him.

There was very little in the room that wasn't broken or destroyed, the bodies of dead and dying elves were all over the place. Kritten was still on his feet and relatively unscathed, the blood he was covered in was mostly not his own. He approached Chulunn and stood dutifully in front of him, a cadre of twelve soldiers behind him. All that was left of the attack force.

"The helicopter is inbound, my lord," he said.

Duncan was cradling Greg in his arms. The imp was unconscious, his breathing shallow and halting.

"How is he?" I asked.

Duncan shook his head in way of response, looking grave. His eyes were watery.

"My healers can help him," Chulunn said. "To the roof, quickly."

I called Buck as we headed to the stairwell.

"Do you have him?" she asked, before I had a chance to speak.

"No. We got Orsa. Annalisa and Alamander got away."

"Disappointing," she said, her voice icy.

"The bird's coming back in for extraction, we need an exit corridor," I said through tight lips.

I wouldn't have said anything nice if I'd engaged with her jab. I was still fuming at Annalisa falling through my fingers... again.

"You're clear for eight minutes," she said and hung up.

The copter was landing as we made it up onto the helipad. It was a good thing the elves were so small, because we were definitely pushing the passenger limit. Four minutes later we were clear of downtown and halfway back to Chulunn's.

CHAPTER TWENTY-FIVE

It was a little after 2 am, just over three hours after we started the tower raid.

Chulunn had a cell in his smaller guest house, located on a basement level. Orsa was inside. Chulunn, Cuda, Duncan, the Feds, and I were standing outside.

Now that she was his captive, he had Conclave's rules to abide by. Even though all his actions were justified by her initial attack on his house, he could not be her judge and jury. It was elf law that she be allowed to speak to the Conclave in her own defense, then they would determine her fate. Things are so much easier with Half-kin. We fight. You're dead. I won. Moving on.

"I got this," I said.

We needed answers from Orsa, which she wasn't going to give willingly, and we didn't have much time to get them.

"I cannot be a part of it, nor can anyone I employ," Chulunn said, looking at Cuda.

He thought I was going to torture her, which seemed like the logical route to take. I've had more experience with it than I care to remember, in some of my younger, darker moments.

"I said I got this," I reiterated.

"She cannot die," Chulunn said, firmly.

"She won't," I said.

He raised a doubtful eyebrow at me. "We will be watching," he said, pointing to a large monitor mounted on the wall by the door, showing four camera angles of the room.

"Don't worry, I'm not even going to touch her," I said with a wink.

I pushed the door open and entered the room. It was a square, maybe ten-by-ten, completely empty, and painted all grey. It had a slightly concave floor with a drain right in the center of it and smelled strongly of disinfectant. Chulunn obviously had some experience with torture, himself.

Once I was inside I fixed Orsa with a stare and closed the door very slowly and deliberately behind me.

She was chained to the wall. Her arms extended straight out at shoulder level, each wrist shackled in a shiny metal cuff that was bolted to the wall. Her legs were spread apart and similarly cuffed at the ankles, each cuff having a thick piece of chain link attached to it. The chains were welded to thick metal plates which were bolted into the wall, giving her a little freedom of movement.

"He sends you, to keep his own hands clean," she said.

She was wearing tight black leggings and combat boots. A heavy black tactical belt wrapped her waist. Her black, long sleeve shirt had rips and burn holes in it. We'd tossed the leather jacket she'd had on because it had been burned to tatters by Chulunn's magic.

"Yeah, I'm the back door man," I said, smiling coldly at her.

"Chulunn must keep me alive and unharmed," she said defiantly.

"Unharmed and pain-free, are two very different things."

I brought my face close to hers. I had to bend over to do it. She was only five-six, or so.

"Where is Alamander's unbinding spell taking place?"

She just glared at me.

"You really won't like what's going to happen if you don't tell me."

"You don't scare me, Dragon," she said fiercely.

"I really should."

"You can't touch me."

"I can do so much worse," I said, bringing my lips right up against her ear, "Prince Ellam Ko," I whispered in it.

Her reaction was, in a word, priceless. The blood drained from her face, her eyes went wide, and her whole body trembled enough to make her chains rattle. Pain doesn't always have to be physical.

"W...w...what do y..you..." she barely managed to stammer out.

"I know you wielded the blade that killed him two hundred years ago, and I have it," I whispered a description of the blade to her in great detail.

She started talking like a coked-out parrot on truth serum. Five minutes later I walked out with all the information we needed.

"Griffith Park Observatory, at midnight," I said to them. It was less than twenty-four hours from now.

"What did you say to her?" asked Chulunn, his tone indicating he was more than a little impressed.

"I'll tell you later," I said, glancing sidelong at Buck and Hooper. "For elf ears only."

Buck remained stone-faced, Hooper rolled his eyes slightly.

"Very well," Chulunn said.

He had taken up my cause of his own volition, sticking his neck out for the Conclave to possibly chop, by attacking other elves, because he understood the stakes. The least I could do was give him some ammunition to fire at Orsa and Pharyn-Cull, in case he ever needed it.

The short version of my history with Pharyn, a long time ago he'd hired me through intermediaries to kill some people for him, as part of one of his Machiavellian schemes. He'd taken me for dumb hired muscle, but I'd been smart enough to figure out what I was involved in, and the parts other cogs in his machine were playing. Orsa had been a big one, and she knew full well what her part was.

Prince Ellam Ko, a legitimate heir to the Red Elf throne, was assassinated by Orsa's hand. The result of the prince's death, and Pharyn's intended outcome for the entire scheme, had been his elevation to the title of duke. After the prince's murder, I'd managed to get my hands on the blade she'd used. A blade that elf magic could prove was the murder weapon. I'd kept it safely hidden for over two hundred years, knowing that one day it, along with what I knew, would be useful, even if I didn't know how. Believe me, I never would have predicted this situation. I'd kept it as insurance against Pharyn, I'd actually considered Orsa mostly irrelevant.

You might think that my telling her wouldn't cause her to break so completely. With the power she stood to gain for her faction of Reds, the Conclave would become irrelevant to her, but right now she found herself chained to a wall at Chulunn's house, her plan's success in doubt. A plan I'd bet my left nut Pharyn was the real power behind.

Now, if their plan failed, she knew I could burn her for the prince's murder, and by extension possibly Pharyn as well. He would stop at nothing to prevent that from happening. Orsa would become less than meaningless to him, a loose end he would have to eliminate to protect himself. He was that kind of self-serving nasty, and she knew it. I'd gambled that her fear of Pharyn was greater than her belief in Alamander. It had paid off.

"Can't believe I didn't figure it," Duncan said, bringing me back to the moment. "The observatory shoulda been goddamned obvious."

"Indeed," agreed Chulunn.

It didn't seem obvious to me. The alignment was going to be a cosmological event only in terms of the planets aligning. The part of it that mattered to us, the alignment of the realms, was happening in the metaphysical sense. The most powerful telescope in the world wouldn't be able to see a hint of the alignment. That required magic.

"Why?" I asked.

"Same," said Hooper.

"The observatory's a power node," Duncan said.

"The hell's a power node?" Hooper asked, saving me the trouble.

"A convergence of Ley Lines," Duncan replied.

"Liwix will know how to tap into it. It could increase her power a hundredfold," Chulunn said.

"Possibly a lot more than that," Duncan said.

"Can you elaborate?" Buck asked.

"They are concentrated lines of Earth's natural magical power that run across the globe, often connecting physical places of ancient mystical significance, infusing them with power," Chulunn said.

"Easter Island, Stonehenge, the Great Pyramids, Chichen Itza, to name just a few," Duncan continued, "Major lines can circumnavigate the planet, and they carry a shit-ton of power if you know how to tap into them."

"Damn," Hooper interjected.

"Yeah," Duncan said, grimly. "Three major lines intersect underneath the observatory forming a node. It's a supercharged energy well, and because it's a fixed point it's easier to tap into."

"There's gonna be a lot of innocent people in harm's way up there," I said.

"No, there won't," Buck said.

She'd been staring at her phone and scrolling, while we'd been talking. She looked up at me.

"As haphazard as your tower plan was, it has proven beneficial in regard to the observatory."

"Haphazard?" I said, a little annoyed. No one appreciates genius.

"Yes, at best," she replied with a touch of condescension. "Due to the staged gunfight, every large event venue, concert hall, arena, and public park in the greater Los Angeles area has been shut down for the next forty-eight hours for public safety concerns. LAPD is sending out press releases now. The observatory will be empty."

"Haphazard for the win, then," I said, giving her an equally condescending smile. "They might have been counting on it being crowded up there, this could throw a wrench into their gears."

"You have an overly generous definition of 'winning,'" Buck said, then she turned and stalked away.

"I'd say don't take it personally, but..." Hooper said with a shrug, then he followed her.

"Who pissed in her coffee?" Duncan said, as he watched them leave.

"Clearly I did."

"How?"

"Don't know, don't care. We got bigger problems to deal with right now."

"Speaking of, I'm going to see Greg. Chulunn's healers kicked me out of the room to give them room to work. I'm going to kick in the door if they don't let me back in now," he said gruffly.

I could feel the pain in his voice. I put a hand on his shoulder.

"Got your back if you need it. I'll meet you there in a bit." I had some explaining to do with Chulunn before I could join him.

CHAPTER TWENTY-SIX

I gave Chulunn the long version of how I'd been involved with Pharyn-Cull, what I had said to Orsa, and how the blade she had used to murder the prince had come into my possession. He absorbed it like a sponge, only asking questions when he wanted granular clarification.

"I'll get you the blade as soon as all this is over. It will take a little time to retrieve it."

"The prince was a good man, though I doubt he would have made a strong king," Chulunn said, when I finished my story. "Regardless, this is high treason."

"It will help you with the Conclave for sure," I said.

"I plan on keeping what you have told me to myself, for the time being."

"You sure that's the right play?" I said, a little surprised.

"Some on the Conclave may find my actions with Orsa distasteful, but the majority will see me as justified. I do not want

I AM DRAGON

to utilize such potent information against Pharyn when it is not necessary. There will come a time when I shall take great joy in twisting this blade in him, but today is not that day," he said, giving me a cold grin.

Having waited two hundred years to use the information myself, I could understand.

Chulunn excused himself, to go contact the Conclave. I headed to meet up with Duncan.

The door to Greg's room was still on its hinges, so apparently he'd gotten in without a fight. It was a large bedroom in the bigger of the two guest houses. I pulled up a chair next to Duncan. It must have been a suite for non-elf guests because Greg could have used the massive bed for a swimming pool if it wasn't for his current state. His wounds had been coated in healing salves and ointments, then bandaged, but angry dark bruising was visible underneath them. His breathing came in short, ragged breaths.

One of Chulunn's healers was sitting across from us on the opposite side of the bed, humming a repetitive chant. A soft yellow glow emanated from his hands, which he held just over Greg's chest. I felt intense heat coming off both of their bodies. The little guy would twitch and shudder every few minutes.

"He's fighting," Duncan said, trying not to choke up and not succeeding very well.

"He's tough. He'll pull through this, Dunc."

He shot a quick glance at the elf, who seemed unaware of our presence.

"What happened?" I asked. I hadn't gotten the story from his side yet, not wanting to bother him with a debrief before we'd gotten Greg taken care of.

261

"We got in fine, took 'em by surprise for the most part. Lucky, cause they had numbers on their side that we weren't anticipating. Chulunn, Cuda, and I had point, and we'd narrowed the odds some, but then that old broad Liwix came out of nowhere. She's got power."

"I know. I got hit with it," I said.

"She was trying to take me out, numbnuts here jumped in front of me and took the shot. Stupid imp. He…" his voice cracked.

It was a crude analogy, but over the course of their time together, Greg had become the supernatural equivalent of a PTSD service dog, to Duncan's broken patient. He'd originally bound Greg to go on liquor runs for him, so he could more easily drink himself numb. Ironically, the longer they'd been together the more Greg had pulled Duncan out of the bottle. Their relationship, wacky as it was, slowly helped to heal whatever had broken Duncan.

I'd tried to help him a few times, but he'd wanted none of it. My kind are the ultimate believers in free will and personal accountability, so it wasn't in my nature to try and force him into getting help, even though I'd thought he could use it. His choices were his to make. Not gonna lie though, I was afraid of the dark places he might go back to if he lost Greg.

"If you want to stay with him Dunc, I understand," I said, "But I really need your help tonight. You still with me?"

"Don't worry, lizard, I'm in it till the end," he said, with fire in his eyes. "That bitch owes me for this." He pointed at Greg, his voice was as hot as his eyes.

"I need you to make something. For the Darkling."

"What?"

I quickly explained what I wanted.

"Yeah, I can do that. Shouldn't be much of a problem."

"Thanks," I stood, giving his shoulder a solid squeeze, then I headed out the door.

Hooper was waiting for me. Yay.

He held up my weapons case. "We took it out of your truck after we nabbed you in the hotel garage. Didn't trust you enough to give it back to you earlier."

It had Drop's prison and the crystal rose in it.

"You do now?" I asked, taking it from his hand.

Honestly, I was relieved I wouldn't have to go back to the death trap hotel to get it. With my luck at that place, there would have been a bloody earthquake and the building would have collapsed on me.

"Barely," he said with a small grin, "How's the imp?"

"Still critical. Chulunn's healers are good, but…" I let it hang.

"Sorry. I hope he makes it. Losing a man is never good."

I'd been expecting more shit about my 'haphazard' plan, not sympathy for an injured friend.

"No, it never is," I agreed.

I started walking towards Chulunn's training space. Hooper fell into step beside me.

"Kevin," he said, "Tell me about him."

"I honestly don't know that much. He's saved my life twice, and I owe him a debt of gratitude for it. He's from the south, wants to be an actor, he killed a vampire."

"He fucking what?" Hooper blurted.

I gave him the condensed version of Kevin's story.

"Black Caste. Jesus."

"It's why he's so invested in protecting me, he's afraid he won't get answers he desperately wants. Kid's been thinking he might be going crazy for years now."

"I know the feeling," Hooper said, his look introspective.

I shot him a sidelong glance with a raised eyebrow, but he didn't elaborate. He firmed his jaw and put his Fed face back on.

"He wasn't lying about his skills. I don't know if I've ever seen a better sniper."

"You had time to check him out already?"

"Somebody shoots me, I make it my business to get into theirs."

"So you know he wasn't trying to kill you."

"You said he doesn't know you're a Dragon. What does he think you are?" he asked, ignoring my comment.

"A badass?" What? I'm sure Kevin did think I was a badass.

"You actually seem concerned about what happens to him, so how about you stop being an asshole, just for a minute, and answer my questions. It might help the kid out of the hole he dug himself into... because of you," he said, shaking his head in frustration.

I was in a bad mood and purposefully being difficult, having just walked out of Greg's infirmary and seeing Duncan in the state he was in. And failing to get Annalisa twice. And not having Shrill back. And Buck calling my plan 'haphazard.' And... I wanted to hit something. Hooper was a tempting and convenient target at the moment, but not a deserving one.

"Fine," I sighed. "He doesn't know what I am, just that I'm not human."

"What did he see?"

"Aside from the aftermath of my fall into the pool, he caught the tail end of a fight between me and Alamander in the hotel garage. He saw some magic being used, and watched Alamander shrug off what should have been a killing blow, that he delivered."

"Anything else?"

"That isn't enough?"

"Just being thorough."

"Why does any of this matter to you?"

"I'm trying to figure out what to do with him. The more information I have the better decision I can make."

He surprised me with what he said next.

"I'm thinking of offering him a job."

"The kid's done being a soldier, Hooper, let him be."

"You know that for a fact, do you?"

Actually, I didn't. From what Kevin had told me I'd just assumed it. Hooper saw it on my face.

"Might help him cope," he said, his expression turning introspective again. I could tell he was speaking from personal experience.

"Hell, maybe you're right," I said, "It beats jail."

"Thanks for the info," he said with a chuckle. He broke off and headed back to the main house.

I continued toward the training house. Hooper was right about one thing, dealing with your demons head-on was usually the best way to excise them. Maybe Kevin wouldn't mind being a different kind of soldier, now that he knew there was a different kind of enemy.

I entered the guest house to see Buck squared off in the middle of one of the sparring floors. She was surrounded by four elves, armed with wood bo staffs. She had a Kali stick in each hand. A slim, round length of heavy wood about two feet long, used in the Philippine martial art of Pakamut, or stick fighting.

In unison, they closed on her. In a blur of staffs and sticks they danced around the floor. Even in her human form Buck moved with the liquid speed I had dealt with firsthand, and her fighting technique was a thing of beauty. She could flex and bend in ways that were rubbery, allowing her to strike from positions that were completely unexpected and seemingly impossible. Circus contortionists would be jealous. She took out all four elves in less than a minute. It was damn impressive.

There were several large heavy bags hanging from ceiling-mounted brackets. Just what I wanted, something to hit. I stripped off my jacket and shirt and went to town on one of the bags. Buck approached and watched me intently. I wanted to think she was getting turned on, but more likely she was studying my skills the same way I'd studied hers. I kept at it for thirty minutes and would've gone longer but after several vicious kicks in a row, the bag broke off its bracket and exploded against a wall in a shower of sand. Guess I was a little more pent-up than I thought. Oops.

Buck was in my face before I could even pick up my towel to dry off.

"Your plan last night was reckless, and little was achieved."

I'd just worked off most of the frustration and anger I'd been feeling, and she reignited it in one sentence. Since we'd declared truce and agreement, I'd thought that between the Feds I'd get along better with Buck. If for no other reason than we had common ground as supernatural beings, but it was turning out to be just the opposite.

"Too little?" I growled. "Because of my plan we know exactly why, where, and when they're going to be tonight."

"For the lives that were lost, that is too little."

"Then we make sure those deaths mean something, by stopping this madness at the observatory."

"And how many more will die?"

"None, if I can help it," I said, my anger rising.

She dropped her gaze to the floor and muttered hotly through clenched teeth. "Arrogant, callous, heartless…" She took a deep breath and looked back at me, her eyes blazing with anger. "What if it's your wizard that falls this time? Or your Fae? Will you shed tears for Chulunn-Bat's kin? Do you even care about those who fight with you?"

Who did this bitch think she was? I got in her face and looked daggers into her eyes.

"Last night wasn't perfect, but it worked. Some of ours died, more might tonight. You'd be a fool to think otherwise. If you can tell me how to prevent it and still get the job done, I'm all ears."

My voice had turned to ice.

"As to who I mourn for, don't ever presume to understand that. You don't know me, kitten."

She threw a right hook with blinding speed. Her fist cracked into my jaw like a sledgehammer, snapping my head around. I recoiled backwards several steps. It got quiet in the room as all the elves near us stopped what they were doing to watch.

"I warned you not to call me kitten," she said, the heat in her voice matching the ice in mine.

A low snarl rose from the back of my throat as I balled my fists. I was as turned on as I was angry. To be honest I was probably more turned on. All of her sexy plus all her strength and skill, how could I not be? Stupid libido.

"You damnable Dragons are all the same, no matter your family line, you think only of yourselves!" She spat in a hissed, angry whisper, trying not to draw any more attention to us.

Wait, what?

Her animosity was somehow personal, she had a problem with me because of what I was, not because of anything I'd done.

"What is your problem with me?" I asked, resisting the urge to charge back into her face. "Have I caused harm or offense to you, or your kin?"

It was another one of those questions, asked only by one supernatural being to another. To find out if you had dishonored, hurt, or killed another's family or friends. It was asked honestly, to learn about any unknown transgression.

"No," she said, harshly. "My problem with you, and all of your kind, is your disregard for how your actions affect the lives of others, and for being arrogant beyond tolerance."

Despite my anger, I failed to stifle a laugh at her last point. As a species we wore that fact rather proudly.

"Hell, that's no secret. You had a Green working for you. Talk about arrogant."

She flinched, her pulse rate quickened, her temperature shot up, and she broke eye contact with me. I stared hard at her as it hit me.

"I'll be damned. The Green, you were involved with him, weren't you?"

"Yes," she said, looking back at me after a beat. The expression in her eyes was far more powerful than anger. It was sadness.

This was the single weirdest thing about Greens. They were the only kind of Half-kin to couple with only one mate for long periods of time. Like more than a year. That's a lifetime for most of us.

"And it's none of your business," she said sharply.

"No, it isn't," I agreed, my anger cooling.

She'd suffered a loss and it was apparently deep. She was projecting her feelings of loss for him onto me, and it was coming out as anger. It shed light on why she was so angry at me for being reckless and arrogant. Traits that probably helped get her boyfriend killed after he confronted Alamander.

"I'm sure he was a good man," I said, sincerely.

I got another emotion out of her... shock. She knew my kind and Half-kin rarely said anything good about one of our own when they got killed. We didn't mourn or feel sorry for them, we blamed them for being stupid, careless, unprepared, incompetent, or all the above. In death, we were always at fault for our own unworthiness to reach the Test. A wave of emotions played across her face as the anger in her eyes subsided.

"He was... mine," was all she said. It was enough. It spoke volumes.

"I'm sorry for your loss."

"Thank you," she said, composing herself. Her expression a touch softer than usual.

I took a few steps back to her. There was no aggression in my stance and my hands were down.

"If I could do this on my own to prevent others from dying, believe me I would. I can't. This is too big, the stakes are too high, and I need help. People may die in the effort, that's the cold hard reality of it," I said.

She folded her arms tightly across her chest.

"I reiterate, I want Alamander alive."

"You want him to pay for what he did to your Green."

"Yes," she said, flatly. "And death is not the price I have in mind for him."

They way she said it was downright chilling. She had her own ideas about blood debt, apparently.

"You handle him then," I said, "I'll focus on Liwix and getting Annalisa clear."

Annalisa being in my care made her my priority and trumped my desire to take another shot at Alamander, and Liwix was going to be a big hairy handful. The amount of power she could potentially wield with access to the node was effing scary. Strategically speaking, taking her out of play as fast as possible was the smartest move.

"No," she said, shaking her head. "The observatory and park grounds are closed, but we still have to ensure what happens there remains isolated, and it will take most of the resources from our division to do it. Hooper and I will have to control that from outside the grounds. Alamander's capture remains your responsibility. Deliver him to me in any condition other than alive and our terms will be null and void. You know that we need no judge or jury to deal with you as we see fit."

"You really need to work on your motivational speeches," I said.

"I want you to understand how serious I am about keeping him alive."

"You're letting emotion get the better of good judgement," I said.

Her expression hardened into something so cold I swear the temperature around us dropped. I didn't let it stop me, she was tying my hands with her emotional BS. Or at least forcing me to fight with one of them behind my back.

"Your personal grudge is not important, compared to what's at stake here. If it comes down to killing Alamander to save Annalisa and stop Dragongeddon, there's not really a choice in the matter."

"There's always a choice. You'll just have to accept the price for what you choose."

She turned and walked away before I could respond.

Bloody hell.

CHAPTER TWENTY-SEVEN

When we regrouped, I found out things had gotten more complicated and a lot harder.

"You're forbidden from further interference in the situation? Why?" I asked Chulunn in disbelief.

"The Conclave is not happy with what has transpired between Orsa and I. I've been ordered to stand down by the king himself."

"You told them what's at stake, didn't you?"

"Of course I did, but there is skepticism among some on the Conclave that unbinding the Test is even possible."

"We've got proof."

"No. We have bits and pieces. Annalisa's kidnapping. Alamander's admission to you. The appearance of In-Ra. Duncan's research. The alignments. All together it amounts to nothing more than theory, conjecture, and assumption."

"You can't seriously believe that?"

He held up a hand placatingly, "I am telling you how the Conclave sees it. I do not share their shortsightedness, but I am bound by their orders."

"Orsa tried to kill you," I said, incredulously.

"Indeed. It's all that is keeping House Bat from being severely sanctioned, and me from being imprisoned right alongside her. In the Conclave's eyes, my actions up to this point have been justified, but I have been commanded to go no further."

There's too much at stake to stop bending the rules now," I said, trying to convince him to stay in the fight.

"I have bent them as far as I can," he shook his head in frustration. "If I break them, their substantial weight falls onto my back, not yours."

"That won't mean dick if Alamander succeeds."

"Would you break your oath of care to Annalisa?" he asked, his eyes flashing at me with anger.

Bollocks. He had me there.

"No. Of course not," I said begrudgingly.

"I too am oath-bound, Randall. I must ultimately answer to my kind, even if I believe they are wrong."

"This is Pharyn's doing," I said, my jaw clenched.

"Of course it is," he snapped. His anger wasn't directed at me now, just the situation.

"What happens to you now?" Buck asked.

"The Conclave is sending envoys within the hour to monitor my actions. My assistance will be severely limited," he winked at me conspiratorially. "At that point."

"Before that point?" I asked, allowing a slight grin to touch my lips.

He turned to Cuda, who was standing behind him.

"Cuda, I believe a training mission with some of my soldiers is required. They seem to be lacking in their tactical combat skills for field operations. Ten would be acceptable."

"Not a problem, boss," Cuda said, with a beaming smile.

Whether they were just too shortsighted to act, or Pharyn's influence and manipulation was convincing them not to, we'd still do what had to be done tonight. The Conclave could thank us and kiss Chulunn's ass afterwards.

"Only ten?" said Duncan.

"The three hundred Spartans led by King Leonidas stopped the Persian army cold. Much can be accomplished by few, when properly utilized," Chulunn said.

"Yeah. Course, they all died," Dunc huffed.

"Then let's make sure we do it better than them, Dunc," I said.

We huddled up, and I laid out a plan. It was much simpler and with far fewer moving parts than last night's multipronged chaos ballet. Everyone seemed relieved about that. Whatever.

As we broke up to rest and prepare, In-Ra caught my eye.

He shuffled to a far corner of the room and slumped down heavily into a chair, head lowered and shoulders drooping as if the weight of the world was crushing down on him. He'd sworn an oath on his life to protect Annalisa, and keep her from discovering her true nature. She'd learned anyway, and even though it wasn't his fault, he looked like he was taking it as his personal failure. I felt for him because I could relate, having failed in my oath of care.

That's why it was Annalisa who I truly felt for in this whole mess. She was going to pay a steep price for what had been set in motion, no matter tonight's outcome. If we failed, she would be enslaved to a mad Dragon who seemed hell-bent on bringing chaos to the realms. If we succeeded, she was going to have to come to grips with the reality of being djinn. As sharp and strong as her mind was, she was ill-prepared to walk down that path. It was going to take an enormous amount of time and effort.

I knew from personal experience how hard it could be. It's a simplification, but one day you think you're human, the next you learn you're a Dragon. It's a bitch of a transition, like puberty but supersized and on steroids. Understanding and acceptance don't happen overnight, which is why our fathers show up to see us so often when we're young. They teach us how to cope, keep us grounded, start our martial arts training, and teach us about our new life. If it weren't for their commitment and dedication during that transition, a lot of young Half-kin would probably end up dead during the transition. It can be that much of a mind fuck. Of course, once you come to grips with how much better you are, it makes it all worth it.

Annalisa was not going to have the luxury of her parents' knowledge and wisdom, and was going to suffer for it. With luck she would have In-Ra, if he made it through the night.

"You cool, lizard? You look like you just swallowed a cow turd," Duncan said, walking up beside me.

My brow was furrowed and I was scowling, thinking about Annalisa. I shook it off.

"Specifically a cow turd?"

"Wombat turd would have been weirdly obscure."

"Yeah, stumpy, I'm cool," I pulled the crystal rose from my weapons case. "Let's free the Darkling."

"Speaking of Wombat turds," he replied.

CHAPTER TWENTY-EIGHT

We had five hours till midnight. Chulunn was not about to let us free Nerufane at his house, and Duncan wasn't keen on using the summoning circle at his place. I couldn't blame them, I wouldn't want a Darkling anywhere near my home either. Unless maybe it was for target practice.

I'd found a spot that was strategically located near the observatory and immeasurably cool at the same time. At the top of Canyon Drive, deep in the hills of Griffith Park, is the Bronson Cave. Carved into the side of a hundred-foot wall, Bronson is not just any cave. In the sixties it was used on a certain TV show as the entrance to, wait for it... the Batcave. It was flat, open, and most importantly, secluded.

Duncan was still wearing his green wizard robe, but heavy denim jeans had replaced the yoga pants, and his Converse shoes had been swapped for black leather engineer boots. The smiley face T-shirt had been switched for a black one with a picture of

Darth Vader's face that read, 'Come to the dark side. We have tacos.' As soon as we got there Duncan went to work, pulling supplies out of an Igloo cooler he'd brought along.

Tat was perched on my shoulder, watching him intently.

"What do you construct, Duncan?" she asked, shifting position to lay on her stomach, resting her chin in her palms.

"A power circle."

"What does it do?" she pressed.

"It focuses and augments magical energy that's fed into it."

"What does, augment, mean, wizard?" she asked him.

Duncan shot me a quick look, *I need to focus, here*, it said.

I turned my head to look directly at Tat, refocusing her attention on me. "How you doing, little one? You ready for tonight?"

"Ready," she replied simply, her eyes fierce.

"I never thanked you for saving my life at the hotel. I wouldn't be standing here now if it wasn't for you."

"Wasn't the first time, nae will it be the last I'm sure. You've saved mine many a time, Anii." She reached out and touched my cheek. "The words are unnecessary, they're understood."

I smiled. She frowned.

"What's wrong?"

"I am troubled by something. Our allies, they do not share the same oath of care that you have given to Annalisa."

"No, they don't."

"Her life is not as valuable to them, as it is to you."

I scowled as she gave voice to a thought I'd had in the back of my mind since the tower raid failed. Tat's point, Annalisa was only in *my* care.

"The surest way to stop Alamander is to slay Annalisa, is it not?" she said, not being morbid or cruel, just pragmatic.

"Yeah," my scowl deepened.

If we failed again tonight the world and the realms were going to suffer horribly. The easiest way to prevent that suffering would be to kill Annalisa as soon as she showed up. It would stop Alamander's plan dead in its tracks.

"Our allies, good, wise, and fair though they be, might take an easier path if things become to dire," she said.

"Yeah," I agreed.

I couldn't allow it to happen, not while she was in my care and I was still breathing. Which meant that I could end up fighting ally as well as enemy if things went completely off the rails. Bloody fuck all.

"We can trust only a few," she said.

"Yeah. I have faith in everyone fighting by our side, but trust... you, Duncan, and In-Ra, that's as far as it goes."

She shifted into a sitting position and folded her arms defiantly across her chest. "I'll nae trust the djinn," she scoffed.

"He's oath-bound to Annalisa on his life, Tat. That's a way stronger bond than being in my care, and you know it."

"You speak true," she said, begrudgingly. "I still d'nae like him."

"We can also trust everyone on Alamander's side. Not to kill her, anyway. She's the lynchpin to their whole plan and they need her alive."

"Aye, they'll protect her fierce."

It was small comfort and the irony that our enemies would keep Annalisa safer than our allies might, wasn't lost on me.

"Glad you brought it up, little one. It needed to be said."

She nodded, and her frown turned into a smile, though not a joyful one.

"Do some recon over the observatory grounds for me. See if you can sense anything."

Faeries are highly sensitive to magical energies. If anyone else was up to magical shenanigans near her flyby, she would feel it.

She floated off my shoulder.

"Be safe," I said, seriously. "I can't have you getting captured again."

"I shall be," she said, then shot into the sky.

I pulled out my phone and made a call.

"Hooper," he said, answering on the second ring.

"I need a favor."

"You're joking."

I wished I were. I didn't want to owe the Feds anything more than I already did.

"Dead serious."

"We're kinda busy right now."

"I appreciate that. I'll owe you a personal favor."

I had nothing else to bargain with. There was silence for a few seconds.

"What is it?" he finally said.

It took me five minutes to explain. I'm not positive, but he may actually have thought it was a good idea after I finished.

"I'll take care of it," he said and hung up.

I stayed in the Batcave brooding for about fifteen minutes until Duncan shouted at me.

"Hey, lizard!"

I hustled out of the tunnel over to his circle. He had gouged it into the ground and filled the outline in with a mixture of charcoal, steel, and copper shavings, from the smell of it. Large, clear shards of crystal were placed at the north, south, west, and east points of the ring. In the center was a large red ruby, sitting on a small wood block that was etched with runes.

"Ready," he said.

I put my fingers to my mouth and whistled. A minute later Tat came streaking back in to land on my shoulder.

"Anything?" I asked her.

"Nay, nothing save for this spot where Duncan prepares his works."

"Let's get this done," Duncan said. "Call him."

I took out the rose and said Nerufane's name to it. It began to glow a soft orange and floated away from my palm. The glow got brighter as it grew into the size and shape of man, finally coalescing into the form of the Darkling.

Shrill sat at his feet. He had a thick metal collar on his neck, attached to a chain leash which Nerufane had a tight grip on. Tat hissed angrily under her breath when she saw Shrill chained. My hands balled into fists, which I wanted to repeatedly slam into Nerufanes face. I refrained.

"Hello, muffin!" Nerufane trilled, flashing his megawatt smile. "It's a glorious night to be free."

I was surprised by how subdued his outfit was. Tailored grey suit, black shirt and tie, glossy black shoes. The only flamboyant thing he had on was a black fedora with a red band. His hair draped down his back in one long single braid.

"Definite improvement over the booty shorts," I said.

"Just precious, Randall," he said, tucking the rose into his hat band. "I've bought myself some extra time and don't prefer to waste it sparing with you, so let's get this party started, shall we?"

"Give me Shrill," I said.

He tugged on the leash, keeping Shrill in place.

"I think, no. I need some insurance you'll keep your word, muffin," he said, pouting his lips.

"He's still in here," I said, holding up Drop's glass prison. "Isn't that enough?"

"Still no, but as a gesture of goodwill..."

He curled his right hand into an arcane shape and said several words in his native tongue. It was harsh and guttural, with none of the high pitch he normally spoke in. Which was nice.

Within seconds the top half of the ball dissolved away, leaving me holding a glass bowl. Inside was a completely inert pool of water. I shook it gently, but it didn't move. Not even a ripple played across its surface. I glared at Nerufane.

"Patience, muffin, patience," he said.

About five seconds later the water woke up. Drop exploded upwards out of the bowl in a spray, shooting above my head then coalescing in midair before landing on the ground at my feet as a two-foot-tall, translucent, blue, liquid-ish human form. He didn't really have a face, just two crystalline green spots where eyes would normally be. He had steam coming off his head and shoulders, which happens when he's angry. He looked righteously furious as he pointed a shaking hand at Nerufane.

"You cock chugging son of a whore! I will rip off your fucking head and shite down your windpipe!" he yelled in his thick brogue accent. Drop was from Invermoriston, Scotland. I'd befriended him there seventy years ago.

"I'll kick your balls so hard they'll come out through your eye sockets!"

Did I mention he swears like a drunken sailor when he's angry?

"My, my, such language," Nerufane said, decidedly unthreatened.

To be fair, Drop's two feet tall and see-through, so it's kinda hard to be threatened by him.

"No time for ball kicking now, buddy," I said sternly. "Put a pin in it, we've got bigger problems to deal with."

Tat landed in front of Drop and wrapped him in a hug.

"'Tis good to see you safe Fae-kin. Be still now, I'll explain all to you in short time."

She gently pushed him back behind me while he fumed under his breath about eyeballs and sporks.

"I have less than an hour now," Nerufane said, his eyes narrowing. "If I'm not free by the time I am recalled I am dead upon my return. This one returns with me to share my fate." He yanked on Shrill's leash for emphasis.

"It's your show, Dunc, get it on the road," I said.

"Stand by the ruby," Duncan said gruffly, gesturing toward the gemstone with his staff.

Nerufane gave the chain some slack so that Shrill could stay near the inside edge of the ring, but his grip on it didn't loosen as he moved into position. Duncan faced him, the ruby between them. He inhaled, and the Phoenix on the top of his staff burst into living flames, the four crystals began to glow like lightbulbs, and the mixture in the groove of the ring lit up like glowing embers. They were enveloped inside the ring by a ten-foot-high wall of translucent white light.

"Extend your arms out to the side and show me the bindings," he ordered.

The diamond-looking enchantments became visible as Nerufane did as instructed. Duncan lifted his staff over the ruby, hovering just a few inches above it.

"Try not to move, elf, this is going to hurt," he said.

He closed his eyes and opened his mouth. A vibrating, resonant hum flowed from his throat as he brought the staff down onto the ruby. It lit up like a big road flare. What happened next was kinda spectacular.

The Phoenix blazed brighter and then burst into hundreds of smaller versions of itself. The tiny birds began swarming around the two men in a moving sphere. They were all the wild colors of fire, reds, oranges, golds, blues, and whites. The colors flowing and vacillating through them as they flew. Individual birds began darting from the sphere and into the bracelets on Nerufane's wrists and ankles. They would rip a diamond off and streak away from it, then the bird and the diamond would explode silently with a burst of light, like a little firecracker. Nerufane grimaced in pain, screwed his eyes shut, and tried not to scream.

I watched him, feeling no sympathy at all. He'd kidnapped my friends, the fact that I wasn't going to kill him meant he was getting off easy as far as I was concerned.

It took exactly forty-one minutes. Duncan closed his mouth and the sound stopped. He removed his staff from the ruby, now blackened and cracked. It crumbled into dust as soon as his staff broke contact with it. The ring of energy surrounding them disappeared, and the crystal lightbulbs winked out. He dropped to one knee, all the color drained from his face.

Nerufane was on his knees looking like a hot mess. His suit was torn to tatters from the elbows and knees down, and his wrists and ankles were covered in angry blisters and welts where the binding bracelets had been ripped away. His hair had come almost entirely out of its braid and was plastered to the back of his sweat-drenched jacket. He shakily raised his arms close to his face, looking at them with exhausted joy.

"Free," he croaked, his voice sounding dry as sand.

The leash dropped from his hand, and Shrill bolted to my side. I dropped down to a knee and broke the collar off his neck, hurling it away. I scratched his head with both hands.

"Did he hurt you?"

"No, he's just a righteous douchebag," Shrill said, his voice a deep baritone.

"Good to have you back, scaley."

"Good to be back, my friend," he said.

"Stay with Tat and Drop, I'll deal with the douchebag," I said quietly.

I walked into the ring to face Nerufane. His skin had darkened to its natural deep blue color. He rose unsteadily to his feet, raised his arms above his head and spun around in a wobbly pirouette.

"Free!" he shouted.

"Which means you can tell me who was pulling your strings."

"Of course I can, muffin," he spun again, his smile beaming. "Because I'm free!"

He wobbled and put both hands on my shoulders to steady himself.

"His name is Dalujac. He is a djinn lord of the current ruling house. Third in the line of succession to the throne."

"How did you end up getting bound by him?"

"Liquor and bad life decisions, mostly," he said, "But that's all behind me now, because I'm free!" he shouted and pirouetted again.

When he came back around, I hit him square on the underside of his chin with a haymaker of an uppercut. It snapped his head back and lifted him off the ground. He landed at my feet like a rag doll.

"That's the shite I'm talking bout right there, boyo!" Drop shouted, "Hit the twaddle-fuck again!"

"Bet that felt good," Duncan said as he pulled a large bottle of water and a couple of PowerBars from his cooler.

"Not gonna lie," I said with a smirk.

As good as it had felt, I'd clobbered Nerufane for strategic reasons not personal ones... mostly. I wanted to make sure he was out of play for the duration. He claimed to have no interest in Annalisa, but there was no way I was gonna trust a Darkling at his word and expect him to just run off and disappear into the night.

"Shrill, did you ever see his master, this Dalujac?" I asked.

"No," he said, shaking his head. "He kept me sequestered in the same room until tonight. I never saw or heard anything."

"Did he feed you?"

"Dogfood," he said, disgustedly. Shrill had discerning tastes.

Duncan pulled a bag of beef jerky out of the cooler and handed it to Shrill. "It ain't filet mignon, but it's better than kibble."

"Oh, teriyaki, marvelous!" Shrill said, tearing into the jerky like a starving man.

"What are you going to do with the wombat turd?" Dunc asked, nodding at Nerufane, as he ate his second PowerBar.

I hefted the turd over my shoulder and headed toward my truck. "Got that covered. Lock and load, everyone."

It was a short drive down the hill from the Batcave and then back up into Griffith Park on Hillcrest Avenue to the Greek Theatre, but Duncan kept his staff trained on Nerufane the entire ride, just in case he woke up and had to be put out again. I would have happily punched his lights out again myself, but, driving and all. Safety first.

I was stopped at the entrance to the theatre parking lot by a couple of serious looking men wearing FBI windbreakers and dark sunglasses. One approached the truck, hand on his sidearm.

"I'm here to see Hooper," I said, before he had a chance to speak.

He peered inside the truck and didn't seem at all surprised to see an unconscious Blue Elf in the passenger seat.

"Wait," he said, then backed off and spoke into a radio he pulled from his belt. A moment later he waved me through.

Hooper stood by the entrance doors to the theatre, a large duffle bag by his feet. I hefted Nerufane out of the car, lugged him over to the Fed, and laid him on the ground.

"This is my first Blue Elf. They all look like this?" he asked.

"No, this asshat is unique in my experience. They usually look more, orc-ish?" I looked at Duncan.

"Gruesome?" suggested Duncan.

"He's a supermodel for his kind," I said.

"What the hell happened to him?" Hooper said indicating his wrecked clothes and wounds.

I gave him the condensed version.

"Interesting," was all he said as he took pictures of Nerufane with his cellphone. He opened the duffle bag and pulled out the cord restraint system they'd used on me.

"You got the stuff, Dunc?"

"Yeah, here," he said.

He handed me a small clear bottle, filled with amber liquid. I knelt next to Nerufane, unscrewed the cap, and poured the contents into the elf's mouth.

"What's that?" Hooper asked.

"Sleeping potion," Duncan said.

It's what I'd asked him to make for me, back at Chulunn's house.

"You really think that's necessary when he'll be wearing this?" Hooper asked, as he started attaching the restraints.

"Blues are sneaky, dangerous bastards, and I don't know all that he's capable of. Don't take him lightly just because you have him restrained."

"You worried about me? That's so sweet."

"I'm worried about him getting free and fucking things up at the observatory. Your Scalestones won't work on him."

"The Stones aren't the only trick I have up my sleeve," he said with a wink.

I reminded myself again not to underestimate Hooper.

"Be prepared to use them. How about the other thing?" I asked.

"It's set up."

"Thanks," I stuck out my hand. "I know it's a big ask, I appreciate it," I said.

He hesitated for a beat and then shook it. "Don't fuck up," he said.

"You and Buck really need to work on your motivational speeches."

"Hooah," he said earnestly. It was the army battle cry, only said soldier to soldier. Coming from Hooper, I knew how much it meant.

I nodded at Nerufane, "As much as I'd like for you to keep him locked up and lose the key, we made a deal. After midnight you can let him go."

"Why midnight?"

"After the alignment happens, win or lose, it won't make a difference if he's free or not."

CHAPTER TWENTY-NINE

The real problem tonight, and what my plan couldn't control, were the variables we couldn't account for. Like the number of Orsa's remaining troops. We hadn't eliminated House Ziwix last night, just the contingent at the tower. Alamander's resources were another unknown. If he'd convinced other Half-kin to join him we would be at a massive fighting disadvantage.

I mulled over all these pensively as we left the Greek and drove up a short hill, entering a tunnel at the top where the two roads into the observatory met. The headlights revealed In-Ra and Cuda standing at the far end. I stopped when I reached them. We got out and circled up in the headlights. It was 10:30.

"Status?" I asked Cuda.

"Chulunn's soldiers be in position round the observatory, mon," he said, "The 1 and I swept the grounds and lower hiking trails. All clear. FBI be on point."

"So far, so good. Let's get up there," I said.

We jumped into the truck and drove the short distance to the observatory lot, parking on the road just before entering it. Everyone got out. As Drop and Shrill moved to exit I stopped them.

"You two stay here," I said, "This isn't your kind of fight."

They could be effective combatants in certain situations, but this wasn't one of them.

"Are ya fucking serious, boyo? I'm ready to bust some skulls!" Drop fumed.

"Not today, buddy. I just got you guys back. I don't want anything happening to you."

"Ya wee softie," he griped.

"You'll get no argument from me," Shrill said. He was willing to throw down if necessary, but he was more thinker than fighter. "Be careful, watch your back."

"Give 'em a proper fuckin' foot up their arses!" encouraged Drop.

I went to the lock box in the back of the truck as the others started toward the observatory. Tat stayed with me.

"In-Ra, a minute," I said to the djinn.

He turned back and joined me at the truck bed. He was in his true form, no longer needing to hide behind a glamour since Annalisa had discovered she was djinn. A curved scimitar hung in a scabbard on his hip.

"Yes, master Dragon?"

I opened the lock box and pulled out the Odachi, the shotgun, and the tactical bag with the extra magazines. I probably should have brought more.

"Do you still keep track of things that go on in Djinn, in terms of royalty?"

"As best I can. I am no longer a..." he paused for a beat, looking a little sad, "A welcome visitor in the realm. It makes information hard to come by."

"Do you know who Dalujac is?"

His eyes widened at the name.

"He is a prince. High in the line of succession to the throne of the current ruling house of djinn. If the rumors I've heard are true, he is not in high favor with the royal court, though I do not know why. How do you know of him?"

"Long story. The short of it, he's been trying to get his hands on Annalisa. He knows who she is."

"By the great flame," In-Ra said angrily.

"If we make it through tonight, I'll give you the full run-down. Won't make much difference if we don't."

"We shall succeed," he said, setting his mouth into a grim, hard line. "There is no other option," He started to turn away. I stopped him with a firm hand on his shoulder.

"There's something else we have to consider. You and I are the only ones here oath-bound to protect Annalisa."

"In truth, it is only I," he said.

Tat huffed loudly. "If you believe that, djinn, you know us not at all," she said, bite in her tone.

"I intend no insult, but she released you from service at the tower, did she not?"

"I'm sure she was spellbound when she said that. She's still in my care as far as I'm concerned."

"Then yes, we are the only ones," His expression turned dark as the light of understanding widened his eyes. "The others might put the safety of the world ahead of hers, if they feel it becomes necessary."

"He understands. Shocking," Tat said, losing none of the bite.

"Throttle down, Tat. He's on our side," I said. I could tell he was surprised to hear me defend him. Tat huffed.

"You believe that our allies would act so?"

"We have to be prepared for it, regardless of what I believe. As much as I want to trust them, the cold fact is people usually make choices based on their own self interests and need to survive."

"What would you have me do?"

"I'm not going to be able to track everyone when the shit hits the fan. Keep an eye on Cuda and the Reds. Try and stop them if they make a move against Annalisa. Can you handle that?"

"Aye," he said, "And the wizard?"

It bothered me that I even had to consider Duncan in that way, but he'd said it himself, he didn't like the idea of the world being overrun by Full Blood Dragons. As dark a horse as it was, I still had to be prepared for the possibility that he might ride it.

"He's my responsibility," I said.

"Ours," Tat chided.

I put my fist up to my shoulder, and she bumped it.

"I shall do my best," he said, with a bow of his head.

We left the truck and quickly followed the others to the observatory. As we approached it, Kritten popped into view on the roof and shot me a high sign. Most of his team was stationed up there. There were two elves on our level, hidden behind veils on either side of the grounds. I couldn't see them, but I knew they were there.

Large spiral staircases on either side of the observatory lead up to its roof. Duncan, Cuda, In-Ra, and I went partially up one of them. Hidden in the shadows, our position gave us a defensive wall for cover and an unobstructed view across the expansive main lawn, all the way to the parking lot.

In the middle of the lawn, about halfway between us and the lot, stood the Astronomers Monument, a tall, spire-shaped sculpture, made of white concrete. The lower half of it featured the full body busts of six of the world's most influential early astronomers. Hipparchus, Copernicus, Galileo, Kepler, Herschel, and Newton. Sitting atop it was a large copper armillary sphere, a pre-telescope astronomical device used for tracking the movement of celestial bodies. It was a giant artistic representation of one, and weighed about nine hundred pounds.

I stared at it, scowling, as time ticked by.

"You feeling anything, Dunc?"

"Nothing except the node," he said.

"What if Orsa lied, mon? Maybe we be in the wrong place," Cuda said.

"They need the node. There's no other place in LA with this much concentrated juice," Duncan said.

I checked my watch. 11:30 on the nose. Where were these assholes? I caught myself scowling at the shiny armillary sphere again. Wait, shiny? That thing was nine hundred pounds of green oxidized copper, nothing should have made it shine. The hairs all over my body stood up at once.

"Holy Christ! You feel that?" Dunc gasped.

"Dunc, how good is copper at amplifying magic?"

His eyes widened, following my gaze. "Good. Really fucking good."

The sphere began to glow. Duncan doubled over, exhaling sharply as if he'd been gut punched. In-Ra had a similar reaction though less severe.

"Mother of God," he hissed, "The energy!"

I felt it, but it wasn't affecting me physically, like them. Being magic wielders, they had a more direct connection to the influx of such massive raw power.

I leapt off the stairs and charged toward the sculpture, Cuda a step behind me. We'd gotten maybe twenty feet onto the lawn when we ran into a colossal wave of force emanating from the sculpture. Our forward movement came to an almost dead stop, it felt like trying to run up Niagara Falls.

A giant circle of black energy materialized on the ground, with the sculpture at its center point. Alamander, Liwix, and Annalisa rose up out of the morass, like they were taking shape out of hot tar.

Annalisa was no longer a willing participant in her fate. She was on her knees in front of them, naked and bound in chains that pulsed with a bright red glow. They were probably a binding, or at least the start of one.

Hovering above the ground between Annalisa and Liwix was a giant crystal, about four feet tall and brilliant ice-blue in color. Energy arced between it and the Armillary Sphere in huge pulses that looked like lightning. From the bottom of it, the same energy hammered into the ground. It was the mother of all Loci, tapping into the node.

I growled and drove forward with all my strength. I managed a half step. Beside me, Cuda was able to take a full one.

The black circle they had risen from began to move, pulling itself apart into smaller circles, maybe a half dozen total. They stayed in a wide ring, still encircling the statue. Shapes flowed up out of them, large ones. *Oh great...* They were full-grown drakes, geared for battle, covered in thick plate mail armor to protect their heads, necks, and legs. As soon as they cleared the circles, they spread their wings and launched into the sky with a collective roar.

Liwix raised her staff and touched the dream catcher to the Loci. With a blast of light it expanded into a huge dome of glowing blue energy, encompassing the three of them and the Astronomers statue, and stopping a few feet from Cuda and I.

The energy wave that had been keeping us at bay disappeared, sending us lurching forward from the sudden lack of resistance. Cuda stumbled to his knees and reached out a hand to the dome to catch himself. He screamed and recoiled.

I barely stopped myself from face-planting into it, my nose less than an inch away. It thrummed with power that vibrated straight through my bones. I scrambled back to Cuda's side.

His hand was a mess, the skin sizzled down to the bone in places on his palm and fingers. There wasn't much blood as it seemed to have been cauterized as well.

"Bloody hell," I breathed.

"Don't be touchin' the dome," he said through clinched teeth. "It hurts... a lot."

Gunfire exploded from the rooftop as the elves unloaded on the flying drakes. One of which was dive-bombing right at us. Its open, screeching mouth launched a fireball at us. I dove into Cuda like a linebacker, tackling him out of the way. The fire wouldn't have hurt me, but Cuda didn't share my resistance to fire. It missed us by a few feet, but it turns out that drake fireballs have kinetic energy too. The concussion blasted us backwards towards the steps of the observatory entrance.

I twisted in midair and managed to land somewhat on my feet. Cuda was totally off balance from my tackling him out of the way and landed in a mountainous heap. I didn't even have time to catch a breath.

"Above you!" In-Ra shouted in warning.

A second drake launched another fireball at us. I whipped the Odachi off my back and cleaved it in two before it struck. The runes along the blade ignited in glowing green as they dissipated and deflected the concussive energy.

I looked up in time to see In-Ra take a running leap from the stairs, scimitar in hand, a golden glow surrounding him as he used his magic to propel him the long distance to the drake. He landed on its back, and in one fluid motion drove the scimitar into a gap in the animal's armor around its neck. It roared in pain, looped over backwards and nose-dived straight toward the ground.

In-Ra lept off the dying creature at the last moment, leaving his blade buried in its neck. He landed safely, but the dying drake bounced off the ground and tumbled onto him, pinning him underneath its bulk.

With a snarl Cuda was on his feet and charging at the downed animal. Ignoring the pain in his hand, he grabbed it by the tail, spun, and flung it at the dome. It crashed into it in spectacularly gruesome fashion. The metal of its armor shrieked and threw sprays of sparks and flame where it hit the searing energy. The animal's flesh melted and burned as it rolled down the side of the dome. It landed with streams of foul-smelling smoke wafting off it.

The dome didn't show a hint of stress or damage from the drake's impact. It just shrugged it off. Bollocks, this bloody thing was gonna be a problem.

I ran to In-Ra. His face was twisted in pain, one of his legs clearly broken. Cuda was looking skyward to make sure we didn't get fire-balled again.

"I'm going high-side to help the elves," Cuda said and sprinted toward the stairwell.

They were pinned down on the roof by three drakes, fireballs raining down on them. Wait, two drakes. Great shot, Kritten. The other two drakes had targeted Duncan. He was pinned on the stairwell steps, countering their fireballs by shooting what looked like glowing crystal shards of purple energy from his free hand. The Phoenix on the top of the big stick blazed with the same purple energy.

"I fear I will not be able to complete the task you asked of me," In-Ra said through gritted teeth.

"Yeah, you're fired," I said as I picked him up. I ran up the steps to the observatory entrance and dropped him against the doors. It was the only place I could get him quickly, that had any kind of cover. It wasn't much, but at least nothing could come at him from his back. I handed him one of my Desert Eagles and two extra mags.

"Do what you can, try not to die," I said and sprinted back toward the dome. I had to get inside the damn thing.

As I neared it, one of the drakes peeled off its attack from Duncan and swooped towards me. I aimed the AA-12 at it and fired two rounds. I had loaded the shotgun with explosive armor-piercing shells, essentially mini-missiles, thirty-two of them in the drum. The first shell blew apart its neck plate. The second blew its head clean off its body. I was still in a full sprint to the dome as it crashed to the ground off to my side.

I emptied the drum at the dome. Thirty shells exploded against it with thundering impacts, creating a fireworks show of flame and sparks. For all that sound and fury, the only result was an angry red spot, radiating hotly against the dome's ice-blue glow. I'd managed to give it a bruise. Hurray.

Things started to get bad right about then.

High above the dome, the sky… opened isn't the right description. It became opaque, and a completely different sky became visible. It was a daylight sky glowing with warm hues of red, yellow, and orange. It looked like a sunrise.

"Randall, it is Djinn," In-Ra shouted at me from his place by the entrance.

Bugger me. The Material Plane and Djinn were in alignment. I had maybe ten minutes before Wyrm lined up, then it became bugger everyone.

From inside the dome Annalisa screamed. She was prostrate on the ground at Liwix's feet. The elf stood with her staff raised high, the tip pointing at Annalisa's midsection. Energy arced from the Loci into the staff then shot downward into Annalisa. She had begun to change, body elongating, muscles growing, horns were starting to sprout from her skull. Her body spasmed with convulsions as the energy wracked her.

By contrast Liwix stood so eerily still she may as well have been a statue. She was draped in a short red cloak, the cowl pulled up over her head, hiding her face in shadow. Only her eyes and mouth were visible, all blazing with a furious red glow. Around her waist was a gold chain, a gold lamp straight from Aladdin, dangled from it.

"The spells that keep her from becoming djinn, the Magus-Sai undoes them!" In-Ra shouted again.

Before I could move things went from bad to worse.

Three elves came crashing down onto the lawn around me, dropped by one of the remaining drakes as it flew by overhead. They might not have been dead, but they weren't moving.

Duncan was on the move, halfway to the steps of the main entrance, trying to get to In-Ra's side. Before he got there he was forced to a stop by a barrage of fireballs spat at him by the creature he was still engaged with. He managed to throw up a shield of energy in front of himself just in time to avoid being incinerated.

Almost immediately things got worse again. More worse? Worser? They got FUBAR.

A fireball hit me square in the chest. I was lifted off my feet and punched backwards like a baseball just hit for a home run. The only thing that stopped me from tumbling ass-over-teakettle down the hill I was flying toward was the concrete wall that I smashed into. *Crack*! Pretty sure that was a rib breaking. The burning pain that flared a second later confirmed it. Fuck my life.

It wasn't just my life though. It was Annalisa's life. It was Duncan's, Tat's, Shrill's, and Drop's. In-Ra's, Kritten's, and whatever elves were left. Every Half-kin on the planet, possibly a good chunk of the world's population. My pain was of little consequence right now. I pushed it down and stood. It still hurt but I ignored it.

I drew the other Desert Eagle and aimed at the drake above Duncan. Its hindquarters were the least protected by armor, and I put five shots into its thigh. It roared and whipped its head around toward me. I put my last bullet into its exposed eye. It faltered in the air but didn't drop. Until Duncan hit it.

He dropped his shield and leveled his staff. The Phoenix, glowing dark purple, opened its wings wide and snapped them forward flinging blades of purple light skyward. They sliced through the drake and its armor like white-hot knives going through an unlucky slab of butter. It dropped to the ground at the base of the main steps, dead before it hit the cement. That left two.

"Duncan, I need a doorway into that dome right now!" I yelled.

Cuda and Kritten came leaping off the roof. The elf landed lithely on the grass and in one fluid motion turned and fired at the drakes that were following them. They veered off and swooped across the lawn toward the parking lot. Tracer bullets erupted at them from the two elves who had been in hiding, as they broke the cover of their veils. The drakes took some hits but stayed in the air, dipping and swerving to avoid the gunfire and get out of range.

"Keep those things busy, Kritten," I barked at him.

He raced to join his two brethren, and their gunfire ripped through the air again, keeping the drakes at bay back over the parking lot. Duncan, Cuda, and I met at the dome. It still had the angry red spot where I had blasted it with the shotgun. I drew the Odachi off my back.

Inside, Annalisa was now still, but she had completely transformed. She was bigger, looking at least a foot taller, though it was hard to tell because she was curled in a fetal position. Her hair was a long, tangled mess of dark copper, standing out against reddish-black skin. Her horns were fully grown, long and ebony black, they flowed out of her forehead and swooped elegantly back over her skull. Her eyes were closed, and her breath came in rapid heaves.

"Tell me you can open this fucker," I said to Duncan.

"I'll open it. You'll have to move fast, and he's gonna see you coming." He pointed at Alamander who watched us calmly from the spot where he'd first appeared.

He was dressed like a medieval knight, elaborate white and silver plate armor covering him from head to toe. A flowing white cloak draped across one shoulder. Strapped across his back was an oversized broadsword, his bow was in his hands.

I looked at Cuda. "Ready?"

"Ready, mon."

"Aim your blade at the red spot, and slice when I tell you. You'll only have a few seconds," Duncan said.

"That's all we need," I said. I was gonna hand him his ass and then make him hold it while I kicked it some more.

Duncan reached into his pocket and withdrew the lodestone that Chulunn-Bat's niece had been wearing, placing it into the mouth of the blazing Phoenix. He tipped his staff toward the dome, and immediately the Phoenix changed from purple to its ice-blue color. Energy began arcing from the dome to the bird. He wrapped both hands tightly around his staff and raised it over his head, pointing its glowing tip at the dome.

"Now!" his voice boomed with palpable force.

With a Gandalf-worthy 'You shall not pass!' swing, he slammed his staff into the dome sending filigrees and cracks through it where he struck. The Phoenix erupted into an upward blast of ice-blue energy. The runes on my blade blazed into view as I drove it into the weakened spot. It pierced deep into the dome, and I pulled the blade downward, cutting it open in a shrieking swath.

Cuda dove through over my head, and I lept in after him. My cut immediately glued itself back together behind me, frying off the bottom edge of my coat as it did. Peripherally, I saw Duncan hurled to the side in a wild backlash of magic energy.

Alamander had a full view of what we were doing, but he'd remained where he was. He must have believed we'd never get in, so he hadn't moved to the best attack position, leaving himself farther from us than he should have been.

He raised his bow, but there was no arrow knocked. The gloves of his armor glowed white, and an arrow of energy flowed from them to the bow. He loosed it at Cuda, who was in front of me. It struck him dead in the chest before he could move. His whole body convulsed as his mouth opened in a silent scream. He toppled to the ground, smoke wafting off his body.

I leveled Incindis at Alamander and triggered its full charge. A roaring tongue of fire lashed at him. He must have remembered his last run-in with the ring because he was prepared for it. He raised a glowing gauntlet in front of himself, and a white shield of energy materialized from it, as tall as he was. It hissed angrily, turning red hot as it absorbed all the flame, never getting close to Alamander.

I was already in motion, charging toward him and firing with the Desert Eagle. The shield shattered into pieces under the onslaught of high-caliber bullets, releasing bursts of fire as it broke apart, causing Alamander to backpedal away from his own defense.

Alamander created another arrow and aimed at me, but before he could fire, I threw a Rondel dagger at him. Well, not him exactly. The blade struck his bow dead center and cracked it in two. I had tried to throw it hard enough to go through the bow and bury itself into his chest, but the impact sent it skittering off trajectory, bouncing harmlessly off his armored side. I dropped the empty gun, and we charged at each other, blades drawn.

We came together in a metallic shriek of metal. We whirled and spun, blocked and parried, blades clashing again and again. He was good. Blood flew, equal parts mine and his. Green sparks flew off the glowing Odachi as it bit into his sword, taking shards of metal out of it. His blade might have been well forged, but it wasn't spellbound like mine.

We came together hilt to hilt, locking wrists, each of us trying to gain the advantage.

"It's not too late, you can still join me, near-kin," he said.

"Hard pass," I growled, "I'll earn my wings the right way."

"By slaughtering your own kin, you fool!"

"You know the reasons why as well as I do. You're insane to try and undo it!"

"Killing each other, so that only one may become what is the birthright of us all? *That* is insanity."

We pushed away from each other and charged in again in a whirlwind of steel. The Odachi pierced his armor and bit deep into his shoulder as I drove him back toward Liwix. He was buying her time, fighting to keep me away from her. We grappled again.

"Is it? I don't see any more of us here trying to help you. Not even one of your own kin."

He laughed. It was strangely sad.

"I am the last of my kin."

"You're what?!"

If I hadn't been fighting him for my life I would have dropped my sword in utter shock. All he had to do was successfully pass the Test and he could become a Full Blood White Dragon. What the hell was motivating him to go through all this if he was so close? His admission made me pause just enough for him to take advantage of it. His head snapped forward, hitting my nose with a solid headbutt.

Stars exploded in my vision and I staggered backwards as blood poured out of my nose, but I never lost my grip on him. In case you forgot, I took a sledgehammer to the face a few days ago. I have a famously thick skull, literally and figuratively.

I gave Alamander a bloody smile and returned the headbutt, releasing my grip at the same time, as he staggered back a step I kicked him in the chest so hard I dented his armor.

He rolled with the kick, falling into a backwards somersault to put space between us, coming up gracefully onto one knee.

"What is wrong with you? Why not just take the damn Test?" I raged at him.

I was furious. He was standing on the edge of Full Blood Dragonhood, everything I'd lived and fought my entire life for, and he was refusing to take it. Chasing some insane fever dream instead.

"My father posed the same question. When he asked me to kill him," Alamander said calmly.

I stopped, frozen in disbelief.

"That is the Test, Randall. The horror of it. Beyond the madness of killing your brothers, at the end, you must kill your own father to become the head of your line, so that you may have sons of your own."

It took me a second to find words. I didn't find a lot of them.

"That's... that's," I stammered.

"Insane?" he said, standing up. "Yes, but that's what is asked of you. What you will have taken away, by your own hand. I faced the Test, and refused it."

As often as I'd thought about killing my father when I was growing up, especially after a particularly bad beating, they were never anything more than fleeting thoughts. Gone after my ego had gotten over the humiliation of another loss. I wanted to beat my father, wanted to be better than him, but I didn't want to have to kill him to prove it. I loved him.

"Do you see now why I cannot stop? The Test is an abomination, and it will happen no more!"

He launched himself at me, and I was grateful for the attack. My mind was reeling, trying to process what he'd just told me. Returning to the fight gave me something to focus on, a reason to move. Otherwise, I might have just stood there rooted in place.

He came at me swinging high. I went low, slashing at the unarmored part of his legs. If I could cut the right tendons, he wouldn't be able to stand. It's hard to fight when you can't stand. At the last second he pivoted, blocked my strike, and stepped in close. His metal-clad elbow smashed into the side of my skull. I took a step backwards to stay upright, and he returned the front kick, sending me flying into the statue of astrologers. Copernicus got fucked up. It might have been Hipparchus. I couldn't really tell.

Alamander leapt at me, trying to drive his sword through my heart. I pushed off the statue and spun out of the way as his blade drove deep into cement instead of my chest. It stuck momentarily and as he tried to yank it out I brought the Odachi screaming down towards his wrists. He bet on being fast enough and lost. I took one hand off at the wrist. He screamed as blood sprayed.

I pressed my advantage, striking him with a barrage of punches, driving him backwards until he hit the inner dome wall and its energy bounced him off, throwing him violently into the ground. He lay there in a crumpled bloody heap. I stomped on the stump of his arm to hold him in place, and he screamed. I stood over him, my hand in a white-knuckle grip on the hilt of the Odachi. One stroke and he'd be dead.

I didn't do it, and it wasn't about my terms and agreement with the Feds, or Buck's threats. The truth is, I didn't want him dead now, I had too many questions for him about the Test and how he'd learned its secrets.

Even if Alamander was telling the truth I still had to stop his plan from succeeding. Even if I had to kill my father one day, the alternative of Dragongeddon was worse. I forcefully repeated that in my head over and over, to get myself to move. Liwix was behind us on the other side of the statue, I could kill her and put an end to all this.

I kicked Alamander in the head, knocking him out, and turned toward Liwix. As I did I was hit by one of the hardest punches I think I've ever felt and found myself flat on my back without even realizing how I got there. I saw stars, then black, then stars again as I fought with all my will to stay conscious. Through blurry vision and disbelieving eyes, I saw Cuda towering over me.

"Sorry mon, truly. This be the chance of a lifetime. I couldn't turn him down."

He grabbed me by my throat and yanked me into the air. I grabbed at his fingers, trying to pry them back and keep him from crushing my windpipe. Shock, disbelief, betrayal, all bored out of my eyes at him.

"Don't do this…" I choked out through the vice grip on my throat.

"Already have."

I swung my legs up over his giant arm, trying to get more leverage to pry his fingers off my throat.

"Why?" I croaked as I bought myself a millimeter of breathing room.

"I got thirty-six brothers left. No reason they need be dyin' just so I can live. We all deserve to become what we truly meant to be."

I managed to pry two of his fingers off my throat, as my vision started to blur. I let go with one hand and desperately reached for the knife in my boot. Before I got a hand on it the dome began to fade, it's energy powering down. Everything changed in a heartbeat.

We were hit by a sensation unlike anything I've ever felt before. I knew Cuda felt it too because his grip loosened, and I frantically sucked in air. Sound dimmed away to almost nothing, movement around me slowed to a crawl. Everything funneled in and hit me as one driving, focused, overwhelming feeling.

Fear.

Believe me I've felt fear before, lots of it. Being in wars and battles all over the planet, thousands of life-or-death fights against men, supernatural beings, and monsters. Most recently almost being thrown to my death. I'd felt fear in all those situations, but it was useful fear. The kind that dials your senses up to twelve, makes your heart race and blood sing, and drives you forward despite the odds against you. It's a tool I've learned how to focus and wield for my survival.

This was something otherworldly, the kind of fear that turns your blood to ice and shoves your heart up into your throat so deep you can barely breathe. It paralyzes you in place or makes you turn tail and run in a blind stark raving panic. I'd *never* felt this kind of fear.

Cuda's arm slowly dropped toward the ground. I unwrapped my legs from it without even thinking about it and slid down onto my knees. My throat was still in his grip but it was more of an afterthought. I stayed there, my gaze pulled upwards to the source of that terrible fear.

Another rift had opened in the sky, above the window into Djinn. It was Wyrm. I couldn't see much, a sunset sky that was a riot of purple and orange hues, like it was on fire. The outlines of three moons in different states of fullness. A smell wafted out that was totally alien, yet deeply familiar on a subconscious level. It was glorious, and terrifying, and not mine to enter. The magic of the Test was letting me know that in no uncertain terms. My legs were trembling underneath me, just from looking into Wyrm.

The two realms hadn't fully aligned with Earth yet. There were maybe a few minutes tops before that happened. I had to do something. I had to move. I couldn't. I was paralyzed.

The giant Loci was glowing like a star, as great pulses of ice-blue energy slammed upwards into it from the node, then arced from it to the armillary sphere. The sphere matched its brilliance, as two great arms of energy ascended skyward, reaching out to the open rifts in the sky.

On the ground smaller tendrils had reached out from the Loci, snaking around Annalisa to wrap her in a glowing cocoon of energy. The lamp on the Liwix's hip was similarly covered in the ice-blue glow.

Move, Randall! Move! My brain screamed. My body wouldn't respond. I just sat there on my knees in Cuda's grip, like a kitten being held by its mother.

The front of Cuda's head exploded as a large-caliber shell drove through his skull. The report of the shot hit my ears a second later. He was dead before his body started falling and his grip released. The shock and gore of Cuda's grey matter spraying all over the side of my face snapped me out of the daze of terror just enough for me to wrench my eyes away from the rift into Wyrm. The favor I'd asked of Hooper earlier had just saved my life, all of ours if I could move fast enough.

I looked at Alamander to make sure he was still out, then picked up the Odachi and swiveled my gaze back around to Liwix as I drove myself to my feet. I focused on Annalisa's still form as I stumbled across the lawn, trying to ignore the over-powering force of Wyrm, which wanted to draw my eyes back up to it. I knew if it captured them I would end up paralyzed with fear again. I managed a few more steps to the Astronomers Monument and slumped against it, fighting a losing battle to the rift's irresistible pull.

Liwix was only a few yards away from me. It might as well have been miles. Stone still, she hovered a few inches off the ground, she and Annalisa were completely cocooned in the flowing energy from the Loci. I wasn't going to make it.

The rifts to Djinn and Wyrm were in almost perfect alignment, the energy tendrils from the armillary sphere close to touching them. I felt something deep inside me, something I'd never felt or known was there, begin to come apart, and rapidly dissolve. It was the binding magic being pulled from me. Every Half-kin worldwide probably felt the same thing, with no understanding of what it was.

I lost the battle with the rift, and my eyes locked on it again. In that moment something unexpected happened. From somewhere deep within Wyrm the distant roar of a Dragon echoed out of the rift. It was faint, but it hit my brain, heart, and soul like a blasting clarion call, filled with the magnificent, overflowing resonance of life. It was indescribable. A sonic reminder of what I am, what I could become, and everything that I've spent my entire life fighting for. I wanted that roar. To one day hear it raging out of my own throat. No one and nothing was going to take it from me. It broke the fear and snapped me out of my paralysis. My system surged with battle-adrenaline. I didn't have to reach Liwix.

I coiled every muscle and leapt upwards toward the armillary sphere, and I roared. No sound like that had *ever* come from my throat before, and it reverberated around the observatory grounds.

As I reached it, I slashed through the statue where the sphere connected to the concrete. Its weight sent it toppling down and away from the loadstone, falling on the far side of the statue. Pulses of energy trailed after it as it fell, crashing into the surrounding concrete sidewalk. It cracked into two pieces, immediately severing the connection between it and the lodestone. The huge arc of energy connecting the two ground out to nothing, and the tendrils reaching for the rifts disappeared, leaving only a sudden and very loud silence.

The rifts to the Djinn and Wyrm Realms flickered and closed simultaneously.

I landed on the ground by Annalisa and my legs gave out, sending me face-planting into the grass. I was utterly spent, having used every drop of battle-adrenaline. I'd felt stronger after surviving my fall into the pool. Still, I'd just stopped Dragongeddon, and I hadn't killed Alamander doing it. Go me.

Liwix didn't share my enthusiasm. My head ended up on the receiving end of a vicious swing from her staff. I felt the crack all the way down to my toes. I rolled twice and ended up on my back. I saw her in triplicate as she stalked towards me, her eyes still blazing red. All six of them.

"Decades of planning, ruined, you stupid animal!" she hissed. "I'll make you pay for it."

She was still using the loadstone, drawing power from the node, and her dream catcher began to glow ice-blue. It grew into a sharp-edged, spinning wheel of vibrating energy, throwing off hissing sparks of light, like a giant buzz saw.

I had nothing left, barely enough energy to move, but I glared at her defiantly.

"Felthi'de dex nath-trulla armeth!" I spat at her.

She shrieked at me in fury, but before she could fling the spinning wheel of death at me, Tat streaked by out of nowhere, hitting Liwix in the face with the most perfectly timed sucker punch ever. Liwix staggered back, but kept her feet. The old elf was tough.

"Your Fae bitch is not enough to save you," she said, her red eyes blazing at me.

She sent the energy wheel screaming toward my head. Before it hit me, her chest erupted in a blaze of purple light and fire, as the Phoenix from Duncan's staff exploded through it. The spinning wheel went skittering past my head, missing by inches as it cleaved a deep gouge in the lawn before flashing out in a pinwheel shower of ice-blue sparks. The light in Liwix's eyes went out, and she toppled face down into the lawn.

Duncan stood there, a cold look of satisfaction on his face. He held the big stick in his hands, the Phoenix statue now just a melted black mass. He padded slowly toward me.

"Thanks, Dunc," I managed to choke out.

A voice inside my head whispered, *'you are not going to die today,'* and a small smile touched my lips as I stared up at the sky, where the rift into Wyrm had been. A moment later Tat landed lightly on my chest, and I winced. She felt like a hundred-pound weight, but I didn't have the heart to ask her to move. Christ it hurt. It was glorious.

"Are you all right, Anii?" she asked.

"All rainbows and glitter, little one. Great timing with that punch."

"Twas most satisfying. Though I would like to have torn the eyes from her wicked face," she said with a fierce grin.

"That's my girl."

Kritten stepped into my view and regarded me with a raised eyebrow.

"Felthi'de dex nath-trulla armeth," he said, repeating my words to Liwix. "You told her to, 'go fuck herself with a flaming nutsack hat in hell.'"

I guffawed out loud as he broke into a wide grin.

"That's not even close to what I thought I said."

"Your elvish sucks, lizard," Duncan said.

"It really does," I agreed.

I managed to prop myself up and look around, turning my head toward Alamander. I wanted to make sure he was being covered by somebody. I was surprised to see Buck standing guard over him, as a few other Feds worked at restraining his unconscious form with another cabling system. Buck nodded at me, and the faintest of smiles played across her lips. I think.

"When did they get up here?" I asked Kritten.

"Not too long after you got inside the dome I think," he replied. "Can't be sure. We were a little busy with the drakes," he said, nodding at the two elves who stood behind him.

"Is this all that's left?"

"Aye," he said grimly, "Seven gone."

"I'm sorry," I said sincerely, "You all have my gratitude."

He knew what that meant. He hadn't saved my life directly, so I didn't owe him a true debt of gratitude, but he was most definitely in my favor, and all things considered it amounted to the same as far as I was concerned.

"If memory serves, drinks are on you, lizard, and you're buying for all of us," Duncan said.

"My pleasure," I said, "And my honor."

"That was the batshit craziest thing I've ever seen in mah life," A very pronounced southern drawl broke in. Speaking of debts of gratitude. "You all right, Mr. Ddraik?" Kevin asked, as he walked up next to Kritten. He was wearing camouflage fatigues and a sniper rifle was slung over his shoulder. He had the dazed look of someone who'd just witnessed a whole lot of impossible.

I don't think I've ever owed one person a debt of gratitude three times over. Kevin had set a personal record with me.

"Hooper was right, you're a hell of a sniper," I said to him. "Thanks."

"Can't even believe I could focus enough to take that shot. I feel like I'm on acid right now, to be honest."

His eyes weren't crazed this time, just amazed. His gaze kept bouncing between the elves, Tat, and In-Ra, as he tried really hard not to stare at any of them. I think he'd turned a corner.

Kritten reached out a hand, and Kevin joined him, together they helped pull me to my feet. All the pain got worse. Glorious, I reminded myself, glorious.

"You should go check in with Hooper before he decides to arrest you again."

"Yeah, I know. Are you..." he said, hesitating.

"Don't worry, I'll be in touch soon."

He nodded and headed toward the Feds. I realized Hooper wasn't with Buck, or the others who were trussing up Alamander.

"Can you drive, Dunc?"

"The dick on wheels? Sure," he said.

I handed him the keys.

"Can we give you a lift back to Chulunn's? I asked Kritten.

"No thanks, we have a ride, but..." he paused.

"What?" I asked.

"Can you transport our fallen back there?"

"Again, it would be my honor."

"We'll collect them and put them in the back," he said with a grim but respectful nod.

"I'll meet you all at the truck, I've got something to take care of first," I said to them.

In-Ra had managed to get himself to Annalisa's side, and I joined him there. He must have used some healing magic on himself because he was handling the pain of his broken leg much better now. He used a little more now and created a glamour, simple clothes to cover Annalisa's naked form. I helped him remove the chains from her ankles and wrists as she slowly regained consciousness. She was full djinn and brimming with power I could feel gently thrumming off of her. She took us both in, then focused on In-Ra.

"I saw you. At the tower." She marveled at him, seeing another of her own kind for practically the first time, since she learned what she was.

"Yes, my lady. I was there, trying to protect you."

"You're like.. like I... I am," she stuttered.

"I am djinn, but very much unlike you," he said deferentially.

"I don't understand," she said.

"I will explain all to you in time, my lady. I have much to tell you, and more to teach you, about who you truly are."

She looked down at herself, her eyes widening as she took in her new form. Wait until she got a hold of a mirror and saw her horns. It was going to be a whole new world for her.

"For now, let me introduce myself properly. I am In-Ra Dosham, Master of Servants to the late Lord and Lady Dahllaside, your parents. I am your sworn servant and protector, and I pledge my life to you."

She was taken aback, not knowing how to respond. It was the first time I'd ever seen that happen to her. Seriously, her picture should have been in the dictionary next to the word poise. Her mouth worked silently, trying to find words.

"Just take a breath, Annalisa," I said, "You've got a long hard road ahead of you," sugarcoating it was not going to help her, and she wouldn't have appreciated it anyway. "In-Ra's a good man. He'll help you travel it."

He looked at me and nodded in thanks. Annalisa placed her hand on top of In-Ra's.

"Then I am in your care, In-Ra. Thank you."

She turned her gaze to me.

"Thank you, Randall, for not giving up on me. Even after I told you to."

Her eyes hadn't changed at all, I was pleasantly surprised to see. I still saw my mother in them.

"That's what you're paying me for," I said with a smile.

"Money well spent."

What? You think I'm not getting paid after all this? After what I just went through? You must be out of your bloody head.

CHAPTER THIRTY

I was wearing an expensive set of black and red Dianese motorcycle leathers that matched the custom-painted Ducati Superleggera I sat on. A Glock 19 gen 5 pistol was neatly hidden in a shoulder holster under my jacket and an ESEE-6P-B fighting knife was tucked into my boot. Always prepared.

I was parked in the driveway of the Saint Marque Hotel waiting for Kevin, who had just finished his last shift. He'd decided to take the job with the Feds. Hooper had let him give two weeks' notice so that he could leave the job on a good note. It had been important to the kid. They'd apparently needed him as Don had suddenly stopped showing up for work, leaving them short staffed. Weird, right?

It had been just over a week since the fight at the observatory. The Feds covered up the damage, terrorist activities was the official story, which allowed them to keep it on lockdown for as long as they needed in the interests of national security. I was impressed by the media bamboozle they pulled off.

Hooper had released Nerufane from his bindings shortly after midnight. He said the elf was unconscious the entire time, and while neither he nor any of his people had seen it happen the Darkling had vanished sometime after that. Good riddance. There was a chance that Nerufane might come after me for some twisted reason, but I didn't think he would. We'd set him free from enslavement, and even to a conniving, vindictive, backstabbing Blue Elf, that counted for a lot in terms of goodwill.

My relationship with Buck and Hooper had warmed some after I'd made good on our agreement and delivered Alamander to them alive. Oh, and saved the world from Dragongeddon, let's not forget that. I wouldn't say there was trust but there was respect. Buck still wouldn't sleep with me. Go fig.

Greg had been awake when we returned to Chulunn's compound with our fallen. He was weak but no longer critical. I don't think I've ever seen Duncan quite so happy. The hug that he gave Greg even made the imp feel awkward and embarrassed. That alone made his recovery worth it. I learned there are few things in life funnier than an embarrassed imp.

Chulunn was going to come out all right in dealing with the High Noble Conclave, but he'd made a bitter enemy of Pharyn Cull in the process. Something we now had in common, I was sure. I made it clear to him that if he ever needed help against Pharyn, or a favor of any kind, I would be at his full disposal. Free of charge.

I'd spent three days after sleeping, healing, and eating. After that I'd taken Duncan and the elves drinking for a victory celebration and to pay our respects to those who fell in battle with us. Instead of getting smashed Duncan had one beer and headed home to look after Greg. I'd never have expected it, but I knew it was a good thing. Maybe his battle with the bottle was over, or at least he'd moved to the winning side of it.

I spent a couple of days with In-Ra and Annalisa, telling them the full story about Nerufane and Dalujac, and doing what I could to help her adjust. He knew that the process was going to be a long one, maybe anticipating a day like this would come eventually, and he'd been prepared. He already had a safe house set up, and with Annalisa's resources it wouldn't be hard to establish more. She had to keep up appearances as the head of her company, but it was more important for her to lay low and stay off the radar for a while. As powerful as she was, she still had to learn how to use it to protect herself. She was facing a whole new world of threats now, all of which were far more deadly than a hostile takeover, or falling stock prices.

Annalisa was a threat to anyone sitting on the djinn throne, or in line for it. There was little chance that any djinn would come to the Material Plane to threaten her themselves, but they could still employ powerful proxies to do their dirty work for them, as Dalujac had already proven. If he'd passed around knowledge of her existence to any other royalty, it was only a matter of time before someone else made a play at her.

In-Ra said he would find out everything he could about Dalujac and pass along the information to me. I told Annalisa I was at her service if she ever needed me. By the time I left them I knew she was in safe hands with In-Ra. I wasn't inviting him to my house for dinner anytime soon, but I put him on the shortlist. I got a million-dollar bonus for a job well done.

In quiet moments, in the days since the observatory, I tried to come to grips with Alamander's revelation about the Test. *Kill my father?* I didn't want to believe it, but I knew on a deep gut level that he'd told me the truth. He'd found out by facing the Test and refusing to take it. As far as I knew, Alamander and I were the only Half-kin on the planet who knew the truth. Cuda had died with the knowledge, if he'd ever had it at all. Now I was faced with an even bigger question, what to do with the information? Did I let all the other Half-kin know? Maybe I should only tell my brothers? Or maybe they were the last people I should tell? Did I keep it to myself and use the knowledge to my advantage? Was it even an advantage? Bloody hell, it was an epic mind fuck.

There were two people I needed to talk to before I took any action, Alamander and my father. The problem was I didn't know if Buck would let me near Alamander, or if he was even still alive to talk to. My father, well, just the thought of having that conversation with him scared the bejesus out of me for a lot of reasons. I ultimately made the very brave decision to keep thinking about it and not deal with it for a while.

I heard the rumble of Kevin's bike as he pulled out of the parking garage and glided to a stop next to me.

"Where to?" he said.

"Thought we'd ride up the coast. Grab some lunch in Malibu."

"Sounds good. I really appreciate you taking the time for this."

"I told you I make good on my debts. The Feds will tell you all about why, I'm sure."

"Yeah, the Feds. I…" he paused, looking uncertain.

"You sure you want to take this job, Kevin? Don't let them force you into it. I've got a little leverage with them now if you want out."

I wanted to make sure he knew what he was getting into. I also figured having him in my confidence would give me eyes and ears into their world if I ever needed it. Better to build that trust now before he started the job and they got into his head, which I knew they'd try and do.

"No. It's not that at all. Trying to be an actor was kinda a thing for… it was just a way of not having to be myself as often as possible. Not having to deal with what happened in country. This job, I think it's gonna help me a lot and answer a bunch of questions, I'm looking forward to it. I always liked being a soldier."

I could relate to that. "So why did you pause?"

"Well, I don't mean to pry. It's just that I'd rather hear it from you than the Feds. What…" he stopped, uncertain again, then forced himself to continue. "I know you ain't human. So, what are you?"

I had to laugh. They were going to tell him anyway. He was going to learn all about the supernatural world, my kind included. Besides, I owed the kid. He had saved my life three times. I gave him a big incisory smile and answered him before I pulled my helmet over my head.

"Me, kid, I'm a Dragon."

The look on his face was worth the reveal.

THE END

Author Bio

BRIAN J. GREEN

Brian J. Green has been writing in some way, shape, or form for thirty-six years. He started on a whim, trying his hand at cartoons because he was a die-hard Looney Tunes fanboy. From cartoons he switched to screenplays and after spending over twenty years in the screen-world, he wanted a change. He decided to try his hand at writing a novel, a format that would allow him the freedom to world-build and fully develop his characters, without the restrictions of worrying about producers, directors, actors, or budgets.

"It'll be so much easier!" He stupidly thought to himself.

Brian has always been a fantasy geek and a huge fan of Dragons, probably from too much D&D as a boy (and as an adult, honestly. He still plays weekly). So, a book about Dragons felt perfect, but not your 'normal' familiar kind of Dragons. He set out to create a story that had familiar tropes, but would flip them on their collective heads, in an urban-fantasy taking place in the present day. His Dragons wouldn't be giant, winged monsters. Wizards wouldn't always be sage and wise. Supernatural creatures from myth and lore would abound, but most often wouldn't behave, or even look like what one would expect. Several (ahem, *many*) years later, the book *I Am Dragon* was born.

When Brian is not using his hands to write, he can usually be found upside-down standing on them, or using them to balance or hold other people up, while engaging in acrobatic shenanigans, or twisting the throttle of one of his motorcycles. As a writer, hand-balancer, acro-yogi, juggler, and lover of all things movement-related, Brian's hands get a lot of work.

Brian lives in Grass Valley, California.

Printed in the USA
CPSIA information can be obtained
at www.ICGtesting.com
LVHW012156011224
798080LV00034B/977